broken beginnings

CITRUS COVE
BOOK 1

CLIO EVANS

For anyone who knows me for tentacles, tails, and fangs and is deeply confused by me writing a straight small town romance

content warning

Parental suicide (off page but mentioned), witnessing a murder, bullying, stalking, CNC, assault, guns, spitting, spanking, exhibitionism, a switch scene, breeding kink, use of sex toys, and more.

If you have any questions regarding content warnings, please reach out to me via Instagram **@clioevansauthor** or via email clioevansauthor@gmail.com

Except she wasn't really free.

Not like how I would be in two years.

Sarah meant she would be free from school but not from this prison of a town. My plan was to get the hell out of Citrus Cove the moment I could.

I hated it here. I hated Texas. I hated the heat, the people, and how they whispered about us. Four years ago, after our daddy walked out, our mama dropped us off at Honey's and then took her own life. The moment he left us, she decided that it was time to leave us too. That earned us two types of reactions—prayers and pity or sneers and snide remarks. Both were the type of spotlight that made me want to tuck tail and run.

It didn't help that Cameron Harlow, resident bully, went out of his way to make my life hell. Ever since we started at this school, he'd spread rumors about me, make fun of my clothes or body, and *accidentally* drop food or drinks on me. It was always something.

"I hate the Harlows." I yanked my hand free. "I don't want to go. If you want to, just go have fun. I know you want to see Colton."

Sarah scoffed at me. "Don't even get started on that."

I fought the urge to laugh at her. She tried so hard to pretend she didn't like him, but she couldn't lie to me.

Colton was okay, at least. He wasn't one of the Harlow brothers—not by blood anyway—but was always with them. Despite his friendship with them, I still tolerated him. I saw the way Sarah looked at him; she could do better, but she could also do worse.

She rolled her eyes, reaching for my hand again. I evaded her grip. Fireflies flickered around the oak tree in the front yard, the quiet street interrupted by her pleading voice.

"Come on. Seriously? I'll even sneak you a drink."

We stared at each other. I knew that was probably a lie.

content warning

Parental suicide (off page but mentioned), witnessing a murder, bullying, stalking, CNC, assault, guns, spitting, spanking, exhibitionism, a switch scene, breeding kink, use of sex toys, and more.

If you have any questions regarding content warnings, please reach out to me via Instagram **@clioevansauthor** or via email clioevansauthor@gmail.com

haley

Fourteen Years Ago

"COME ON, it'll be so much fun!"

My sister dragged me out the front door into the sultry humid night. Sarah was two years older than me and determined to take me to the party at the Harlow boys' house, even though I would be much happier doing literally anything else.

I didn't want to go. In fact, anywhere that Cameron Harlow set his big-ass boot was a place I didn't want to be.

"I don't want to," I hissed at her. "People are just going to be throwing up everywhere. It's hot. Besides, I'll be the youngest there."

"You know Sammy will be there, and he's younger than you," Sarah said. "Besides. Honey isn't home tonight—she's working an overnighter. It's just us. And I want to celebrate being *free*. One more week until I graduate."

Except she wasn't really free.

Not like how I would be in two years.

Sarah meant she would be free from school but not from this prison of a town. My plan was to get the hell out of Citrus Cove the moment I could.

I hated it here. I hated Texas. I hated the heat, the people, and how they whispered about us. Four years ago, after our daddy walked out, our mama dropped us off at Honey's and then took her own life. The moment he left us, she decided that it was time to leave us too. That earned us two types of reactions—prayers and pity or sneers and snide remarks. Both were the type of spotlight that made me want to tuck tail and run.

It didn't help that Cameron Harlow, resident bully, went out of his way to make my life hell. Ever since we started at this school, he'd spread rumors about me, make fun of my clothes or body, and *accidentally* drop food or drinks on me. It was always something.

"I hate the Harlows." I yanked my hand free. "I don't want to go. If you want to, just go have fun. I know you want to see Colton."

Sarah scoffed at me. "Don't even get started on that."

I fought the urge to laugh at her. She tried so hard to pretend she didn't like him, but she couldn't lie to me.

Colton was okay, at least. He wasn't one of the Harlow brothers—not by blood anyway—but was always with them. Despite his friendship with them, I still tolerated him. I saw the way Sarah looked at him; she could do better, but she could also do worse.

She rolled her eyes, reaching for my hand again. I evaded her grip. Fireflies flickered around the oak tree in the front yard, the quiet street interrupted by her pleading voice.

"Come on. Seriously? I'll even sneak you a drink."

We stared at each other. I knew that was probably a lie.

The moment we got there, my sister would leave me high and dry. I would sneak my own drink. And if Honey found out about that, we'd be dead, but...

Sarah's eyes pleaded.

"Fine," I caved.

"It'll be fun," she promised.

For you. "Sure, whatever," I muttered.

I followed her to the beat-up Corolla and climbed into the front seat, cranking down the window. Her AC was busted, and it was too expensive to fix.

One day, I'd have all the money in the world. I wouldn't have to worry about broken air conditioners or cranking down windows because I'd be able to afford a brand-new car. Maybe I could even take care of Honey, too. All I knew was that my life was not meant to be here in this town.

"Why don't you go to college?" I asked her as she started down the street.

"It's too expensive. Besides, who needs that? I have my job at the cafe."

Citrus Cove Cafe was known for the best cherry pie in the county, but that wouldn't help her make more money. I fought my inner demons, never knowing what to say. I could hear Honey's voice in my head. *Some people like small towns. Your sister is one of them, and there ain't nothing wrong with that.*

"Yeah, but..." I drifted off. It was useless arguing with her, and yet I couldn't stop myself. "Do you really want to stay at the cafe your whole life?"

"Not everyone wants to be rich and famous, Hal," she quipped. She continued down the road but looked at herself in the rearview, tucking back her blonde waves. "Or whatever it is you think you want to be."

"Eyes on the road, diva. And I don't want to be anything. I just want to be out of this place. I'd do anything to leave."

"You act like we're trapped here. We're not. We're on our way to a cool party and we're going to have the night of our lives. Maybe you'll find someone to make out with."

I made a face. That sounded gross.

Black Velvet crooned in the cabin. Once we hit the town limits, she gunned it down the never-ending dirt road that took us to the Harlow barn. The wind whipped my curls, turning my hair into a tangled mess that left me feeling frustrated. I could never seem to tame them, even when I pulled them back.

My stomach twisted as I saw a slew of parked trucks and cars, all crammed together haphazardly in the grass. "Half the town is here," I protested as she parked.

"Relax." Sarah was already getting out.

I unbuckled quickly and slammed the door, shaking my head as she practically skipped toward the barn. Music played through speakers, people from school milling around, drunk and laughing. I paused for a moment and watched as Katie Mays, one of our most popular cheerleaders, ran toward the fields and threw up.

Gross.

This would not be fun for me.

I tried to keep up with Sarah, but as we made it into the barn, she slipped away. I cursed under my breath as the music got louder, people dancing all around me.

I didn't understand why people came here anyway. The barn was old and hardly used anymore; the Harlows had finished building their new home next to their vineyard and farm.

Must be nice.

"Hey, Haley," an unfamiliar voice said.

I glanced up, seeing a guy leaning against the wall. He had dark hair and an even darker gaze. I'd seen him around but couldn't put a name to his face.

He moved toward me, but then an arm slipped around me.

I didn't even have to look, to know that it was *him*. I came toe-to-toe with Cameron Harlow—blue eyes, pompous grin, and all.

"Let me fucking go, you ass," I snapped, my cheeks flaming hot.

Cameron was wearing an open button-down, exposing his chest and abs, along with faded jeans. If he wasn't the bane of my existence, I might have thought he was hot. But I knew better than to have a crush on the devil.

"Just the girl I was looking for," he said. "Haley Bently came to my party!" he shouted.

That earned claps and laughter, two girls that hawk-eyed him glaring at me. A guy laughed as he passed him, handing Cameron a five-dollar bill.

"You smell like beer," I snarled, shoving him away. "You really bet on if I'd come here or not? Get a fucking life."

"No, other people bet on it. But I know you wanted to," he said, sliding his arm around my waist again.

I shoved him harder this time. "I hate you. Just let me go, so I can go watch people throw up or something."

He was a lot taller than me and a lot stronger, so that shove did nothing. He chuckled, looping one of his fingers in my blonde ringlet. "Why are you so angry all the time? Is it because your mother died?"

His words stung, but I'd learned how to numb the whip of them. "Wouldn't you like to know? You're never gonna leave this town. You'll grow up and die here, just like the rest of your ugly family."

That sparked a cold fury in his icy gaze. If there was one way to piss off a Harlow, it was dragging the rest of their kin.

"What the fuck would you know? You don't even have a family."

5

"I do too," I said. "And I'm sure as hell going to make mine a lot prouder than you'll ever make yours. You're a good-for-nothing idiot who can't tell his left hand from his right."

"You don't even fucking know me," he snarled.

"And you don't know me."

He lifted his beer and dumped it straight over my head. I never broke eye contact, even as it ran down my face. I felt the tears well up, the humiliation of it all, but I held strong, forcing myself to stay still even as those around us laughed and catcalled.

"You're going to end up just like your mama. Alone and forgotten and dead," he whispered. "A guy like me shouldn't even give you the time of day."

Beer ran down my neck, soaking my dress. My hands curled into fists.

Something in me snapped.

I pulled my fist back and punched him straight in the face. I gasped as I felt my knuckle crack against his nose, pain flaring through my hand.

His head whipped back, but he recovered quickly. He grabbed my jaw, squeezing tight. He parted his lips to sneer something but was interrupted by a harsh voice.

"*Cameron.*"

A broad hand grabbed him by the shoulder and hauled him back. Hunter Harlow, the oldest of the three, grabbed Cameron like a kitten. Hunter gave me a startled glance.

"What the fuck is wrong with you, Cam? What the fuck? Sorry, Haley," he huffed, shooting me an apologetic look. "If you need anything, just let me know—"

"I don't need anything from any of you."

With that, I turned around and marched out of the barn. I ignored the snickers from classmates and the curses I heard coming from Cameron's older brother.

"*You're going to regret that,*" I heard him say. "*You're such a dumbass.*"

It was going to be a long walk home, but at least I wouldn't have to deal with anyone else. It wouldn't be much longer until I left this place, and then I'd never have to come back again.

CHAPTER ONE

Present Day

IT WAS ONLY the end of April, but the heat had already settled over the Hill Country in a sticky, unwelcome blanket. Everything from the grass to the trees seemed to have wilted from the fury of the sun, ugly and soon to be dead. I peeled my thighs off the leather as I gunned it down the road, trying to focus on anything other than what I was running from.

Why am I doing this again? I'd asked myself that question a million times on the long drive from Baltimore to Austin. It's just that the answer was one I didn't want to think about.

The road dipped and curved, inching me closer to the one place in the world I'd sworn I'd never crawl back to. Miles of fences and farmland passed me, dotted by the occasional house or windmill or a scatter of cattle.

It wasn't long until the views became ensconced by trees, the hills growing curvier. The heat might have been early, but bluebonnets still lined the sides of the road, their deep blue a mirror of the open sky. It had been a long time since I'd seen those flowers, and I wasn't entirely sure that I'd missed them.

At least I was rolling into this hellhole in style. I patted the dash of my Corvette, going well over the speed limit. In this part of Texas, if a cop stopped me, it would be to admire the car.

It'd been twelve years since I graduated and moved on from Citrus Cove, leaving everything I'd ever known behind. My grandmother, my sister, the small-town mindset that I'd fought damn hard to beat, and the sting of all the bad memories.

Welcome to Citrus Cove. Population 2,877.

Well, 2,877 plus me.

I passed the quaint sign and sighed. As strange as it was, I felt like I was coming home.

Tears stung my eyes again. I was tired of crying, though. My teeth dug into my bottom lip, the pain grounding me in the present.

This place had fought me. It shoved down who I truly was over and over. From the bullies I'd gone to school with to the scowling church ladies, it nearly drained me. Hate was stronger than love, especially when it was backed by self-righteous, close-minded people.

I was no longer the little girl I'd been when I lived here. I grew up and found myself. Writing was something that I'd always excelled at in school, and it came in handy as an adult. I wrote travel articles for a well-known international magazine— a dream job that took me to Venice, Paris, Hong Kong, Sydney, Rio de Janeiro, and more. I made a career doing something I truly loved, and it didn't hurt that I made more money than I could have ever dreamed of.

After experiencing the world, Citrus Cove was just a forgotten, washed up, dot on the map.

And yet here I was.

Running back to a place I hated.

A place that I swore I'd never come back to again.

My stomach grumbled and I glanced over at my passenger seat. A pile of granola bar wrappers sat there. I was hungry for something other than oats and fig jam, and hoped that maybe I'd be gracing my grandmother's doorstep in time for dinner.

It had been too long since I'd seen Honey. Another stab of guilt, one that I was too numb to truly feel at the moment.

Being a travel writer gave me every excuse to never come back. It was easy to skip Christmas when you were in another time zone on the other side of the world, and even easier to placate any grumbles with gifts. Honey, bless her, loved it when I sent her magnets for the fridge.

For over ten years, I was free from this town and its hate.

I shouldn't have come back.

But where else was I supposed to go?

After everything I'd been through the last three weeks, I needed to hold my grandmother and sister.

The Bently Girls. That's what Sarah and I had always been called. *Those Bently Girls are nothing but trouble. Those Bently Girls are a curse. I heard their grandmother took them Bently Girls in because no one else in the family wanted them.*

Now, Sarah was married to some man I vaguely remembered from high school. She wasn't a Bently Girl anymore, hadn't been for a long time, and was the mother to twin boys that I only knew through pictures.

She was a stranger now, but it was easier that way. All I could do was hope that maybe we could patch some things up. I'd at least like to meet my nephews...

I chewed my bottom lip as I slowed to crawl down Main Street. The sun set, casting a golden glow over the sleepy southern town. Citrus Cove *had* changed, but only bits here and there. Some new shops, fresh paint on old ones, new light poles. As an adult, I could see more now. The community, the connection, the way the people who lived here banded together during hard times.

Well, if you were one of them. If you weren't, then you were shit out of luck.

"I'm an adult," I reminded myself. "I'm in control. No one can take that from me." That had become my mantra, even if it felt like bullshit.

Here in Citrus Cove, there was no crazy killer. There were no dead neighbors. And god, did I hope there would be no more nightmares.

Maybe it was the fact that I couldn't stop thinking about the blood on my hands, the way she died slowly in my arms. I needed Citrus Cove and its safe, quaint, quiet ways. No matter how hard I tried to hide it, my roots were still here, drenched in the sweet tea and bible verses I'd purged from my mind.

My phone buzzed in the passenger seat, text messages coming in. I already knew it was Emma checking up on me and my twenty-three-hour drive from Baltimore to this small town south of Austin. She was one hell of a friend. Ready to pack everything and leave her luxurious lifestyle for boots and sunscreen just to support me.

Coming out of downtown, I took a right and then a left. Twelve years, but driving to my Honey's was still an autopilot motion. *Honey.* When my sister and I lived with her, we'd started calling her Honey, and it stuck. It was ironic, considering her spine was made of steel and her temper sharper than barbed wire. But her patience and strength in raising us after my mother passed was something I'd never forget. Even if the three of us bumped heads. Even if she called me every holiday and berated me for not being home.

I also knew, even if I felt nervous about it, that I'd be

welcomed home. I forced another deep breath as I eased down the street, my heart hammering as I pulled into the drive. I felt sick to my stomach being here. *Maybe this was a mistake. Maybe I should have just stayed at Emma's.*

Honey's pale yellow pickup sat in front of me. She'd owned that thing since the '70s, and it ran like a 2023 Chevy.

One breath. Two breaths. Three.

I was already here. There was no point turning back now. I turned off the engine and reached for my phone. As I'd guessed, Emma had texted me.

Emma: *I know you're driving but let me know when you make it. Should be any minute now.*

Emma: *Yes. I've been keeping count.*

Emma: *Donnie misses you already.*

A picture of her hairless dog with his tongue sticking out popped up, and I grinned. He wore a Tiffany-blue collar covered in crystals.

Me: *I made it. I'll keep you posted. Still don't know if I'm even staying here tonight.*

Emma: *If they're unfriendly, just grab a hotel room. You don't need extra stress right now babes. If it doesn't work out, we can fly to Paris for the month.*

She was right, as usual. She was *always* right.

I opened the car door and stepped out, my legs feeling like Jell-O. Lights on inside the house gleamed through the closed curtains. It was a small house with a whitewashed porch, an oak tree that stretched high above. My eyes scaled up to where some branches had been cut, keeping them away from the roof.

Someone was taking care of her. I was grateful for that, at least.

I stood frozen for a few moments. Just staring. Remembering. Doing my best to make my body stop trembling.

If I stayed out here like this too long, one of the neighbors would see me. The gossip would already start.

That spurred me forward. I walked to the porch and climbed up the front steps. Heat crept up my spine, my stomach rolling.

I hit the doorbell and waited.

Within a few seconds, I heard the shuffle of her footsteps. The front door flew open, and my grandma stood in front of me.

Our gazes locked, ice blue on deep brown.

"*Honey.*"

There was something in the silence between us, a bridge that fell over the gap time created. I felt everything—all my worries, fears, pain—all of it in that moment. I'd missed her so damn much and hadn't realized it until now.

It was the final straw. I broke. The floodgates opened.

"Oh, dear heavens," she whispered.

She pushed the screen door open, but I was already crying. Her arms wrapped around me, and I sank into her, feeling everything in me snap.

Her scent was an immediate comfort. I held on to her, even as she pulled me inside and shut the front door. At seventy, she was still stronger than a damn ox.

"I'm sorry," I sobbed. I leaned against her, feeling myself drowning. Falling. The murder flashed before my eyes, along with all the sharp words that I'd been harboring for so long. It was a lethal mixture, the kind that made me want to curl up and hide.

But she wouldn't let me do that. Honey would make me get up. She'd make me stand.

Another reason I needed to come home.

I couldn't let myself go right now. I needed the people in my life to force me up, even if I didn't feel like I could do it.

"Sweetie, I don't know what's happened, but you're home now," she said. She gripped my cheeks, making me look at her. Through the blur of my tears, I noted that her hair was bright silver, brighter than before. She was wearing a bright pink nightdress, her reading glasses hanging around her neck. "How long are you here for?"

"I don't know," I whispered.

"Your room is almost how you left it," Honey said. "Some things are in storage, but you'll be right at home. Have you eaten dinner yet? You're thinner than a sheet."

She didn't mean those words maliciously. They were simply a fact. When I'd left, I'd taken nothing with me. I'd eaten a box of granola bars on my drive down. As for the comment on my weight, I'd damn near forgotten how common they were in the South. If it was anyone but my grandma, I would have gone off, but I didn't have the energy.

"My weight is fine. But I haven't had dinner, no," I said, wiping my tears. I felt hollow. "I drove straight through from Baltimore."

She shook her head, clearly concerned. "I'm going to make you some leftovers, and we're gonna sit so you can tell me what's happened."

* * *

I sat in her picturesque kitchen, taking everything in. She'd redecorated, which was unsurprising. Growing up with Honey, she'd redecorated at least once a year. All the place mats were checkered yellow, a vase of flowers at the center of the table. Magnets that I'd sent peppered the fridge, along with a few photos of Sarah's boys.

She put down a plate of grilled chicken, vegetables, and a soft roll. Then a small plate with a slice of apple pie in front of me, and for a moment, all my worries melted away.

"I won't fight ya if you eat your dessert first."

I grinned because that was exactly what I was going to do.

"Got these apples from the Harlow farm," she said, clearly pleased. Her chair creaked as she sat down, settling in as I took my first bite. "One of those boys cut me a deal."

I doubted they were actually boys anymore. I fought the glare, not wanting to signal just how much hate I harbored for my old high school bully. It didn't hurt the way it used to, but I would never forget that bastard.

I had bigger things to think about than the past. Tina, my boss, had been very gracious with me since the murder. And in all technicality, I could turn this trip into a 'work' one if I wrote an article about Citrus Cove. I wasn't going to worry about any of that right now though.

It was one day at a time.

Another patch of silence settled between us. Honey scrutinized me as I kept eating.

"So, Haley Marie Bently," she said. I stiffened at the use of my full name. "What brings you back to Citrus Cove? I know you don't like it here. You got me worried. You didn't even call before coming. I could have been going with Mr. Johnson."

"Honey," I hissed, scandalized. Despite the horror of what I was about to tell her, my mouth fell open. "What do you mean, Mr. Johnson?"

She arched a gray brow, her bright blue eyes twinkling with amusement. "I'm old, not dead. I've got needs. So does he since his wife passed away last year. We drink sweet tea and get naked sometimes."

"*Honey!*" I wheezed.

She reached out and patted my hand the same way she had the first time she'd given me the birds and the bees conversation. Her smile lit up the room, but then I felt the dark clouds return.

She knew me.

She knew I wouldn't have come if I wasn't hurting.

Her hand squeezed mine, encouraging the truth from me like she always had. When I was ten and stole a newspaper by accident and then tried to burn it to hide the evidence (catching a tree on fire), she squeezed my hand like this. When I'd come home with a shiner and a bruised rib because I'd picked a fight with one of the McConoville kids, she'd done this too.

I leaned back in my chair. The story was on autopilot at this point. I'd lost track of how many times I'd told it to the police and Emma and my boss and the landlord and gods knew who else.

"Three weeks ago, I was leaving my apartment when I heard a scream. I went down the hall to a door that was partially cracked. I opened it right as a man slit a woman's throat. He was wearing a mask. He ran at me, attempted to stab me. I moved out of the way, but the knife still got my arm. It's mostly healed now, so don't worry. It was evening so other people were coming home from work. Someone shouted and startled him. He ran off, leaving me with the woman as she died. I held her as she took her last breath. She'd clearly been tortured. All right down the hall from me."

The sweetness of the pie with the words coming out of my mouth didn't feel right.

I'd watched the light leave her eyes. And I'd wondered— how long had she been suffering right down the hall from me? I should have realized something was wrong. I didn't know her, but I'd returned misplaced mail to her before. I'd passed her coming and going on my adventures.

Elizabeth Jacobson from apartment 1208 was dead. It wasn't my fault, but I'd been living with guilt every day since. Hating myself because I could have potentially stopped that man, or I could have paid more attention. I could have helped her.

I'd untied the ropes around her wrists and closed her eyes. After I was able to come out of the initial shock, I called 911, and everything from the rest of the night was a blur. All of the questions. The police. Someone prying her from my arms. Her blood covering me. Emma picking me up. Her shoving me into the shower, throwing out my ruined clothes, and making me eat. Tina calling me, concerned and then giving me time off. The landlord offering to give me a month free if I kept quiet about what happened.

I hadn't slept well the last three weeks bunking on Emma's couch. Finally, yesterday, I got up and decided that I had to get out.

There were some things about that night that I hadn't told anyone, not even the police. Running was the only way to escape.

Honey's eyes glistened, and she gave a slight nod. The scent of warm apple pie and honeysuckle filled the kitchen, accompanied by the leftovers of grilled chicken and mashed potatoes she'd made me eat before dessert.

I'd missed her, I realized. The revelation was just another wound. It hurt, but at least it hurt in a better way than all the other stuff haunting me.

"You can stay as long as you want. You're always welcome in my home. You know that, sweetheart."

And that was just like her. She wasn't going to push for more right now. She wouldn't ask me a million questions. She wouldn't question why I hadn't called her three weeks ago or why I'd just followed the wild whim of showing up on her doorstep.

"I thought you'd be mad at me," I whispered. "And I wasn't sure about Sarah... I haven't spoken to her in a long time."

"I can't speak for her," my grandmother said tightly. I frowned. What happened between them? "I'm not mad at you, just incredibly disappointed." Her tone became kinder, although still firm. "But for other reasons, sweet child. Reasons that are neither here nor there right now. What matters is that you're home. What happened to you was awful, but it's over now. It's time to heal. You're safe."

Safe.

"Now, eat the rest of your dinner too. A piece of pie isn't a full meal."

I snorted, but didn't argue. I could feel the weight of everything rolling through me, but then it lifted. I breathed out, my shoulders relaxing for the first time in a month.

That was why I had come home to Citrus Cove.

I was safer here than anywhere else in the world.

CHAPTER TWO

cameron

I SET my laptop down on the oak-top bar as I settled on the stool, overlooking the empty tap room. It was days like this that I got to really take in the beauty of the place. The finished wood, the gorgeous bar, the exposed beams.

I'd done a damn good job. Renovations were a nightmare, but the fruit of that labor was worth it.

Citrus Cove Wine & Ciders was going on its third year. It was stressful. I worked more than I ever had before, even when I'd been in construction. But I loved it. It was another way for the Harlow legacy to live on and helped our farm flourish tremendously.

Plus, I got to be my own boss. That was one thing I learned early on about myself—I didn't do well working for others. This place was a wild dream turned into reality, and that was best for me and any unlucky sap who might have been my boss in another universe.

The winery would open in a few hours and would be busy, given that it was Friday night. Being down the road from

Austin meant we got some out-of-town traffic, which was good for business.

My family owned an orchard and vineyard that we'd been growing and tending for over eighty years. There was even a big old oak tree at the center of the farm that every couple within the family carved their initials in once they found love, a Harlow tradition. My great-great-great-grandfather started that when he'd found the first love of his life, Essie. She'd passed not long after they married, and he fell for Anna. They'd carved their initials into the oak tree too. Between his first marriage and second, he had ten children. All of those children carved their initials into the tree when their time came.

I was thirty-two and sometimes wondered when it would be my turn. Almost every Harlow in the family seemed to find their one true love, except for me and my two brothers. I'd joked with my mom before that we'd be the end of the line, which always earned me a swat. Mama Harlow had made it abundantly clear that she expected grandchildren at some point, even if she said it with a slightly hopeless and exaggerated expression.

I pulled up our book-keeping program and did a quick run through of expenses. How in the hell had I ended up with such an adult job? And why was doing expenses something I looked forward to?

I mindlessly categorized everything, adding tags, approving things, sending invoices, gawking at how much supplies cost to keep our business going. This place was my pride and joy, even if it pained me sometimes. I let out a low whistle in seeing how much I'd spent last week, feeling my balls shrivel just a little.

Still, we were in the green.

Now, if only I could stop working so damn much. I needed a good fuck, a good beer, and a massage. Most of the time when the whole family was around it wasn't such a big deal, but recently, I'd been manning the winery, farm, and watching my parent's dog, Benny.

Speaking of.

"Damn it," I muttered, glancing up at the clock. I needed to stop by and let Benny out at some point. I had time though, and it was just a quick ride down the road from here.

I lost track of time working. It wasn't until I heard tires outside on the gravel that I leaned back and rubbed my eyes, rolling my neck and shoulders.

"You've got that glassy-eyed look, partner."

I looked up, seeing my co-owner and best friend of twenty years.

"Colt," I greeted as he slammed the door shut behind him. He came over to the bar and leaned over, running his hands through his blond hair and fixing his baseball cap. "Might as well get some of those ponytail holders and wear it up," I teased him. "It's at your shoulders already."

"You're just jealous. I've got the looks," he quipped, wagging his brows.

"And I've got the brains."

He laughed. "And yet, who's the one that makes all our ciders and wine, huh?"

"True," I snorted.

Colt was part of the reason this whole dream had come true in the first place. The two of us made a damn good team.

I glanced out one of the massive windows, eyeing the sunshine warily. We hadn't been lucky with the rain this year, which worried me for the farm. It would be hell for all of us if we didn't start getting some rain soon. All I could do was hope that April and May lived up to their legacies and brought us more showers. "It's hot already, and it's not even May," I muttered.

Colt glanced out the windows and shrugged. "Texas," he

said. "Click your heels three times, and then we'll get flash floods. You know that."

I rolled my eyes, but he was right. I didn't want to hope too hard for the rain because then we'd end up with a damn flood. Which would also fuck with the farm.

Colt slid onto a stool, giving me a look. *That* look.

Did I even want to know? "What do you want? What are you dropping by for? How did you know I was here?"

"I saw your truck. And you're always here. All the time. I think you should start keeping boxers in the office."

"Fuck off, man," I sighed.

"I'm here to gossip, actually," he said with a coy smirk. One that didn't sit well with me. "And to make sure you're not working yourself to death. Have you talked to Hunter lately?"

I narrowed my eyes on him. Gossip in Citrus Cove was a regular commodity, but I didn't like the hint of mischief I heard in his voice. I'd known Colt my entire life, and his misdirection questions rarely worked their magic on me. "He's out of town for another few days. When he gets back, I'll take a load off. I'm splitting my time between here and the farm." It had been a lot. Too much, in fact, but I wasn't one to complain. Once Hunter was back, he'd jump in, and everything would be alright again. "Mom and Pops are in Tampa for another week, and then they'll be back home."

"Getting that Florida sun," Colt said. "Jealous."

"We've got plenty of it here," I mumbled. I couldn't fault my parents for taking a vacation though, even if it was the third one in six months. They deserved to do whatever the hell they wanted after raising three boys—four if we counted Colt, which we all did.

"And Sammy?"

I snorted. "Sammy does all our social media, is a 'cook influencer,' whatever the fuck that is, and plays live music three times a week. I can barely get a text back. But yes, he's covering the bar, too, until everyone gets back into town."

"You know, I think his cooking videos are just porn. I saw his video one time on Instagram, and he fingered a grapefruit. The comments were wild."

"Probably. Wouldn't put it past him." I loved Sammy, but he was a wild card.

Colton made a disgruntled noise, drumming his fingers on the bar top. He had a hard time sitting still, and I was surprised he even sat down. "You should hire someone else."

"We live in a small fucking town and are too far for people to want to drive," I grumbled. "We've had this conversation like every week."

"Right. So, maybe someone new in town..."

"Get to your point."

He hesitated dramatically.

I raised a brow, unamused. "Spill it. You already have someone in mind."

He grinned. "Of course I do. Brains, remember?"

"Colt, I swear to god."

"I'm gonna tell your mama you did. I heard that Haley Bently is back in Citrus Cove. And according to her grandma, she's here to stay for a while."

My blood ran ice cold. "Really? Interesting."

Haley Bently.

After all this fucking time.

I kept my voice as neutral as possible. Colt knew some of the history there, which was why he was being so damn nosy and mischievous about her arrival. But he didn't know it all. And hell, I didn't want him to. "How in the hell do you know that?"

"Well, you know all the ladies tell me everything." He wiggled his brows, and I shook my head at him again. "And also, I stopped by Mrs. Hamilton's to make sure that oak hadn't done any more damage since the wind storm a few weeks ago. Those branches damn near took off her roof."

I nodded, letting out a soft grunt. That was why I'd live here for the rest of my life. We all looked out for each other. You couldn't get that in the big cities, especially like the ones the infamous Haley-hates-small-towns-Bently ran off to.

Why had she come back? I couldn't help but wonder. She hated this place. I remembered that much about her. Maybe she'd gotten married but now was getting a divorce and wanted to see Honey. Maybe she'd decided to move to the other side of the world. Maybe...

There were so many maybes, and all of them meant jack shit. Just the mention of her set my blood to boiling, and not in a good way.

"I doubt a city girl like her is looking for a job," I said, clicking on my laptop mindlessly. I wasn't even sure what I was working on. What was I even clicking on? Emails? The same email button over and over again just to pretend to be busy?

That time of my life was a sore wound. I'd bullied Haley because I was a moron. My mama raised me better, but I'd been an idiot. More than an idiot. I'd been an asshole.

The older I'd gotten, the more I'd come to realize how much I'd probably hurt Haley just by being an ass. And I hoped that none of it stuck with her, but if it had...

Another flash of guilt rolled through me. I tried to shake it off. I needed to stop making assumptions, right? I'd changed. I'd grown up.

"She could always go work for Sarah. That cafe needs help," I said.

Colt's eyes darkened. It was barely there, a spark that had never gone away, not even after Sarah Bently got married and had twin sons. It was Sarah Connor now, wife of David

Connor, a man that both of us despised. A man that I'd throw hands with on sight, law be damned.

It lasted a split second, and he didn't miss a beat. "She's already been here for a week, and the grapevine says she wants to work. I'm gonna invite her out tonight."

I felt a prickle of heat along the back of my neck. If I told Colt no, he'd dig his heels in. And then he'd pick me apart. The best way to handle this was like I didn't care, even if the idea of her being around me made me nervous, cranky, guilty...*Damn it.* "Fine. Whatever. I need to get some work done, Colt."

"Yeah, yeah. Get some more coffee going in the back so you're not a grump tonight. I'll see you later."

"Hey, can you let Benny out?" I asked.

"Do you want me to just take him the rest of the week?"

"Man," I sighed. "I would have but he hates being away from the house. He's old and set in his ways, otherwise I'd bring him here. You can try if you want?"

Colt nodded. He'd always had a way with animals, so I wouldn't be surprised if Benny actually listened to him. "Alright. I'll let him out and give him a run around. Maybe he can ride with me for errands. And I'll see you in a bit."

"Thanks," I said, mentally checking another box on my to-do list.

I stared at my screen as he left, my focus ruined.

All I could think about was how I'd always done everything right in my life. I'd always been kind...well, most of the time. Always been good for the most part.

Except to Haley Bently.

When she was new to our school, I'd done everything from sticking gum in her hair to stealing her books. Starting rumors about her. All because I didn't want anything to change, and a new girl meant change. Fuck, I'd done some terrible things.

And then I'd found out that her mother passed, and when I'd tried to make it right, I'd made it worse.

That girl hated me. Even though I grew to regret my behavior—I'd done the work to manage my own emotions and not take it out on others—I was enemy number one to Haley Bently, and I understood why.

And to think that it was all because I was a selfish, arrogant kid who didn't think about how my actions would hurt her. Back then, Haley somehow became the girl I pined over but instead of self-reflecting, I did stupid things.

It pained me, looking back. If I could go back in time and punch myself, I would. I'd knock myself clean out. Hell, Hunter had done so at least once.

I'd talked a lot with my therapist in the years since about why it was only ever Haley. I'd learned a lot about how insecurities could manifest as anger, and how someone can be a catalyst and end up taking the brunt of those unmanaged emotions.

That was over fourteen years ago, but I still felt the sting of embarrassment and shame.

I'd learned so much since then. And had unlearned so much misogynistic, toxic male bullshit.

One day, I'd find the right woman. And when I did, I'd do anything to make her happy.

But I didn't need Haley working for me. I needed someone who didn't hate me. Someone that wouldn't set my teeth on edge.

In fact, I was entirely certain that she would turn down Colton's invite. Why would she ever want to come near me after all I'd done to her?

CHAPTER THREE

"SO, ARE YOU REALLY STAYING, HAL?"

"Yes," I sighed, grimacing as I talked with Emma. We'd been talking so long that my phone was hot against my ear. "For now, at least."

A week had passed since I'd landed back in Citrus Cove. Since then, I'd done nothing but eat my grandma's apple pie, talk to Emma, post on social media to keep up appearances, and do some minimal research on places I could write about in this area. I was getting restless, Sarah had ignored all my attempts at reaching out, and part of me was resistant to going into town.

Somehow, I'd built it up in my mind over the last twelve years that Citrus Cove was evil, and working through my mental blocks was taking longer than I'd planned. It wasn't like the little shops on Main Street had freezers full of bodies.

"Damn," Emma sighed. "I'm going to have to move out there, aren't I? I can't live in Baltimore if my best friend is in bumfuck nowhere Texas. That's cruel."

I laughed, leaning against the kitchen counter and peering

out the window above the sink. There were small clay angels on top of the ledge that Honey collected. I reached up, tracing one of their wings as I spoke. "You don't have to, of course. And it's not that bad. We're close to Austin, at least. And not that far from San Antonio."

"Austin sounds okay, I guess," Emma mumbled. "I'm going to have to get sunscreen for Donnie."

I barked out a laugh. "Oh my god. Can you imagine?"

"I'm going to have to. I really miss you. I get that you travel for a living, but this feels different. Hell, we've lived in the same city for a decade, Hal. And especially with everything that happened, I don't like being far apart."

I sobered up quickly, pressing my lips together. Emma had been with me through thick and thin. The absence of Sarah had been filled by her. In fact, there had been countless times that Emma had played the role of family. "I just need some time," I whispered. "I can't stop seeing her in my head, Em. I dream about her. I dream about him. About him finding me. They haven't made any progress on the case."

"*Stop*. He won't find you. It was just the wrong place, wrong time. I'm thankful everyday that it wasn't you. I don't care if that makes me a selfish bitch."

I bit back tears, not willing to go back to that place in my mind. Not willing to replay what the killer said to me. What I'd told no one.

"Right," I said hoarsely. "Brain doesn't always compute logic, as you know."

"I know," she said. "I do. Do you want me to send you anything from your apartment? You took nothing with you."

"Actually, maybe," I hummed. I'd gone through my suitcase once now and was already getting sick of the same thing. And my closet from when I was a teen? I wanted to burn everything

29

in it. "Maybe some clothes. I can always buy more, but I hate doing that. And maybe some things like... I don't know. My passport."

"I got you. I'll run over there today or tomorrow. But really, get out of the house. And since you're taking some time off, do something fun. Be spontaneous. Be like your grandma, out there getting *nekid*."

I cackled again, fighting back tears. I'd told Emma about Honey and Mr. Johnson, and she'd yet to let it go. Honey was, according to her, *goals*.

"I love you. Keep me posted."

"I love you too."

We ended the call, and I stood there silently, embracing the peace.

The first night, I slept like the dead. The second night, I took in the song of cicadas and whip-poor-wills through the night, much different from the hum of cars below my apartment. Since then, I'd gotten used to the quiet buzz that was living in a small town.

I missed my apartment in the city. Popping down to the cafe across the street, grabbing an overpriced latte, and going back up to my desk to write an article or make a post. That had been my life for so long. And if I wasn't at home, I was on a plane headed to a beautiful city. I'd taken a whole three months to explore Australia a few years ago. My list of countries I hadn't visited was growing smaller and smaller.

I'd be a liar, though, if I didn't admit being here was a breath of fresh air.

A knock at the front door jarred me from my daydreaming. My heart leapt to my throat as I turned, staring toward the foyer for a few moments.

It wasn't like a murderer would knock on the front door in broad daylight.

Right?

Stop being paranoid.

I crossed the kitchen to the foyer and arched up on the balls of my feet, peeking out the glass slivers of the door window.

"Fuck," I mumbled.

Whoever he was, he was tall and hot. I hesitated and then opened the door.

I was met with a grin that could have blinded me. "Haley Bently. Your grandma told me you'd rolled into town, but I haven't seen you around."

I stared at him wordlessly, trying to remember who he was. His eyes lit up with more amusement as he realized I didn't recognize him.

"It's Colt. Colton Hayes. We went to school together. You look amazing."

"*Colton,*" I said, thoroughly shocked.

High school Colton and Adult Colton were not the same. High school Colton had been too tall and lean, with big feet and glasses. Adult Colton looked like Adonis had a baby with a model and added dimples just for good measure.

Jesus Christ.

He nodded with an earnest grin, holding up his arm and flexing his muscle. He was wearing a gray T-shirt, his abs exposed right above his jeans. "I've been working out. Can grow a beard now too."

"Congrats," I said, snorting. I leaned against the doorframe, raising a brow. "It's a surprise to see you."

"I can say the same," he said as he relaxed. "I gotta ask. Is that car yours?"

I looked at my prized Corvette and nodded. "My pride and joy."

"Don't suppose you'd let me take it for a spin?"

"Not a chance in hell," I laughed.

He snapped his fingers, giving me a boyish smile. "Worth asking, anyway. I wanted to invite you to the winery. It's a little outside of town, but it's where everyone hangs out. The old Harlow barn. We turned it into an awesome venue. There will be some familiar faces, I'm sure."

"Oh." I frowned. I wasn't sure I was ready for that. The idea of seeing people I knew so long ago made me itchy.

"No pressure," he added quickly. "Although... your grandma said you might be looking for a place to work temporarily. And I know they're hiring for the bar."

Goddamn it, Honey. One offhand comment and she was convinced I was looking. I was still a travel writer; I was just taking a break until I pulled myself back together. Tina knew about everything that happened and had practically kicked me out to take some time. Plus, she'd worked with me for years. She knew I'd be back in it as soon as I could be.

I snorted and shook my head. "I don't need a place to work. I still have my job. I'm just taking some time off. Although..." I trailed off. It wasn't like I was going to divulge all my secrets to Colton, of all people, but if I didn't find something to do in this small town, I'd go crazy. "I have been restless, so maybe..."

"Could be a nice temporary fix," he offered. "Easy peasy. No pressure."

I studied him warily. "And you work there?"

"I'm the co-owner," he said. "But the big boss will be there. I'll introduce ya."

"Kind of you," I said. I let out a low hum, thinking it over.

I didn't need to work. But if I was planning on staying long term, sitting in my grandma's house would make me go insane. The idea of working at a bar again sounded nice enough. Different, busy, and would keep me from going stir-crazy. I couldn't stay in the house and write articles all day anyways, especially if I couldn't travel.

Maybe it would help me forget about the murder. I swallowed hard.

"What's the place called?"

He looked proud, like he'd just reeled in a big fish. "Citrus Cove Wine & Ciders. Come on over at 6:00 p.m. Taco truck on Fridays. Live music. Remember Sammy Harlow? He sings and plays guitar and is *actually* good. I promise it'll be fun."

"I'll think about it." I certainly wasn't making any promises.

He nodded and then stepped back off the porch. "It's good to see you, Haley. I hope you're here for good reasons."

I said nothing as he left. He got in his pickup truck and disappeared down the quiet street.

He was still Colton. Friendly, easygoing, and more observant than should have been allowed. I'd never hated him, just his best friend.

I sighed and rolled my shoulders.

6:00 p.m.

That gave me a couple of hours to find something good to wear.

If I was going to make a grand entrance, it was going to be the kind no one would forget.

* * *

Citrus Cove Wine & Ciders sat on the edge of Harlow Farms. There was a massive wooden sign with fresh paint on it and a dirt road that led to a full parking lot.

I pulled into an empty spot at the very back and listened to the radio for a few more seconds, finishing out the chorus of one of my favorite songs. I turned it down and got out, glancing up at the peach-colored clouds. The sun was starting to set, the throbbing hum of cicadas rising up in an anthem.

It was hard to beat a Texas sunset. I might not have been

the happiest to be here, but I couldn't help but smile as I took it in.

My stomach did the little flip it always did before a party or social event.

I grabbed my purse and slung it across my body as I slammed the car door. I was wearing a sleeveless cherry-red dress with sandals that gave me a little extra height. My flaxen hair fell in long curls, framing my heart-shaped face. The curls used to be unruly and the source of so much stress, but I'd learned how to tame and embrace them over the last ten years. Coconut oil was a godsend; flat irons were from hell.

I looked hot. I knew it, felt it, and let the confidence slide over me like chainmail.

My stomach fluttered with nerves as I crossed the parking lot, heading toward the front doors. I could still see the bones of the old Harlow barn, but it was remodeled beautifully. The scent of wood hit me as I stepped inside. Tall ceilings, a massive bar that was bustling, and long rows of seats that led toward open glass doors. I could see the deck out back, the old barn filled with the sound of music over the chatter.

It was nice. If it weren't in the middle of hell, I might have even recommended it as a place to visit in the Hill Country.

A soft whistle drew my attention. I looked to my right, spotting Colton at a table. He waved at me, gesturing for me to come over. I darted toward him, immediately greeted by those sitting around him.

A couple of the faces I recognized, a couple I didn't.

"Haley Bently in the flesh, everyone," Colton announced, patting me on the upper back.

Two women were cozied up together. Seated next to them was another couple.

"Jesus Christ, you are stunning. I don't know if you

remember me, I'm Katie," said the platinum blonde to my right.

"Of course I do." I returned her smile. Katie Mays. She was a year older than me, sweet, smart, a good girl through and through, even if I'd seen her throw up at least three times in my life. "It's good to see you again."

"It's good to see you too, hon. Oh, look!" She grinned at me, the corners of her eyes crinkling as she held up her hand, flashing a big shiny rock.

"Oh, come on, Katie," Colton groaned. "Already with that damn diamond?"

The woman who sat next to Katie wiggled her brows. "I like it when she shows me off, Colt. My name is Anna," she added, smiling at me.

"Y'all haven't even finished your first drinks yet, and you're already being *inappropriate*," the other woman at the table teased. "I'm Tabby. This is Marco." Tabby held out her hand, which I shook as Marco nodded in greeting.

"I'm not sure I remember you," I said.

"Oh, Marco lived here for a couple years and then moved to Austin, which is where we live now."

"Nice," I said. "Austin is lovely."

"It'd be even nicer if the house prices weren't so damn much," Marco grumbled.

Tabby patted his chest and winked at me. "We just bought a home. We're feeling it."

"Rent's never cheap," I agreed. "And neither is a mortgage."

I fell into the ease of conversation. Everyone was so easy going, and the atmosphere was pleasant. I found myself glancing around every now and then, still taking in the building. It was hard not to think about all the parties that were secretly (not so secretly) thrown here years ago.

It was weird being back. But it didn't feel as terrible as I expected it to.

"Austin beats many other places though," Anna said. "You're from...?"

"I've been living in Baltimore for a while," I explained. "I travel a lot though."

"Yes," Katie said, beaming. "I follow your articles online. And your Instagram."

"Oh!" I was surprised.

"She's trying to play it cool, but we actually planned our honeymoon based on your recommendations," Anna said with a knowing smirk. "Went on a trip through Europe and even stopped at that cafe in Greece."

"Oh, I love that," I said. And I did. Warmth bloomed through me, and I felt myself relaxing even more. It was rare that I ran into someone who knew anything about my articles, so I felt giddy hearing that they'd followed my recommendations.

This isn't so bad.

I made small talk with them for a few minutes until Colton interrupted us. "I see the boss man. Let me go get him so you can get that *temporary* job."

Katie snorted. "Colt, surely you don't mean—"

"Doubt we can steal you away from the glamor of traveling. Tonight, he could really use the help," Colt interrupted her.

Katie scoffed at him, giving me a wince. I didn't know what to make of that, and didn't have time to ask. Colton steered me away from the table, leading me through the folks waiting in line at the bar.

"Haley!"

I turned around at the familiar voice, looking over the heads of strangers to try to seek out who I knew. I turned abruptly and yelped as I ran straight into a wall—a wall holding an entire flight of ciders.

I gasped as they flew forward, spilling all over my dress. The glass crashed to the floor, shattering over the wood and nicking my ankles. A series of curses lit up around me.

Big, firm hands grabbed my arms. "Are you okay?"

I looked up.

And straight into the eyes of my old high school bully.

CHAPTER FOUR

cameron

IF HALEY BENTLY were a rattlesnake instead of a gorgeous woman, I'd be a dead man.

Hell, maybe I was a goner either way.

Dark brown eyes burned with venom, cider running down her pretty red dress.

I pulled my hands away, blood rushing in my ears. *Holy fuck, that did not just happen. I did not just dump a whole goddamn flight on her.* My entire body felt like it was on fire, a mixture of stress, embarrassment, and something I couldn't put my finger on.

"Nothing to see here," I barked, looking around at the crowd. Everyone returned to their drinks, the chatter resuming. I turned my attention back to her, painfully aware of the anger rolling off in waves.

Her jaw stiffened as my gaze ran down her body.

She'd come out of nowhere. One moment, I was thinking about how busy our night was going to be and how I needed to get these drinks to a table; the next, I was colliding with *her*.

Haley was just as stunning as she'd always been, except

gone were the awkward teenage motions. Her shoulders were pulled back, her face tilted up defiantly. The gossip through the grapevine said she was a woman who traveled the world. She wrote articles and made a living doing what she always wanted, and I could see that. Maybe a lot had changed, but that flash of temper in her gaze sure hadn't.

Drops of blood swirled with the cider on the floor.

"Fuck," I muttered. Some of the glass cut her ankles.

This was the worst way I could have ever run into her again.

"We got towels!" Colton called. I looked up, seeing him and my younger brother, Sammy, rushing over with towels.

"You're bleeding. Let me get the first aid kit. Can you come with me?" I asked.

I reached for her, but she took a step back, evading my touch. "No, thank you," she said sharply as they made it to us.

Colton and Sammy looked dumbstruck, both standing there like fucking idiots. They were *ogling* her. I wanted to punch both of them.

Sammy was the tallest of all of us, but he ducked his head as he greeted her. "Hi, Haley," Sammy said, running his fingers through his dark hair. "It's good to see you. You okay?"

I didn't like how he looked at her.

Hell, I didn't like the way Colton was looking at her either. I was a man, and I knew both of them as well as I knew myself. They thought she was drop-dead-gorgeous, because she was, and were curious. And when she looked at them, it wasn't with an ounce of hatred. It was with a bit of wariness, but nothing like the heat she held for me.

My jaw set hard, my temper already rising up. Not at her of course. But at the two knuckleheads that had yet to peel their eyes off her.

"I'm okay," she said, peering up at my brother. "It's good to see you, Sammy. I think you've gotten even taller."

He grinned. "Six five, and that's not a lie."

She snorted. "I believe you."

"Oh, this isn't how I planned it, but this is the boss," Colt said casually.

A little too casually.

What game was he playing? I glared at him, but he ignored me.

Haley glowered at him too. "Colton, I'm gonna skin you alive and roast you."

He laughed. She continued to glare.

"Haley, I think you're prettier than the last time I saw you," Sammy said, his compliment warm and sincere.

That made her lighten up. She smiled at him. "I see how it is. Good cop, bad cop."

"I'm just saying," Sammy teased. "You're stunning. Sure you aren't staying in Citrus Cove forever?"

"Sammy Harlow, when did you become such a flirt?"

Their easy banter infuriated me. My temple pulsed. My hands flexed.

I couldn't take it anymore.

Without another word, I scooped up the girl who hated me more than the church ladies hated Satan. I moved toward the back of the house, taking her kicking and shouting through the doors.

"Cameron Harlow, you put me fucking down before I kick you in the balls! *Put me down!*"

My grip on her tightened. "Easy, darlin'. I just want to get you patched up." My voice was a Southern laissez-faire, but that was nowhere near the way I felt. This was crazy. I was carting her off like a fucking caveman. What the fuck was I doing?

I made it to the office and kicked open the door, finally setting her down. The top of her head came up to my chin, but the way she carried herself made me feel like she was taller than I was.

"You've got a lot of fucking nerve." She seethed. "How fucking dare you manhandle me like that? This isn't the Wild West."

It was about to be. Something about her had always riled me up—back then it was a lot of things but now that I was an adult, I recognized what it was.

Lust. Pure and simple and dangerous.

"I want to make sure you're okay." I enunciated every word.

"And I'm fine taking care of myself."

Bullshit.

"Sit," I said, pointing at the chair.

The office was simple and well-kept, the chair one that my mother had picked out. She had an eye for anything decor related.

"I don't need your help," she snapped.

"I *need* to make sure you're okay," I grunted, going to my desk and digging out the first aid kit. "I'm sorry about the dress." It was a pretty dress. A really pretty dress. In fact, Haley was the type of gorgeous that would keep you up at night.

Fuck. I felt like a teenager all over again. I fumbled as I opened the first aid box up, pulling out everything I could possibly use. Did I have everything I needed? I should have thought about getting a bigger kit. What if—

"Cameron, I'm fine. I don't want your help. You're the last motherfucker in the state that I'd like to see right now. I'm going," she snapped, heading toward the door.

"Woman, if you don't sit down and let me make sure you're okay, I'm going to call your grandma and tell her you need stitches."

Haley made a noise somewhere between a gasp and the hiss of a cornered cat. "You wouldn't dare."

"I fucking would."

I raised my gaze, meeting hers. Her cheeks were flushed, her arms crossed but not covering her breasts, which... I could see the outline of her nipples.

God help me, I was going to hell.

I cleared my throat. "Are you cold?"

She stared at me and then looked down, shaking her head. "Hate is too kind of a word for what I feel right now."

Yep, that'd been the wrong thing to ask. Fuck. Where was Mr. Smooth right now? The guy that could flirt with every lady in the room? I knew how to seduce. I knew how to woo. But everything I'd learned since the last time I'd seen her flew out the window.

I was fucking up all over again.

I'd sworn to myself if I ever laid eyes on her again, I'd make things right. I'd show her I wasn't an asshole. And that I was sorry for all the shit I'd done to her.

But here I was, making a mess all over again.

I looked down at her ankles again and cursed silently, grabbing the whole damn kit and rushing to her. "Sit. Please."

She looked down and paled, her shoulders stiffening. "Oh."

"*Oh* is right," I said.

The glass had gotten her good. She sat down in the chair, and I went to my knees, not caring if I got her blood on me. This was my fault. All my fault. Plus, I kept a change of clothes in the truck.

I reached for her left ankle and slid off her sandal, wincing as I opened up a pack of antiseptic towelettes.

"It's a lot of blood," she whispered.

I looked up at her. She was getting paler with each second.

I fought the urge to tuck back a loose golden curl, my chest squeezing. She was so goddamn beautiful she took my breath away. *Earth to Cam, dickhead.* "Does blood make you faint?"

"Didn't use to."

She sounded very far away now. I stared at her, not sure what to do. And what did she mean by "didn't use to"? What happened?

Her eyes glazed over, her lips pressing together.

Fuck. I'd rather see her pissed off and cursing than looking like this.

Since I already fucked up any chance I had of making it right with her, I said the first thing that might break her out of that trance. "Remember that time I dumped beer on your head at the party?" I asked as I pulled her foot into my lap.

She let out a hiss, her expression becoming deadly. "Yes. How could I forget? That's one of those things a girl remembers. Remember that time I punched you in your face?"

Despite the situation, I smiled. "You had a damn good punch, too."

Her ankle was slender in my grip. Blood was still rushing in my ears, and rushing *down*. She smelled sweet, like honey-suckle and jasmine.

"Hunter beat the shit out of me for that," I said, letting out a humorless chuckle. *Get yourself under control.* She went still as I wiped up the blood, cleaning the nicks from the glass. It looked like none of the shards had stuck, at least. "I deserved it. Do you want me to call an ambulance? Or take you to the emergency room?"

She was silent for one beat. Two. "No," she said firmly. "No emergency room. No questions. I don't need that right now. And yeah. You did deserve it. I could never get the scent of beer out of the fabric and had to work overtime for two weeks to afford another." She snorted. "To think I had to work so damn much for something so cheap. And that I thought Honey was ignorant that we'd gone out that night."

I was torn between snorting and wincing. Snorting because anyone that could pull something over on her grandmother had to be a mastermind. And wincing because I would never stop feeling like an idiot for the things I did to Haley.

My family wasn't necessarily rich, but we'd never hurt for money. If I ruined a piece of clothing, I never had to work to get another. I'd caused more damage than I ever realized.

"You sure no hospital?"

"Yep," she said. "Just do your best, and I'll leave. Better yet, let me go, and I'll take care of it myself. I'm perfectly capable of putting on my own Band-Aids."

"I want to make sure you're okay," I insisted. "I'm sure you're capable of it, but this is my business, and I feel bad for what happened. I wasn't paying attention."

"I don't need your pity."

For fuck's sake. I couldn't win.

I pulled out a stack of Hello Kitty Band-Aids and scowled. Fucking hell, I really couldn't win. "How in the hell did these get in here?"

She stared. I stared.

"Is this a joke?" she whispered.

"No. I swear I didn't put these in here." I was going to murder my co-owner, who also happened to be in charge of medical supplies, who also happened to be the one that invited Haley tonight.

"I can't walk out there with those on. I've already been humiliated."

"You? Darlin', no one is going to think anything of you. I'm the one that ran into you."

"Did you do it on purpose?"

That hurt. I looked up at her, feeling a spark of anger, but it was quickly doused by frustration with myself. "No," I said, my jaw tight. "I'd never do that. I promise you that I'm not the monster I was in high school. I'm not an asshole."

She was absolutely unconvinced.

Another silky curl slipped free, and I fought the urge to push it back. I had a feeling if I tried that, she'd break my jaw.

"I think you might have to go with these," I said, hissing through clenched teeth. I dug through the rest of the box to no avail. "I bet Colton put them in there as a prank."

"Just hurry up. I'm going to go home and get cleaned up. I don't want my grandma to see blood."

"She's tough," I murmured. My hands moved a little faster as I strategically placed what felt like a hundred Hello Kitty Band-Aids on her ankles. She let out a soft breath as I placed the final one and stood. She snatched up her sandals and shook her head, muttering under her breath about men.

I looked up at her. If I were a good man, my cock wouldn't have hardened in my blue jeans from looking at her from this angle.

But maybe I wasn't a good man. My zipper felt like it was about to burst, and I prayed she couldn't tell from where she was.

I was on my knees in front of Haley Bently, and she looked so mad she could spit, but I was so turned on that I felt like I could come just kneeling here.

"Thanks for nothing. Stay out of my way while I'm in town."

She left me kneeling there.

"Fuck," I breathed out.

That had been a disaster. I closed my eyes, thinking back. Back to that damn party so long ago. It was just a blur, but I remembered two things. Her looking prettier than a peach and

45

my brother truly beating the shit out of me for the first time in our lives. The memory hit me hard.

"Hunter! I was just joking!"

Hunter shoved me back against an oak tree, his fist hitting me in the stomach hard enough that I threw up. I'd never seen him this mad before.

He slammed me back up against the tree, his fist knocking straight into my jaw. My ears were ringing, my muscles going weak. I was drunk, and he was stronger than me.

He lowered his voice, pulling me close. "If I ever catch you speaking to or harassing a girl like that again, I will bury you, Cam. Mama raised you better than this. No brother of mine will behave like that, do you understand?"

I stared at him, hot blood running from my nose.

He gripped my hair, letting out a low snarl. "Do you understand?"

"Yes," I whispered. "It was just—just a joke."

"That girl doesn't have money," Hunter snapped. "She can't just go get new clothes. Her grandma is supposed to be retiring this year and is instead working three jobs so she can raise them. I've never seen you be cruel like that, and I'll never see it again. Because if you ever are, you will meet God."

"Hey, what the hell was that?"

I looked up to the doorway and blinked, seeing Sammy there. Like me, he was tall and lean, but where my dark hair was cut short, his was long and wavy. He glared at me the same way Hunter had all those years ago. Of course, we'd all fought, forgiven, and forgotten. We were brothers. Harlows through and through.

"What do you mean?" I grunted, finally standing. At least I was no longer sporting a hard-on.

"What do you mean *what do I mean*? What just happened

with Haley? She just fled the building like you'd done something wrong. This isn't high school anymore, Cam."

"Fuck off," I snarled, immediately sour. "I didn't do anything wrong. I patched up the cuts since she was so damn insistent on not going to the doctor. And someone replaced all our Band-Aids with children's ones."

Sammy crossed his arms as I cleaned up. "You're working too much."

"Then pick up the fucking slack," I growled. We both held our breaths for a moment, and then I sighed. I raked my fingers through my hair, trying to find some sort of balance. Just breathing the same air as Haley had turned me upside down. "I'm sorry. I'm stressed. Seeing her was... was something else. And I'm trying to keep everything afloat until Hunter gets back. Mom and Dad should be back next week too, so I won't have to worry about the farm anymore."

"If you need more help, just ask," Sammy said. "I can try and shift my schedule around this week. But Colt thinks you should hire Haley, and I agree. If she's willing, of course."

"I think that Haley would rather work for Satan," I sighed, looking down at my hands.

Sammy snorted. "Maybe you should send her some flowers. And a gift card."

"Maybe," I murmured. "I need to get cleaned up and get back out there."

"We got everything cleaned up. All the glass and cider. I'm glad you got the type of floors you did—it was easy. And Colt and I worked the bar. We can both stay for the rest of the night."

I nodded, relaxing just a hair. "Why her?"

"Why Haley?"

"Yeah. Why should I hire her? Both of you seem to think so. I'm sure there are others that would apply."

"Sure, if you want to put them through the TABC course and get them an underage license to sell."

I snorted. "Oh, come on."

"Or—even better—I heard Betty Jacobs wants to take a break from her Sunday school lessons. You could hire her. Can you imagine? She'd be scoffing about how everyone in here was a sinner and needed to repent while pouring them a glass of red."

Both of us grinned like idiots. The idea of old Betty slinging shots was enough to make me rethink sending Haley some flowers and offering a truce.

"You know pretty girls sell alcohol. And Haley Bently is hot as fuck. The city years did her good."

"I think she's always looked like that," I mumbled.

Sammy arched a brow, his eyes narrowing. "Right. My point is, we live in a small town. Everyone already has a job. And no one wants the high schoolers around. They'll just sneak drinks and do stupid stuff."

He had a point.

I hated that, but he did.

Haley was really the best option. I doubted she'd say yes. She had no reason to, especially since I was someone she had a grudge against.

"Take off for the night. Wash off her blood, for god's sake. And Colton and I will work."

I gave my brother a long look. At some point, he'd become a full adult, and it still startled me sometimes. Especially when he was telling *me* what to do. "It was supposed to be my night," I sighed. "Both of you were scheduled off. All of us already work five nights a week..."

"We're getting too big for that." Sammy shrugged. "It's a good sign. Year three and maybe it's time to hire help that isn't family. Besides, all the extra help is out of town. It's the three of us holding down the fort. And fuck it. If you don't hire her, I will. She likes me."

"I'll handle it." Because the idea of my brother getting close to the only girl I'd ever bullied made me see red.

I would earn her forgiveness.

Starting with that dress.

CHAPTER FIVE

I MANAGED to sneak upstairs without Honey noticing. I shut the bathroom door behind me and breathed out. It was small and clean, the shower curtain patterned with magnolias and the walls painted baby pink. I'd picked up some of my skin-care products earlier this week at an outlet, and the bottles lined the small sink top, the familiarity of them grounding me.

Citrus Cove would never be home to me. I didn't know what I was thinking, going over to get drinks with people I barely knew.

What the fuck just happened?

Fucking Cameron Harlow, that was what.

I shucked off my dress angrily and sat on the toilet seat, fighting tears as I looked down at my ankles. I'd never been one to blanch at the sight of blood, but I'd nearly lost it. The entire time that Cameron put these on, I'd been spiraling.

Well, until he pissed me off.

For once, I was glad that I hated him so damn much. It was the distraction I'd needed to stop thinking about the blood. The murder. The woman I'd held as she died.

My body shivered. I closed my eyes, trying to think about anything else. Somehow, I ended up thinking about the first time Cameron was ever mean to me.

"Everyone welcome Haley Bently. She's our new student."

Mrs. Abbott had a Southern drawl to her words as she announced my presence. I stood in front of the small class, thinking about how my old school had been so much bigger.

I didn't understand why Mom said we had to stay with my grandma. She'd kissed us goodbye a couple of days ago, and every time I'd tried to call her, she hadn't picked up.

"Go ahead and take your seat, Haley," Mrs. Abbott said, giving me a gentle push.

I walked down between the seats, picking a chair in front of an older boy. This school was small enough that some classes had multiple grades in it. I blushed as he stared at me, his eyes reminding me of bluebonnets. He had dark hair and tan skin.

I settled into my seat, swallowing hard. I hated that I'd to come to a new school, but at least there were some cute guys.

The teacher started going on about homework and lessons. This was our history class, and they were in the middle of Texas history. I listened to her as I pulled out my notebook.

I had to make good grades so I could go to college and get out of this place. I wanted to make Mom proud.

I felt something hit the back of my head and frowned, reaching around to pat my curls. I couldn't feel anything, so I turned, seeing the boy grinning ear to ear.

I frowned and then turned back, refocusing on Mrs. Abbott. Pow.

This time, I reached back and felt something sticky. I squeaked as I pulled my hand away.

Gum.

No. No, no, no. If something sticky got in my hair, it would take days to get out.

I turned in my seat. "What the hell?" I asked.

He raised a brow, letting out a soft giggle as he slid his pack of gum under his binder.

"Haley, is there something wrong?"

"If you tell on me, you're dead," he whispered.

"This isn't kindergarten," I snapped, turning back in my seat. "He just put gum in my hair."

The class erupted into giggles. Heat flamed in my cheeks, my heart pounding.

"You're dead," he whispered. "No one will be your friend now."

He'd been right. Finding friends had been harder than ever for me after that. And getting that fucking gum out of my hair had been a nightmare. Sarah had to cut it out, leaving my hair uneven for a few months until it grew back out.

I breathed in. Breathed out.

What a shithead.

I'd stopped shaking. I leaned back, looking up at the ceiling.

After tonight, I felt like the new girl all over again. But at least I wasn't thinking about the killer anymore.

IT'D BEEN three days since I'd gone to Citrus Cove Wine & Ciders and a week and a half since I'd rolled back into the sleepy Texas town. The glass cuts were mostly healed, and I was settling in a bit more.

I still hadn't heard from Sarah.

"Morning, sweetheart."

I looked up from the coffee pot as Honey came into the kitchen. She was already dressed, her perfume disrupting the heavenly scent of burned coffee beans.

"Going somewhere?" I asked.

"Oh, yes. Pour me a cup. I have to go up to the DMV and prove I can still drive. It's ridiculous."

I fought off a laugh. "Are you taking your pickup?"

"Of course. What else would I drive? I ain't walking."

I poured her a cup of coffee and handed it to her, smiling. "Are you sure that thing still works?"

"Better than that pretty car you got," she teased.

It *was* pretty. My Corvette was one of my favorite adult purchases I'd made.

I took a sip of coffee as she settled down at the kitchen table, holding her mug like it was a lifeline. She looked tired.

"Are you okay?" I asked, frowning.

"Your sister called," she said, her voice tight. "The boys are coming over this afternoon."

"Is that a bad thing?"

"Of course not. I love them. They're a bit rowdy, but they keep me spry."

"Then what is it?"

She was quiet. I could see her weighing what to say and what not to say.

"She and David are having marital problems."

I narrowed my eyes. "Marital problems" was a broad statement. "What kind of *marital* problems?"

"I've been asked not to say." Her lips tightened, her eyes burning with what could only be read as anger. There was a lot more simmering under the surface. "He's a son of a bitch," she finally murmured, soft and full of rage. She took a long sip of coffee, looking out the window. She reached out, fussing with the sheer white curtain.

"Is she okay?" My heart fluttered. We might be estranged, but I still loved her. Missed her. And wished that we hadn't grown so far apart. But we lived different lives. "I'll watch the boys if you'd like. They're my nephews."

"Sweetie, they don't know you."

My heart clenched. She wasn't wrong. If I had any regrets over how I'd lived my life the last decade, it was that I'd missed out on a relationship with my nephews. I still wanted to be the best aunt they could possibly have. But, that wouldn't happen unless I started to get to know them both.

"You know I don't mean that in a mean way. But those boys just know your name."

"We've talked on the phone a couple times."

"When they were five. They're ten now."

We were both silent. I turned and poured myself more coffee, blinking back tears. Guilt welled up from all the wounds I thought twelve years had stitched up. But stitches could tear, and being here was doing just that.

I went to the kitchen table and sat across from her, reaching for her hand. I squeezed it the way she'd squeezed mine many times before.

"I've been gone," I said. "I know I've been gone. And I know I've missed holidays. I know that I just left."

"I don't understand why you did." She wouldn't look me in the eye, her gaze fixated on the window.

"I had to," I whispered. "I had to get out for myself. I needed to get out in the world, to find myself. I felt trapped here. There are parts of me that never fit into a place like this, and leaving was the only way I could save myself."

"I know," she said. "And I'm proud of you and all your success. You've traveled the world. You broke the mold of our family. Went to college and got a good job. You've done it all on your own. Never asked for a dime."

"I have done it." I swallowed hard. "You did everything you could for me. Don't think I don't remember how much you worked. Three jobs to get us by. When mom died, she left a lot of financial burdens behind. You got through that, kept this house, and raised your granddaughters while grieving her. Any strength I have is because I've learned from the best."

She nodded, her shoulders deflating. "I tried to do my best by you two. Lord knows I did something wrong with your mom. I wasn't there for her when she needed me. Sometimes, I worry that I messed up with you. That I kept you tied down, put too much pressure on you. I worry about Sarah." Her voice broke, and she drew in a breath, looking back at me. "I love you. More than I have words for. And I know you'll fly away again, but I'm happy you're home. If even only for a short time."

"I'm happy I'm home too," I whispered. "This was the only place I could go."

"You're always welcome," she said, grabbing my hand in return and squeezing. "*Always*. No matter what you do or how you and Sarah fight, you're always welcome in my home."

"Thank you," I murmured. I drew back, wiping my eyes before tears could fall. We both collected ourselves. "So. How can I help with the boys?"

"Well. You can be here when they come over. We'll order some pizza and see what happens."

"Sounds good," I said.

A knock echoed through the house, followed by the doorbell. I started to stand up, but she waved her hand, popping out of her seat before I could.

"I got it," she said.

I settled back in, humming to myself as she opened the front door. I heard her laugh, the voice of a man's soft baritone following.

Within a couple of minutes, she came back holding a gift bag from Saks Fifth Avenue, her eyes glittering with mischief. "You didn't tell me you and Cam were going."

"Going?" I echoed, scowling. "Going to hell?"

"No," she cackled, setting the bag on the table. "Said you came over to his winery Friday night. So that's where you were, hmm?"

I recognized the interrogation. She slid the bag toward me, clearly wanting me to open it. "A gift for you. He said it's his 'truce offering.' If that's from Saks Fifth Avenue, then it sounds like you got yourself a boyfriend."

She wiggled her brows at me, and I shook my head. "Don't go getting any ideas. I'm sure he just reused the bag." I hadn't told her about what happened Friday night and wasn't planning on it.

I stared at the bag for a moment, cursing under my breath. I stood and pulled out the tissue paper jutting from the top, drawing out a note.

Second dress I've ruined. I'm sorry for both. I don't know how to make it up to you, but hopefully this can be the start.
- Cam

Holy fuck. I looked into the bag and just blinked.
This motherfucker.
He hadn't reused the bag.

I reached in and pulled out a cherry-red dress that was the same color as my other, except the material was a lot softer. I immediately reached for the price tag, but he'd ripped it off.
Bastard.

I let the fabric unfurl and sucked in a breath. It was perfect. Perfect size, perfect cut. A V-neck in the front and the back, and it had pockets.

He'd bought me a dress with pockets.

Honey was already digging back into the bag. She let out a low chuckle. "There's another."

Fucking bastard.

I cursed again, and she raised a brow. "Haley Marie."

"I'm grown," I protested. I was seething.

"Yes, and still a lady in my house."

My eyes almost rolled, but I knew better than that. Instead, I draped the red dress over the back of the chair and pulled out the other, highly aware of the way she hawk-eyed me.

A soft gasp left me. The dress was the same deep blue as the one from all those years ago, but a lot nicer. I held it up, admiring the eyelet pattern and the sweetheart neckline. I would look damn good in this. It was casual but stunning and exactly the kind of dress I would have picked up.

Honey peeked around, giving me the *knowing* look. "He's got taste. I've always liked him. You know he and Colton cut those big branches and saved the roof on this house, for free?"

No, I didn't know that. Because I didn't live here in a small town where people just helped each other. And I didn't keep up with my family.

"What time are the boys coming over?" I asked absent-mindedly.

"Around five. I got my appointment."

"Right. I'll be home by then," I said, shoving both dresses back in the bag.

"You better be nice to him," she scolded.

"I'll be sweeter than a peach."

CHAPTER SIX

cameron

"YOU THINK I can just be bought, Harlow?"

Haley slammed the gift bag down on the counter in front of me, crossing her arms. I regarded her over the top of my laptop, trying to focus on the situation and not how damn gorgeous she looked. Morning light poured into the winery, catching the ends of her curls and turning them golden.

"Good morning to you," I mused.

"Seriously. What the fuck is this?"

"I ruined your dress." And was determined to do whatever I fucking could to replace it. I'd buy her ten thousand dresses if it would take that hostile look out of her eye.

She let out a frustrated noise. "And? I can buy my own dress. I'm not a teenager anymore. Besides, the cider came out in the wash."

I shrugged, trying to ignore the way my heart pounded a little faster. My stomach twisted, but I kept my poker face of steel. "Consider it a gift. No big deal."

"It's an expensive gift."

"And?"

"I don't need it."

"Then donate it, Haley."

"You can return it and get your money back," she said, tapping her foot on the concrete floor.

"I threw the receipt away," I responded, giving her an innocent smile. Well, as innocent as it could possibly be. Her expression told me I wasn't fooling her.

"And what if they don't fit?"

I raised a brow now. "Have you tried them on yet? I have a good eye." Giving gifts and being prepared for anything were two of my love languages.

Not that I was in love with her.

Her gaze narrowed, her lips pressing together. My gaze fell on them, on how soft they looked.

"They'll fit," she finally said.

We both stayed silent, simply staring at each other. I shifted in my seat. It seemed that everything I'd felt the other night when I saw her was real, despite my attempts at convincing myself otherwise. Heat crawled up my spine, the kind that made me feel like I was baking on a blacktop in the July sun. It spread through my body, and I swallowed hard.

Was I blushing?

Fuck.

This woman was making me blush.

Her brows furrowed. She finally spoke, ending our stand-off. "What is this? What are you doing? And how come you just showed up on my grandma's front porch like that? I don't know what you think you're doing, but it's not going to work. You can't buy your way to my good side. Not after everything that happened."

I snorted now, pushing my laptop aside. "I've been showing up on her doorstep for years, Haley. That's what we do around here. I try to help everyone I can, in fact." I drummed my fingers on the counter. She was already getting under my skin again. "What do I have to do to prove that I'm not evil? And that we might even be good friends?"

She let out a laugh, a low, sultry one that went straight to my cock. "Stop harassing me," she said. "Stop being..."

"Being what?"

"Annoying. Rude. Mean. An asshole. A fucking small town stupid bastard that I want nothing to do with."

Ouch. "I'm trying to make it up to you," I said, my jaw stiffening. "And I'm asking—what do you need from me? Because right now, you're the only person I'd like to hire to help out around here because I'm drowning. Slowly and painfully."

"Good," she sniffed. But her eyes flickered with something else. "I don't actually need a job."

"I know that. I've heard about how well you've done. You've made a name for yourself."

"I have a job in Baltimore. One that pays me a lot of money. One that let me buy a Corvette my first year," she continued. "I won't even be here for very long. Maybe just the summer."

I fought off a smile. I was proud of her, but I was sure if I expressed that, it would piss her off. So I just kept my words simple. "Cool."

"It would be temporary. But..."

I raised my brows again. There was a "but".

Everything before "but" was bullshit, right? Did that mean I had a chance?

"I'd like to be out of the house more. And I've worked in bars before. It's not hard. I could do it easily."

"Okay," I said, doing my best to play it cool.

Haley Bently was going to work for me. Which meant that she'd be around me more. Which meant I might get to show her the real me and make up for every time I'd ever hurt her.

60

"I'd only do three days a week. I'm still going to write while I'm gone from Baltimore."

"So you'll be here all summer?" I asked, curious.

In fact, I was curious about a lot of things and had gotten almost no answers. She'd blocked me on social media, and then when she left Citrus Cove, she'd cut the entire town from her life. I'd thought about making another account to follow her, but that felt like crossing boundaries.

I did, however, sometimes read her travel articles. I had a list of places I wanted to visit one day because of her. Not that I would bring that up now, or admit that I knew what she did for work. Or how good she was at it.

She shrugged and surprised me by taking a seat opposite, sliding into the barstool. "Maybe. Maybe not. None of your business."

All I could think about was that I was sitting with her.

"So, you're a writer?" I choked out, reaching for my sweet tea. The glass was sweating from the heat, just like me.

Her eyes narrowed. "Yes, I write for a travel magazine. I also freelance for websites and such. Most of what I write is about destinations and hot spots I've visited. Good restaurants, how to get deals, and all of that."

"That's really cool."

"I love it," she sighed, relaxing just the slightest. "It's taken me all over the world. I've seen things I always only dreamed of. And I love it when I find the right vacation for a couple, family, or even an individual. It opens their eyes to what's out there. New cultures, new people, new cities."

I could see that she loved it. Her smile reached her eyes, lighting up the whole room. I'd never seen her like this up close, and it was as if all my worries were being chased away.

How do I keep her smiling like that?

"What's your favorite place you've been?" I asked, leaning forward a little.

"Oh, that's hard. I loved the beaches in Australia. But nothing can compare to this Texas heat, so it's not like it bothered me. I was driving through the tablelands in Queensland one day and stopped by this roadside restaurant. It was such a hidden gem. That's my favorite, when I find the small places no one knows about."

"That sounds wonderful," I murmured, enchanted.

She nodded and then frowned, as if realizing she was sitting with me. Her back went straight, her shoulders stiffening. "I should get going. I'm seeing the boys tonight."

"Sarah's?" I asked.

"Yeah."

I nodded, pressing my lips together. She was observant and noticed my change.

"What is it?" she asked. "My grandma had that same damn look."

"I can't get involved," I said. Because David Connor had tried to get a restraining order on me multiple times over the last few years. He was permanently banned from all the bars in Citrus Cove and knew if he stepped foot on my property, I'd probably shoot him. And if Colt was around? He was a dead man.

But I didn't tell her any of that. It wasn't my place to, and while I no longer really knew Sarah, I worried about her. I worried about Jake and little David. They were young and helpless, and it ate me up that their father was such a bad person.

She rolled her eyes, blowing out a breath. "Fine. Thanks for nothing."

"Wait, so do you want the job?"

She slid off the stool and grabbed the bag with the dresses. "Yeah. Wednesday, Thursdays, Fridays. Five to close."

"Yes, ma'am," I said, amused.

"Thirty an hour plus tips."

"Fuck," I muttered. "That's a lot."

"I'll throw an article out there for your business and I'll unblock you on Instagram," she said, smirking. "See you Wednesday."

With that, she left me sitting there.

Hell.

Sammy had been right though. The truce gift worked.

I spent three hours in that damn store yesterday. Finding the right color of dress, the right size, second-guessing myself. Letting myself sink into the fantasy that I was buying gifts for my future wife.

It was fucked-up, maybe. But something about her stirred me up. I'd dropped $1,500 on two dresses without blinking. It hadn't been about the money though; it had been about finding the right dresses. All because I wanted her to know I was sorry. It still didn't feel like enough.

But maybe I was one step closer to proving to Haley that I wasn't the asshole she thought I was. And I couldn't complain about her working here, not when that meant I got to be around her more.

I picked up my phone and called Sammy, humming to myself.

"Yeah?" he answered.

"Want to trade shifts? I'll work Wednesday if you work Saturday."

"Sure, I guess. Why?"

"Training the new hire."

He snorted. I narrowed my eyes.

"I just have one question for you, Cam."

"What?" I gritted out.

"Should I consider her a no go? As in no flirting, no asking out, no taking to bed—"

I hung up on him, fuming. What kind of question was that?

I shoved off my stool and grabbed my drink, snapping my laptop closed. I needed to take a walk. Maybe through the orchard. I could go check on the trees and grapes and... anything that would distract me from thinking about her.

I fished out my keys from my back pocket and made my way out to my truck, locking up the barn behind me.

Within a few minutes, I was pulling up to my parents' house. I grabbed my baseball cap and fit it over my dark hair, studying myself in the rearview mirror.

I was slowly going crazy. It felt that way anyways. I shouldn't have been feeling this possessive of Haley. She hated me. I'd bullied her for years when we were growing up and made her life a living hell. But damn it, I didn't want someone else to take her out.

I wanted to take her out. I wanted to take her to dinner, to find out what she liked and disliked. It was the same obsession I'd had when I was younger, except now I was grown and not a complete dumbass.

Fuck, if only I could go back.

It was a shot in hell that I'd ever hear her say yes to a date, but I was going to try.

I slammed my truck door and stretched for a moment before going to the house. I hoped they were enjoying Tampa, but I was never going to agree to housesit again if Hunter was out of town too.

Plus, it felt strange when they weren't home. The pale white wood gleamed in sunlight, the front porch decorated with all sorts of plants. Honeysuckle climbed up the lattice on the side of the house, the familiarity calming me.

Our house had been here for what felt like forever. The foundation was as rooted as the trees that grew in the orchard, the farm a heart that gave our family its lifeblood. I was proud to call it home, proud of the memories that I had here.

And for once, even though I missed my parents being in town and Hunter too, I was happy for the silence.

I went up the steps and unlocked the front door, greeted by their black Lab, Benny. Part of the reason I was splitting my time between here and the taproom was because of him. At eleven years old, he was getting up there in age. At least Colt was able to help out some too.

"Come on, boy," I said. "Going for a walk."

He scampered out behind me as we went back down, his nose on the ground as we rounded the house and went down the path that led through my mother's garden. She'd always had a green thumb, able to grow almost anything.

I pushed out the small gate and started into the orchard, letting out a breath. One that I felt like I'd been holding since Haley left.

Fuck.

I had to win her over. I had to keep trying. I'd taken a step forward today with her, and now I just had to make sure I didn't trip and fall.

CHAPTER SEVEN

BUTTERFLIES FLUTTERED through my stomach as a knock echoed through the house. Honey gave me a knowing look, arching a silver brow.

"Want to answer it?"

No. Yes? I felt like throwing up. "Sure," I said. "I'll grab it."

I was about to see my nephews for the first time in person. *I'm such a bad aunt. Fuck.*

"I did talk to Sarah, and she knows you're seeing them," Honey said.

I nodded and went to the front door, pasting on a smile as I opened it.

Jake and David were on the other side, both tall for their age and grinning. Behind them was a man I'd only seen in pictures, their dad. Other David was what I'd labeled him in my mind. He had brown hair that was cut short and a menacing glare. Crooked nose, the scent of alcohol wafting off him.

What the fuck? Had he been drinking? I felt a series of red flags go up in my mind but smothered them all so I could greet my nephews.

66

"Hi," I said, smiling at the two of them.

"Aunt Haley!" Jake beamed, throwing his arms around me hard enough to knock my breath free.

My heart squeezed a little. "Oh my god, you're so strong!" I exclaimed. "Honey and I got some pizza, and we'll watch a movie. Hopefully ones you like. And I may or may not have gotten some ice cream too."

He grinned, one of his teeth missing, and then slipped past me.

"Hey, David," I said to my other nephew.

"Davy," he corrected.

"Davy," I repeated.

He gave me a wary smile, glancing up at his father. His dad rolled his eyes. "Stupid nickname."

What the fuck did he just say?

Davy's expression fell, and he moved past me too.

Which left me standing alone.

"You shouldn't be here," David growled.

I raised a brow and glanced behind my shoulder, making sure the kids were out of earshot because *What. The. Fuck.* I caught a glimpse of them hugging Honey.

"I'm not sure why it matters to you," I said lightly. Why was he being such an asshole?

Other David continued to glare at me like I was the dirt on the bottom of his ugly boots. "No one wants you here, and you're just going to be a bad influence on my sons."

"On *my* nephews. And you're the one that was just a complete ass to Davy for no reason."

"It's a stupid fucking nickname. He'll learn that eventually."

"What is your problem?" I whispered, glaring. "We've never even spoken before."

He snorted, leveling me with a disgusted glare. I took a step

67

forward, shutting the door behind me. I didn't want the boys to hear me or him.

I may not have been in their lives for the last few years, but I still felt a protective streak a mile wide.

"You smell like alcohol," I said, keeping my voice low. "Are you under the influence right now?" The idea of him drinking while driving my nephews here was enough to make me want to kick him down the stairs.

"You mind your fucking business," he snarled, stepping closer to me.

Rage rolled through me, hot and heavy and fierce. I might have been half his size, but I would put him down if I needed to. I'd taken enough lessons with Emma to at least have some basic self defense.

Was this how he was around Sarah? Around the kids? Around Honey?

Was this the *marital* problem she mentioned?

"I told Sarah that you being back would be a problem. No one wants you here. You abandoned them and ran off to be some worldly whore."

Worldly whore. I might have laughed had I not seen the hate in his gaze. I ground my teeth together, keeping my shoulders back. He wasn't the first man to say something like that to me and wouldn't be the last. And brother-in-law or not, I had no inclination to be nice.

"Are you drunk?" I asked again, keeping my voice low. I didn't keep the edge of judgment from it. Fuck him if he was.

"Fuck you," he said, taking a step back. His eyes darkened with hate, and he turned, stumbling down the steps back to his car. A different truck pulled up to the house, but I didn't take my eyes off him as he shot me the bird, getting in his front seat and cranking the engine. He leaned his head out the window and glanced at the newcomer, scoffing. "Of course that fucker shows up. You should leave before something bad happens."

He rolled up his window and backed out, peeling down the street and leaving a cloud of black smoke in his wake. A shiver went up my spine, my gut clenching.

"What the fuck was that?"

My heart lurched as I looked over at none other than Cameron. He was crossing the yard, wearing a brooding scowl. He wore a denim shirt that was unbuttoned and a black tee underneath that fit him a little too well.

I eyed him warily. I hated him just a smidge less at the moment, but was going to blame that on timing. "What are you doing here?"

I didn't have an ounce of rage left in me. I could feel it all draining away, the interaction with David sapping me. I felt a bit of relief that Cameron showed up when he did.

"I'm here to drop off some paperwork for the job," he explained, coming to the bottom step. The toes of his boots hit the whitewashed wood, his belt buckle gleaming in the warm, peachy glow of the setting sun. He held up a folder with papers inside of it. "I don't have your number, so I wanted to bring these over. It has what we agreed upon and my contact info. Was he bothering you, Haley? Are you okay?"

My eyes lifted toward the street again. I was unable to shake the feeling that everyone knew what the hell was going on except me. I hardly remembered David from school, but he'd never had the mean streak I'd just caught a glimpse of. Not to mention, I'd never done a damn thing to him. The hate I'd just met made me feel like I was the wicked witch from Baltimore.

"Hey. Haley."

I looked at Cameron, blinking a couple of times. The last of the sun was turning his dark hair a pretty shade of russet, his well-kept beard a little redder than I realized.

"My nephews are here," I said suddenly, but I went down the steps to meet him. I stopped on the one right in front of him and still wasn't as tall as him. But I liked seeing him eye to eye like this.

He had pretty eyes.

Stop that.

"I got that. What did he say to you? I caught the tail end of it. And it didn't sound like he was saying anything pleasant." His jaw clenched, his posture still stiff.

"Is that a surprise?"

There was a standoff of information happening. We were silent for one beat, two.

"I don't have time for this," I muttered, letting out a frustrated breath. "I need to get back inside and spend time with David—Davy—and Jake. They don't know me, and I'd like for them to."

Why in the hell was I telling him that?

Cameron swallowed hard, his expression finally relaxing. He handed me the papers and then shoved his hands in his pockets. "It's not my place to tell you about your family, Hal. There's a lot that has happened since you've been gone."

Hal. The corner of my mouth lifted. "Starting with you having some sort of reckoning?"

"I had that the moment you left."

That wasn't what I thought he'd say. My heart skipped a beat. "Can you please tell me what I'm missing here with them? With Honey and with Sarah? I know I've been gone, but..."

It was hard not to think about how close we were still standing. One wrong move, and I could topple onto him. All the tension I'd felt through today was becoming hotter than a live wire.

I couldn't be with him. Not like that. No matter how much he'd changed or how hot he was.

Cameron was off-limits.

"He's not allowed at the winery," Cameron said softly, his voice holding a Southern bite. "In fact, the two of us aren't supposed to be within ten feet of each other. I was ready to fight the moment I saw his truck in your grandma's driveway. Normally, Sarah drops them off, and he doesn't come here." My heart continued to squeeze, his words worrying me. "Sarah has a lot on her plate. And she's alone. Colt checks on her, but they aren't friends like they used to be. A lot has changed. There's a lot of pain here. And I'm sorry you've landed right back in the middle of it. That's all I can say."

"That's quite a bit," I said, gripping the folder he'd handed me hard enough to almost bend it. A whoop echoed from the house, breaking me out of this moment and bringing me back to the present. "I gotta go, Mr. Harlow."

His brows drew together. "Please, do *not* call me that. You make me sound like an old man."

"I mean, you *are* older than me. *And* my boss."

His eyes narrowed, and he shook his head. "Older by two years. You call me Mr. Harlow, and I'll call you Haley Marie."

I bristled at the use of my middle name. "How on earth do you know my middle name?"

"I've heard your grandma use it on you a time or two." Amusement gleamed in those baby blues.

"Do you talk to her a lot?" I asked, genuinely curious.

"I talk to everyone a lot. Perks of living in a small town."

I snorted. "I can't tell if I like it or not. It's not like this in Baltimore." My stomach twisted as the words came out of my mouth.

It would be hard to get away with murder in Citrus Cove. Everyone saw something in this small town. Always asking about each other. Watching each other out of boredom.

"Hey, are you okay?" he asked.

I exhaled, nodding. "I'm alright."

"I don't want to keep you too long, but before you go, I have a question that Colt asked me to ask you, also. But it's not work related."

I raised a brow at him.

He shifted uneasily. "There's a party happening tomorrow night kind of late. It's just a small get together. Nothing crazy. But you're more than welcome to come hang out and have a beer and just...get your mind off things. If you'd like."

My lips pressed into a thin line. A felt a mixture of different things. The first was—a party where Cam was? After all this time? Did I really want to even put myself in that situation? I wasn't a girl anymore and he seemed to be somewhat not an asshole, but...All of the memories still came rushing up from where I'd left them.

"I don't know," I said softly.

"I understand. The offer is there."

"Where is it at?" I asked. "The barn?"

"Colt's. He doesn't live far. I'll send you his address if I can get your number..."

I stared at him for a moment. We were going to work together, so might as well right? I held out my hand. "Give it here."

He gave a soft smirk, one that had me narrowing my eyes on him, and handed me his phone. I entered my contact information, sent myself a text, and then handed it back.

"Oh, also–Katie and Anna will be there. You should come. I promise I won't dump beer on you."

I snorted and he winced. It wasn't funny. That night so many years ago impacted me for the longest time, but really it was just the tip of the iceberg. Somehow, I'd turned into a fine adult, but I still felt a flash of anger in thinking about the things he'd said to me. Whether it was making fun of our mother being dead or dad leaving us or just the general struggles of being a fucking outcast, he'd made my life hell.

I didn't like thinking about the past. It dredged up so many emotions and I'd done just damn fine holding my grudge against this town and Cam.

Why couldn't he still be the bad guy? That would be so much easier. Instead, he'd turned into someone I *almost* wanted to know.

It pissed me off.

I was about to say something back to him, but I heard the shuffle of feet.

The front door suddenly opened, and Cam took a step back, his demeanor changing. "Hey, Jake. You're looking strong, bud."

"Thanks, Cam! What are you doing here?"

"Oh, just dropping off some papers for your aunt. Boring adult stuff."

Jake made a face. "Gross. I hate adult stuff."

"Me too, although this wasn't too bad," Cam chuckled. "Gave me an excuse to see you, right?"

Jake grinned. "I guess." He looked at me. "Haley—Aunt Haley, sorry—Honey wants to know if you're gonna *ever* come inside or if you're livin' on the porch now."

I barked out a laugh and turned, tucking the folder under my arm and heading toward the door. "Sorry, Jake, I'm coming in now. I don't know about tomorrow, but put me down as a maybe. I'll see you, Cam."

Calling him Cam suddenly made him feel a lot less like a villain in my mind. I heard his voice behind me, soft and baritone.

"See you, Hal."

CHAPTER EIGHT

LAST NIGHT WENT BETTER than I could have expected. My nephews ended up spending the night after we turned Honey's living room into a pillow fort. I learned all about Jake's aspirations to be the president of Legoland, and how Davy wanted to learn more about rocks. My nephews were way cooler than I could have ever imagined, and getting to know them more was a little bandaid on my heart.

Honey drove them back home this morning. I'd sent Sarah another text that was left unanswered and spent the rest of the day writing an article on hot locations for trips in Baltimore.

Now, I was pulling my Corvette down a driveway and cursing myself for going to this damn party. It was stupid. I felt stupid. I felt like the outcast again, showing up for whatever fucking reason.

I'm an adult. I'm a badass. I'm a goddamn grown woman.

If I had a bad time, I'd just leave.

Still, my stomach wouldn't stop twisting. I'd been too nauseous to eat earlier, wishing that Emma was here to be my wingman. She'd always been able to walk into social events without batting an eye, dragging me with her. Even if I wasn't exactly introverted, Emma was so damn extroverted that it was easy to tag along with her.

But, she wasn't here.

"Fuck me," I groaned as I pulled into the grass.

I didn't see Cam's truck. Was that a good sign or bad one? I considered putting the car in reverse and getting the hell out of here. *What am I doing here? Why am I doing this?* Colt appeared in front with a grin and wave.

"Goddamnit," I mumbled.

I forced a smile as he came to the door and turned off the engine. I got out and he spread his arms, offering me a quick hug.

"Glad you came," he said. "How are your ankles?"

"Oh. They're fine," I said, glancing down. I'd opted for casual and was wearing sneakers with jeans and a yellow baby-doll blouse. "I take it you're the one that put Hello Kitty bandages in the first aid kit?"

Colt winced. "Maybe. Sorry?"

"You should be."

"Hello Kitty is pretty iconic though."

"*Colt*," I snorted.

He grinned. "I'm sorry that happened the other night," he said. "We have a fire going in the back. It's just a few of us. Marco and Tabby couldn't make it."

"I mean, it is a Tuesday," I snorted. "Who's running the bar?"

"Sammy and Cam," Colt said. "They're closing down and joining us. We don't stay open late on Tuesday usually. Maybe once we get some good help." He winked.

Bastard. I fought the urge to ask him why he'd made me run into Cam as I followed him around the house and to the back-yard, which was just an open plot of land. There was a bonfire going. Katie looked up, waving her hand at me. Her and Anna were both seated with beers.

"Hey," I said, smiling at them.

"Want anything to drink?" Colt asked.

"A beer is fine," I said. I went over to Katie and Anna and stole a fold out chair. Crickets chirped in unison around us, the only sound aside from the crackle of the flames.

"How's it going?" Anna asked.

"Good," I breathed out.

"Are you okay?" Katie asked. "The other night was kind of crazy with Cam carting you off like that..."

I snorted and shook my head. "I don't know why he did that. But yeah, I'm fine. The glass got me, but it wasn't bad. How has your week been so far? I realize I don't know what either of you do."

"Katie is a firefighter," Anna said, giving her a teasing look. "Citrus Cove cheerleader turned lesbian firefighter hero."

"Honestly, that's badass," I laughed. "I'm happy for you."

Katie smiled. "Thanks. Me too. Anna is a vet and works at the clinic."

"The only clinic," she sighed.

"I would cry every day," I said. "I don't know if I could work with animals."

Anna nodded. "It's tough, but I love what I do. There are tragedies, but there are also good things too."

The sound of tires on gravel almost made me turn my head, but I was trying very hard not to look. I felt like sprinting away when I heard Cam's voice, followed by a bark.

He's not that bad.

"They brought Benny," Anna said excitedly.

I finally turned my head as a black lab came lopping around the corner straight for us. He paused to give me a sniff and then went to Anna, plopping his head on her knee for pets.

CLIO EVANS

While she was busy calling him a good boy, I found myself turning to look again as Cam and Sammy rounded the corner holding cartons of alcohol.

Colt came out the back door with a beer and snickered. "Look who finally fucking made it."

"Shut up," Sammy snorted. He looked up and saw me, his eyes lighting up. "Hey Haley. Hey Anna, Katie."

"If we're greeted as one entity, does that mean we're official?" Katie snorted.

"More official than my ring?" Anna teased her.

Cam stood still for a moment and then cleared his throat. "Taking these in."

Colt brought me the beer, which was ice cold, and dragged out more chairs as the fire flickered.

"This is great," he said. "I can make the fire bigger and if it catches, I got Katie here to take care of it."

"You will not make this fire bigger," she said, giving him a short glare. "Don't make me work on my one night off, Colt, or I'll cockblock your next date."

"And how would you do that?"

Anna laughed. "You really want to be on her bad side?"

Colt gave the three of us a boyish grin and then settled in a chair with his own beer. Benny betrayed us and went around the fire pit, plopping at his feet.

Sammy took the other chair on the opposite side, which left one more. The only open one next to me.

Fuck me. What am I doing here again?

I hated the way my pulse shot through the roof as the back door swung open and shut. Cam walked over to us and stood awkwardly, and then we finally made eye contact.

"May I?" he asked.

"Sure," I said.

Katie leaned over. "Want to swap?"

78

"No, it's fine." I couldn't help but blush now. I appreciated her asking, but her question was heard by all.

"How was the sleepover?" Cam asked.

All eyes moved to the two of us now. "It was good," I said. "The boys are...boys? Jake wants to be the president of Legoland. Davy wants to know more about rocks. They're both cool."

"They are," Colt agreed.

"Should I get my guitar?" Sammy asked.

"Yes," Anna said quickly.

Oh god. This was awkward for all of us. Everyone knew our history. It was a small fucking town and we'd all gone to school together, except for Anna, who still seemed to be filled in.

"Where's the restroom?" I asked politely.

"I'll show you," Colt said.

"No, I've got it," Cam said immediately.

I stood up quickly, clutching my beer. "I'll find it."

He hopped up as I passed him, following me to the back door.

"Cameron fucking Harlow," Katie called.

That did nothing to deter him. I felt a prick of rage as I stepped inside with him in tow. I spun around as soon as the door clicked shut.

"What the fuck is your problem?" I asked.

"I'm just trying to help—"

The tears came up out of nowhere. I bit them back, trying to keep myself under control. "I don't need your help. It's a small house."

He winced, running his fingers through his hair. "Hal, I'm just trying to—"

"I shouldn't have come," I sighed, taking a step back from him. "Everyone here knows the high school me and how fucking stupid I was."

"You weren't stupid."

"And how fucking pathetic—"

"Haley," he growled. "You weren't the pathetic one. I was. I fucked up. I was so fucking awful to you. None of them should have stayed friends with me, but they did because I've changed. But none of them think you are pathetic or stupid. They think I am."

"You are," I muttered, glowering.

"I am," he said. "I hurt you. Repeatedly. I said awful, terrible things to you that anyone would have been harmed by. It pains me to look back at that time because I should have been better. You didn't deserve the way I treated you."

"I didn't," I whispered, the tears burning again.

I won't cry. I won't fucking cry. Not in front of him.

"If there is anything I can do to make it up to you, I'll do it."

A heavy silence fell between us. I stared at him, my heart beating so loud I could hear it.

"Anything," he whispered.

I looked at the beer in my hands and let out a humorless laugh. He caught my gaze and then shocked me by getting down on his knees in front of me.

"Pour it," he said.

"Cam," I sighed. "I don't need to be petty."

"It would feel kind of good though, right?"

Doing the same thing he'd done to me all those years ago? I turned it over in my head, mulling on it as I held his baby blues.

Yeah.

Well.

There was a time and place to take the highroad, but he was right.

I tipped the beer and poured it over his head. It rushed

down his face and dripped down his shirt, glistening as it doused him. I waited until every last drop had been poured out.

He opened one eye, squinting at me.

I couldn't help but smile. He smiled too.

"You're a bastard," I sighed.

"I'm going to wear this beer proudly the rest of the night."

I let out a hard laugh and shook my head. Fuck. I'd really just done that. "Let me get you a towel," I said.

"No," he said, wiping his eyes. "I'm dead serious. Badge of honor."

I held his gaze a beat longer and I couldn't fight the grin now. "Alright. Get up and go outside. I'll be out in a minute."

He did as I asked and stepped back out. I heard a few snickers and then Katie and Anna laughing at him, and it felt good.

It felt really damn good.

CHAPTER NINE

THE CITRUS COVE WINE & Ciders's parking lot was empty except for my red Corvette and Cam's big-ass truck.

Seriously, there was no need for a truck that big. Right? I shook my head as I went to the side door of the restored barn as he'd instructed. I was grateful that we weren't meeting early given that I didn't leave Colt's until about 2 A.M.

What initially was one of my most awkward encounters in a long time melted into a really fun get together. And no one asked me why I dumped my beer on Cam's head. There seemed to be some sort of silent agreement that no one needed to ask questions or pry.

I lifted my hand to knock, but it flew open. Cam stood there, his gaze meeting mine.

"Hi." I'd been thinking about him all day. All fucking day.

It was annoying. Logically, I knew that it was ridiculous to think about him like I was, but I couldn't seem to stop. I hadn't called a truce last night, but...I was tempted to.

I was starting to realize that maybe he'd changed. That maybe... he wasn't so bad. Even if I wanted him to be.

"Hi," Cam breathed out. We both stood there until he cleared his throat. "Allergies are getting to me or something. Come on in."

It was a lame but cute excuse. I slid past him, stepping inside.

Whoever decorated this place really had done a good job. The last two times I'd been here, I'd been pissed about something, so I hadn't taken the time to look again. It was nice and cozy, sleek where it needed to be and folksy where it could. There were pictures on the walls of the history of the vineyard, showing how the farm had grown over the years. I spotted a picture of the famous Harlow oak tree too. I admired the exposed beams that were clearly the frame of his family's old barn.

What was it like to have a history like that? To have people that worked to build a future for their kids? I'd always been a little jealous of that, even if I'd never wanted to admit it.

"I know you said you've bartended before," Cam said, following me to the bar itself. "How long ago was that?"

"It's been at least seven years," I said, setting my bag on the counter. The last time I worked at a bar, I was making my way through college, surviving on ramen and beer. "But I'm a smart girl. It's like riding a bike."

"I'm not worried, but I'll show you the ropes. We'll work together tonight, and it should be slower than the rest of the week. We'll have our regulars. Fridays are when it gets super busy, Saturdays and Sundays too. Wednesday and Thursday are the sweet shifts. Mondays and Tuesdays, I keep it closed because it's just been family working. Well, family and Colt, but Colt is family. Might as well be a brother."

His rambling was cute. I listened to him as he continued, watching as he raked fingers through his dark hair.

"Hunter will be home soon, and so will my parents, which

will take a load off. I've been working between the farm and here, and it's too much." He rubbed his tired eyes and sighed; his shoulders slumped. He looked exhausted.

"Hey," I said, frowning. I couldn't help myself. I stepped closer to him, touching his arm. It took every ounce of control not to squeeze the firm bicep there. *Are you nuts?* "Are you okay?"

"Yeah," he said, but his tone was unconvincing. He swallowed hard, his eyes falling on my lips and then rising back to my gaze.

And there was that burst of tension again. The kind that made me want to lean forward and kiss him.

"I just didn't expect you to wear one of the dresses. It looks really good on you."

I grinned. I couldn't help it. Because yes. I had worn one of the dresses—the blue one in particular because god damn it, it was perfect. And it had been a power move on my part to wear it, although maybe that was what he'd secretly hoped for.

I searched his gaze and realized that he meant what he said. Heat bloomed in my cheeks. I crossed my arms, studying him closely.

"I never thought I'd hear a compliment from you," I said.

His gaze flickered. "I'm sorry," he said. "I keep thinking of all the ways I can make it up to you. I want to know you. And I want to prove to you that I'm not—"

"If you want to be absolved of the guilt from so long ago, then so be it. Just let it go," I said, frowning. "Dumping beer on you last night might have helped..."

He smiled, but I could still tell he was bothered. I pressed my lips together, considering everything.

Was I going to forgive him?

Really forgive him?

"It's been twelve years. And no, I didn't want to see you

when I came here. I'm dealing with a lot right now, and meeting the man that made my life hell for so long isn't exactly a cherry on top."

"It doesn't matter that it's been that long. I still think about it. I still think about you."

My heart skipped a beat.

"I hurt you. I hurt your feelings. I know you hate me," he continued, his eyes darkening. I frowned, not liking the storm I saw there with those words. "You have every right to. But—"

"I don't hate you, Cam. Well, I did hate you for a long time. A really, really long time. But I'm giving you a chance. Else I wouldn't be standing here, would I?"

It was true. I was giving him a second chance. There were way more pressing issues to think about than holding a grudge against him, and...

Maybe I wanted to know *this* Cam. The one that made my life hell sucked, but this guy in front of me? If he was really how he seemed, then I could forgive him.

Maybe.

"I can let it go if you can," I said.

He pressed his lips together. "What else can I do?"

"Well, you can work with me tonight." I gave him a small smile. "And maybe we can just start over. A new beginning. You did buy me a couple of nice dresses. And let me dump beer on your head. And working here will keep me from going stir-crazy." *And will keep my thoughts from the murder.*

I held out my hand, and he stared at it for a moment before lifting his. His palm was rough against mine. A shiver went through me. We shook hands, standing there like idiots until finally, I pulled free.

"You're full of surprises," he murmured. "I'm still going to work on making it up to you. But thank you for giving me the chance."

I nodded, turning before he could see the blush creeping into my cheeks. "Right," I said, moving toward the bar. "Show me the ropes, cowboy."

"As you wish, sunshine."

* * *

Cameron was right about it being an easy night, which I couldn't complain about. A few hours into my shift, and I'd finally memorized most of the taps. I'd made small talk with those that came in, recognizing some faces and giving them the general update on my life—always leaving out the murder—before sending them off with an ice-cold cider or glass of wine.

"Only got about thirty minutes left until we close. The shift went by quick with you around. I didn't think about this, but when we have a day off, we should do a tasting," Cam said as he bumped his hip into mine playfully. He had his sleeve rolled up, and I raised a brow as I caught sight of a tattoo on the inside of one of them.

I reached for him without thinking, grabbing his forearm and turning it. "Oak tree?"

"Yes," he chuckled. "The Harlow family oak tree, to be exact."

"The legend." I gave him a teasing grin.

"It's not a legend," he quipped. "I'll take you there some-time if you want."

"Isn't that just supposed to be whatever girl you marry?" I asked, bumping him with my shoulder.

"Yep." My stomach fluttered. His answer surprised me, and he was gone before I could get anything else out of him, moving down the bar to greet someone as they walked up.

"Hey, miss, could I get another cider?"

I turned, offering the man on the other side of the bar a smile. He was the only one on this side and was sitting alone.

"Sure," I said.

"Thanks. Long night?"

"Not too bad." I reached for his empty glass. "What cider did you want, sir?"

"Oh, no need to call me that," he said, smirking. I held his gaze and felt a chill crawl up my spine. He had short sandy-blond hair and icy-blue eyes, but there was something about him that set those alarm bells ringing. "What's your favorite one? I'd love to try whatever you enjoy."

I glanced down, looking at the different taps. "I'll pick one for you, then." I had no fucking clue, but I wasn't going to tell him that.

"Thanks. What's your name...?"

"Haley," I answered as I filled his glass. I set it on the countertop and slid it toward him. As I started to pull back, his fingers laced around my wrist, giving me a tug that had me losing my balance. "Hey," I growled.

He let go quickly, letting out a chuckle. "Sorry. You just have small wrists."

I swallowed hard, putting on my best poker face. "What's your name?" I could feel a storm cloud brewing to my right and refused to look down the bar at Cam, even as I felt him closing in.

"Andy," he said, taking a sip of his cider. He slid off the bar and slid cash over, giving me a wave. "Sorry if I frightened you. I work in the jewelry industry—force of habit."

He left right as Cam stopped at my side. "What the fuck was that?"

I turned, keeping my voice low. "It's fine. He was just a little weird."

"He touched you," Cam snarled. "I'm going to beat the—"

"Hold your horses, cowboy," I said, placing my hand on his chest. "There's no need to beat him up. He was just weird, and I handled it."

Cam narrowed his eyes. "If he bothers you again, you'll let me know."

"Is that a question or—"

"It's a demand. If he bothers you again, you'll let me know."

I glared at him. "You can't manhandle everyone."

He set his jaw and was about to argue, but my phone began to buzz in my pocket, drawing my attention. I pulled it out and saw Emma's name.

"Can I take this?" I asked. "It'll be quick."

"Sure," he said, blowing out a sigh. "Of course. I don't even think you've taken a break tonight."

"Thanks," I said, slipping by him.

I went through a doorway and down the same hall I'd been carted through Friday night by Cam. I snorted as I thought about last Friday. I'd given in so quickly to being friendly with him, but it was hard not to. He really wasn't as bad as I thought he was...

I picked up the call. "Hey, Emma—"

"Where are you right now?" Her voice was panicked, the tone setting my back straight.

"I'm at a winery—a place outside of town—"

"Does anyone know you're there? Are you alone?"

"People know I'm here. Emma, what's going on?"

She let out a soft cry, her voice breaking. "Oh god, Hal. I'm so sorry. It's so bad. The police are on the way, but I finally went by your apartment. Everything is wrecked, and there was writing on the wall and-and—fuck. I'm so sorry." She was sobbing.

"I don't understand," I whispered. "Emma, are you hurt? Are you okay?"

My phone buzzed in my hand as I asked her. "I just sent pictures," she choked out. "Everything is destroyed, babe. And

I don't know—someone is after you. Someone is after you, Haley."

Someone is after you.

My hands began to tremble as I pulled the phone back, my ears ringing as I looked at her text messages. Pictures poured in of my apartment, and she was right. Everything was ruined. The couch was gutted and slashed, the coffee table smashed, clothing strewn everywhere and torn. Tears filled my eyes as another picture came in. They'd painted on the walls.

Whore. Slut. I'm coming for you. Bitch.

It should have been you.

You're next.

I heard my name being called repeatedly, but it sounded so far away. I pressed my back against the wall, feeling like the whole world was caving in. Everything was falling apart.

My worst fear had come true.

The killer wanted me dead.

I should have known. I *had* known. The way he'd looked at me, the hatred. The burning rage.

And the words he'd told me. The same ones he'd painted on the wall.

You're next.

CHAPTER TEN

cameron

"GOODNIGHT, BILL," I said as the last customer went out the door. He gave me a friendly wave as he went to his car, and I scrutinized him to make sure he wasn't stumbling. I'd forced him to down a couple glasses of water and he seemed fine.

I locked the door, the silence after a successful night leaving me with an excited buzz.

It was no surprise at all that Haley picked up working the bar with ease. I thought about her as I went back to the bar. She'd taken her break but hadn't come back, which left me feeling uneasy.

I passed through the doorway and froze. Down the hall, Haley was sitting on the floor, hugging her knees, her head down. I could see her body trembling from here.

A streak of panic shot through me.

"Fuck," I said, rushing down the hall to her.

She didn't look up at me. Her phone was lying on the floor, a voice desperately talking, but I couldn't make out the words. Her breaths were slow and shallow.

"Haley?" I knelt next to her slowly.

She startled, her head lifting and eyes wide. Mascara ran down her cheeks, her eyes red and cheeks flushed. She let out another sob, and I couldn't stop myself. I sank down on the floor and reached for her, pulling her hard against me. Her entire body shook as she cried, curling up against me.

"Hey, hey, hey," I said softly. "It's okay. It's going to be okay."

Her silence sent a bolt of fear through me. She began to shake more, her face burying into the crook of my neck. I held her, not knowing what the hell was happening but knowing that whatever it was, I was going to help her. Seeing her cry like this, it felt like my own heart was shattering into pieces.

I needed to know what happened. Had someone died? Was someone hurt?

"Hello? Hello? Whoever you are, pick up the fucking phone!"

I picked up Haley's phone and pressed it to my ear, my heart pounding in my chest. "Who the fuck is this?"

"Who am I? Who the fuck are you?" A woman's voice was shrill on the other end of the line. "I'm Emma, Haley's best friend, and if you don't tell me who you are, I'm going to order an airstrike on your country bumpkin ass."

I snorted despite the situation, my jaw setting. "Doubt you have that power, but your message has been heard. I'm Cameron."

"Cameron." She paused. "Please do not fucking tell me you're Cameron *Harlow?*"

"So you've heard of me?"

"Many things," she said, her voice dry. "Where is Haley? She's gone silent. I have police here at her apartment, and I need to know she's okay."

"She's okay," I breathed out, pulling her a little tighter to me.

Now was not the time to think about how perfect she felt against me or how she smelled like jasmine. They were fleeting thoughts, and yet my mind cataloged this information regardless.

I could feel her finally calming some, her shaking slowly decreasing.

"I've got her. What the hell is going on?"

"I need to talk to her," Emma said.

I looked down at Haley, and she lifted her head. She looked at the phone and then took it from me.

"I'm fine," she whispered, her voice shaky. She was definitely not fine. "Can you keep me updated, Emma? I need to go. I need to get home. I need to make sure everyone here is safe."

I could hear Emma chattering. I watched Haley's expression. Her strength was something that I'd always admired, but I realized I hadn't truly seen it until now. I'd found her broken, but she was already putting herself back together.

Haley pulled the phone away from her ear, handing it back to me. "Emma wants to tell you something."

"Yes?" I asked her, holding it back to my ear.

"If anything happens to Haley while I'm not there, I will find you and grind your balls with a nutcracker."

"I won't let anything happen to her," I promised. "I've got her."

Emma was silent for a moment. "Okay," she sighed. "Her apartment has been completely destroyed. It's all gone. I'm going to do what I can here, but I need your help there."

"You've got it," I promised again.

I wasn't going to let anything happen to her. My arm tightened around her.

The call with Emma ended, and I put the phone down.

Haley drew in a shaky breath and wiped her eyes. She looked at me, swallowing hard. I reached up, wiping away a tear she'd missed. "Tell me what's going on," I whispered. "Are you okay? What happened?"

"I can't," she said, shaking her head. "I can't talk about it yet. I need a few moments to collect myself. I just fell apart on you and—"

"Hey. Take a deep breath. It's going to be okay."

"I don't want anyone else to know," she said, her eyes filling with tears again. She held them back. "You can't tell anyone."

"I can't make promises until I know what's happening."

"I can't talk yet."

"Haley," I said, my hands settling on her hips. "I've never seen you like this. And I'm ready to kill anyone who put that look in your eyes."

She flinched at the word "kill" in a way that made my heart squeeze. Fuck. Everything I said always made things worse.

"We can take a minute if you need it, and then we'll talk. Deal?" I said.

"I need a drink," she whispered. "I left you hanging. You had to close up alone. I'm so sorry."

"No need to apologize. How about this? We can make a plan."

"A plan?" she echoed, her voice hoarse.

"Yes. We're going to get up. You're going to go wash your face and take the time you need. I'm going to get some water and whisky, and we're going to sit and talk about what the hell is going on. And I'm going to do every single thing I can to help you."

Her face softened. "Okay."

"Okay." I shifted to the side and got to my feet, bringing her with me. "The bathroom is the door on the left. I'll get your drinks."

"Okay," she said again. "You're not going to leave?"

"I'm not going anywhere."

She nodded and turned, leaving for the restroom. I ran my fingers through my hair, my mind spinning.

I went back to the bar and pulled out a bottle of whisky, pouring her a double shot. I made her a glass of ice water and added a lemon wedge, thinking about what could possibly be happening. I had that gut feeling, the kind that told me it was bad.

Within a couple of minutes, I felt her presence. I turned as she came over to me. She eyed the whisky.

"Water first," I said, handing the glass to her.

She smiled a little. Just a little. Enough to tell me that she was going to be okay.

She took a couple of gulps, and then I handed her the shot. She threw it back, making a face. But her shoulders relaxed, her expression slowly losing that shell-shocked look and turning into something else entirely. Anger.

"A few weeks ago, I was leaving my apartment," she said, looking up at me. "I was about to lock my apartment door when I heard a scream. It was the kind you just couldn't ignore. I went down the hall, and my neighbor's door was ajar. I opened it right as a man slit my neighbor's throat. She was my age."

"Fuck," I whispered. I turned, pulling out another whisky glass and pouring myself a shot. The idea of Haley walking in on that horrified me.

"He ran at me. Tried to stab me. Nicked my right arm. Ran off because another neighbor shouted in the building. It was night time and people were getting home for the day. I went to her and held her as she died. What I didn't tell anyone was what he said on his way out. He said I was next. I don't know why I didn't tell anyone. Fear. Shock. I don't know."

Rage worked through me. The idea of a man harming her, trying to kill her, threatening her. All of it was a nightmare, and I wished I could do anything to stop it.

She raked her fingers through her blonde curls, her brows drawing together. I poured her another shot, and we both downed them. The burn was a welcome one, warming me straight through.

"Fuck, Haley," I whispered. I shook my head. "He was probably just making threats."

"No," she whispered, her voice becoming hollow again. "That's why Emma was calling. She went by my apartment for me and was going to pack up some items and send them to me. When I left for Citrus Cove, I left in a hurry. I barely packed anything because I just wanted to get out. I wanted to escape this fucking nightmare. But she went by tonight, and my entire apartment was ransacked." She pulled out her phone and shoved it toward me.

I took it, and what I saw made my stomach roll.

Her apartment was clearly a nice one. But now it was destroyed. I scrolled through the photos, my mind racing. When I got to the writing on the wall, I shook my head, that rage returning.

"If he got into my apartment, he knows who I am. He knows where I live. He'll be able to find out things about my family, about me, about everything. I'm not safe, and by being here, I'm just a danger to others. I'll take off in the morning."

"And go where?" I growled, looking up at her. "Somewhere you'll just be alone? That's crazy."

"I can't let anyone else get hurt," she said.

"No. That's stupid, Hal. I'm sorry, but it is. You need to stay here where you're safe. We can go to the police."

"You think *Bud* is going to be able to do jack shit about a killer?" she snapped.

"Bud's a decent sheriff," I said, my voice brusque. She had a point though. Citrus Cove was a small town and not exactly the kind of place where a killer ever ended up. "I think that if you leave, you're just going to put yourself more at risk. And I think you should sleep on it."

She snorted, tipping her head back and looking at the ceiling. "Since when do you care, Cam?"

I set my whisky glass down and stepped up to her, meeting her toe to toe. Her breath hitched as she met my gaze, our bodies almost touching.

"I care about you," I whispered. "It may be crazy. I may not have a single shot in hell with you. But I care, Hal. I care a lot. And I like you more than I should."

She swallowed hard, her gaze dancing with something I couldn't quite read. "It is crazy. Because if I didn't know any better, I'd say you want me."

"I *do* want you. I want you like a garden wants the sun. When I see you, I can't see anything else. I want you and no one else. Maybe I've always wanted you." I didn't care if I sounded like some crazy country poet saying those things, I meant every word.

"So you *bullied* me? Because you liked me?"

"I wasn't raised to express my emotions in a healthy way, I was terrible to you for a lot of reasons, Haley. Reasons it took me years of therapy to figure out. Some of those reasons had nothing to do with you. One of those reasons was that I liked you but I also felt threatened by you. And my teenage, dumbass, hormone-riddled brain didn't know how to process more than one feeling at a time. I'm not that guy anymore, though. I've grown up."

"Threatened by me? What did I ever do to threaten you?"

I sucked in a breath. This conversation had gone through my head a thousand times, and now it was here. Being honest fucking sucked sometimes, but I was going to be truthful.

"You didn't do anything. It was more that you represented change. Nothing ever changes in Citrus Cove. People are born, live, and die here. But one day the Bently girls show up out of nowhere. And, let me tell you it took dozens of hours and thousands of dollars of therapy to figure out why it was only ever you I was terrible to, but you coming to town, it meant that things don't stay the same forever. I didn't know that was why at the time, but you represented the possibility of more, but also the possibility of loss. And we had just lost my grandmother and I couldn't deal with something new. All that, and I had a stupid boyhood crush on you. But I'm not a boy anymore."

"No, you're not," she said, the corner of her mouth tugging. "You've grown up."

I lifted my hand, her cheek warm against my palm. She closed her eyes, the shared touch sending a bolt of need through me. But tonight was not the night to act on that feeling. I needed to make sure she was safe first.

"Tomorrow, we'll go to the station," I said softly. Her eyes opened, a hint of fear there that I wish I could take away. "I'll pick you up. We'll get some breakfast. Make an event of it."

She nodded. "Alright. Okay."

"And I'm gonna drive you home. We'll get your car in the morning, after."

She pressed her lips together, her eyes narrowing. "Has anyone ever told you that you're kind of bossy?"

"Many times," I chuckled. "It's a flaw, but people put up with it."

Her gaze softened. "I guess I'll put up with it too."

My chest squeezed, every primal urge in me rising up, urging me to kiss her.

But not yet.

When I finally got to kiss the woman of my dreams, it was going to be perfect. Because after tonight, I'd realized two things.

One, Haley was meant to be mine.

Two, I was going to spend every waking moment showing her that I was meant to be hers.

CHAPTER ELEVEN

I WOKE UP, fixed the bed, took a shower, got dressed, and made a pot of coffee, all before the sun rose. Last night, I'd barely been able to sleep, and that uneasy feeling didn't seem to want to go away.

I poured myself a cup of coffee and sat at the kitchen table, scrolling on my phone absentmindedly. When I had spare moments, I set up posts for social media to auto schedule for me, which took a load off. I checked my messages from Emma, appreciating that she'd created a digital folder with all the information we needed to take to the police. She was organized like that.

All in all, it felt like I'd lost everything. The wound was deeper this time. I'd watched someone die, and now all of my belongings were destroyed. The police were working the case, but so far, they hadn't found anything.

I was frustrated and scared. I felt sick. But even with the two hours of sleep and the feeling of despair, I felt a flicker of hope.

I steeled my nerves as I heard Honey upstairs.

My worry for her meant I'd keep my mouth shut for now. It wasn't that I didn't trust her but that I couldn't stand the thought of putting more on her shoulders. Not after everything she'd done for me.

Within a few moments, she came down, raising a brow. She was already dressed for the day in calf-length pants and a boat neck floral shirt. "You're up early. Long night?"

"I got home around midnight." I didn't want to relive last night.

The other thing that kept me up was Cameron Harlow.

He'd been there for me last night. Kept me sane. Held me while I fell apart and didn't judge me.

"Do you want a cup of coffee?" I asked, starting to get up.

"I'll get it," she said, waving her hand at me. She was grumpy right when she woke up, and I fought the urge to laugh at her despite everything.

"What? I can't pour you a cup of coffee?" I teased.

She snorted, shooting me a knowing look. "Not when you're being sneaky."

I turned my head before our eyes could meet. How the fuck did she always do that?

The sound of wheels on pavement had me pulling the curtain back to peek out. Cam's truck stopped where my car was normally parked. I started to get up, but she waved at me again, already heading toward the front door.

"Damn it," I mumbled.

Part of me hoped I'd be able to slip out before she was up so I didn't have to come up with an excuse as to why Cameron Harlow was at our front door this early on a Thursday morning.

I heard Honey and Cam chatting at the door, followed by her soft laugh. She ushered him into the kitchen, giving me a smug look behind him.

"Morning, sunshine," Cam said, offering me a smile. He held two to-go cups of coffee in his hands. "Got a little caffeine for us."

"Morning," I said. "That's perfect. Let me put this in the sink and grab my bag, then we can go."

"Where are you two going?" Honey asked, raising a brow. She glanced at the clock on the oven. "It's awfully early for a date."

Cam glanced at me warily. I'd begged him not to tell anyone what he knew, and it seemed he planned to do as I asked.

I could have told her then. And maybe I should have. But it was too early in the morning to tell my grandmother that someone was possibly out there who wanted to kill me.

Cam saved me last night. I'd broken down, and he'd held me, and then I'd pulled myself back together because I had to.

"We're going to do some training," Cam said, clearing his throat.

"Training, huh. Don't think I didn't notice her little race car is missing," Honey said, smirking. "Want some breakfast, Cam?"

"No, ma'am," he chuckled. "Her car was making a weird noise last night, so I brought her home. I'm taking her to the shop."

"Mmhm. I've been on this earth for a while now, Cameron Harlow."

He gave her the most innocent smile he could muster, and it took everything in me to not laugh. I finished the last sip of my coffee, snatched my bag off the table, and gave Honey a kiss on the cheek.

"I'll be home in a while, Honey," I said.

"Sure, sure. You kids have fun."

The two of us made it out of the house and to his truck. I

climbed into the passenger side and slammed the door shut, and so did he before we both burst out into laughter.

"She's onto me," Cam said as he cranked the engine.

"She's always been intuitive," I snorted. "I just didn't have it in me to tell her this morning."

That sobered both of us. He reached over, giving my thigh a gentle squeeze. "It'll be okay."

I hoped so. I really hoped so.

I was silent on the drive to the police station. It was all of five minutes before we were pulling into the parking lot. My stomach twisted.

"I don't know what I'm going to tell them," I said.

"Tell them everything. And maybe they can contact the station in Baltimore. I'll be with you the whole time," Cam said.

We both got out and went inside. He surprised me by pressing his hand against my lower back, offering comfort that I hadn't realized I needed.

The receptionist lifted her head. "Cam Harlow," she chucked. "You and David go at it again?"

I raised a brow, looking up at him. He winced. "No, Tammy, I'm here for another reason. Actually just here to support Haley. Is Bud in?"

"*Sheriff Johns* is," she corrected.

Cam snorted. "You know he plays golf with my dad, and I've known him since I was in diapers."

"Right, but he's still the sheriff in this building, Harlow. Go on back. You know his office."

Cam slipped his hand into mine and led me down a gray hall. My stomach twisted.

"Did you and David *fight* fight?" I whispered under my breath.

"We went a couple rounds, yeah. He never won." There was a hint of pride there.

I shook my head as we came to a doorway. A man in uniform was sitting at a desk, his balding head shining in the yellow lights. He looked up, raising a brow.

"I'm not here for me. I'm here for her," Cameron rushed out.

I fought the urge to laugh at him.

The sheriff chuckled. "You just gonna stand there, then?"

I let out a breath and stepped inside, Cameron following me. There were two chairs that looked like they hadn't moved since the '80s, and we each took one.

"I'm Haley Bently," I said. "Sheriff—"

"Just call me Bud," he said.

"Bud. Someone is trying to kill me."

Both of his brows shot up so far I thought they might end up on the top of his head. "Hell of a way to start an introduction. Start from the beginning, Ms. Bently."

* * *

I kicked Cameron's tire as hard as I could, letting out a frustrated noise. "That was a load of horse shit," I growled, looking up at Cam.

He winced as he went to the driver's side. "Sorry, Hal. I thought there would be more they could do."

More than jack shit. The only thing that Bud said he could do at the moment was reach out to the Baltimore department. As of right now, there were no suspects, the killer had been meticulous and left nothing to connect him to the crime, and the BPD had no hard evidence to connect what happened to my apartment to what happened to the neighbor. And since I left Baltimore, I was now out of their jurisdiction, and they wouldn't have someone keep an eye on my place.

No leads. No help. It felt like there was nobody in my corner. No one but Cam and Emma.

I yanked open the passenger door and climbed into Cam's truck, sinking into the leather seat.

"What now?" I was fighting back tears. I'd barely slept last night, was worried about watching my back, and had somehow ended up with Cameron Harlow as my wingman in this entire situation. My entire world had been flipped upside down.

"How about we go get breakfast? I think some food might help the situation."

I narrowed my eyes, stealing a glance at him. He looked a little more rugged this morning, and I found that I liked him like that. He was hot. Hotter than he'd ever been in high school.

"Sure. I don't think I can deal with Honey right now. Sarah won't even return my text messages, my brother-in-law is apparently a drunk bastard, and my nephews are just now getting to know me. And now I have to deal with a police department that doesn't have any leads, all while watching my own back because apparently "you're next" isn't substantial enough to protect me. And now all I'm going to be able to think about is *when* he'll find me. I really wish I didn't have to deal with any of this and just crawl into a hole and disappear." I blew out a breath, slumping in my seat.

"But then I'd miss you," he whispered.

His voice was soft and gentle, but his words sent a bolt of pleasure through me. I blushed and looked away. He was trouble. That much hadn't changed.

"I won't let him get to you," Cam continued. "I promise."

I stared at him for a moment and felt a flicker of guilt. "You don't have to get involved in this," I said. "You don't have to be my protector."

"I know that."

"You don't even have to take me places."

"I know."

There was a steady silence between us and he gave me a soft smile.

"I'm still going to, though," he said. "I'm here for you. And while you are perfectly capable of handling things, it doesn't hurt to have someone else, right? And also, your best friend did threaten me. Not that she needed to in order to keep me around."

I chuckled, despite everything feeling like it was spiraling. "Alright. I just don't want to be a burden to you."

"You could never be one. What are you doing tomorrow?" He backed the truck out of the station and hit the road, taking us to whatever breakfast place he had in mind.

"Trying to hunt down a serial killer."

"Hal, come on," he said, his voice part plea, part amused.

"I don't know," I said, fighting a smile.

"I was thinking..."

"You do that a lot, it seems."

"I was thinking maybe I could take you on a picnic. And we could do that wine tasting. And cider, if you'd like."

"For work?" I asked, raising a brow.

I was going to give him a hard time. A harder time than necessary. I wasn't new to flirting or dating and while I'd mentally been going back and forth on my feelings about him, I still felt the chemistry.

His jaw clenched, his eyes narrowing on the road. "Not for work."

"Oh? For what then?"

"Well, you know..." He trailed off.

I was fighting giggles now. "Are you going to keep speaking in caveman or say, 'Hi, Haley. Would you like to go on a date with me?'"

He barked out a laugh, stealing a glance at me. His grin was wicked. "Hi, Haley. Would you like to go on a date with me?"

I looked out the window, doing my best to hide my smile. There was a giddiness running through me that made me want to kick my feet because god damn it. *He wants me.*

"You sure you aren't playing a prank on me?" I asked.

"Far, far from it," he breathed out. "Fuck. I'm not an idiot. Well, I can be sometimes. But I want you, Hal. And I want to know you. And I want to prove myself to you."

I bit my bottom lip. "Sure, then," I said casually. That tone was a straight-up lie though. My heart pounded in my chest. I felt like a schoolgirl.

I didn't need someone's approval or desire, but it felt damn good having it. Especially from him.

I could see his reflection in the glass, and the way he instantly relaxed.

"I do have a condition," he added.

I laughed, turning my head. "And what's that, boss?"

"You let me drive your car. Just once."

"Not a chance in hell," I snorted.

"What if I beg for the chance to?"

I shook my head. "You'd have to get down on your knees."

He was silent as he pulled into a small parking lot outside a robin's-egg-blue building. The sign out front said Citrus Cove Cafe and was one of the new places I hadn't seen before in Citrus Cove.

He got out of the truck and shut the door. I frowned, wondering if I'd said something wrong. I'd been teasing him, mostly. I unbuckled right as my door opened, and I let out a squeak as I looked at him.

Cam took a step back, and I watched as he lowered himself, his blue-jean-covered knees hitting the gravel.

"Cam," I hissed.

"On my knees, sunshine. I'm begging you to let me take you on a picnic and spoil you and for you to let me take a ride in that Corvette."

I blushed from head to toe, if that were even possible. My entire body warmed, my heart drumming in my chest. "You're such an idiot," I said, breaking into a giggle. The entirety of the last few weeks had been a nightmare, but my old enemy was the ray of sun striking through the darkness.

I slid out of the seat and landed right in front of him, stumbling enough that he rose up and caught me.

"Fuck," we both whispered.

His body was warm against me. I grabbed his arms, feeling his biceps, even if I didn't mean to. He shook his head, his eyes never leaving me. "You're perfect, you know that?"

"And you've got a silver tongue," I whispered.

"I mean it, Hal. You're so fucking beautiful it hurts. And you're smart. Stubborn." He lifted his hand slowly and slid it behind my neck. "All I want to do right now is kiss you."

"Don't," I whispered, swallowing hard. "The whole town is going to be talking now."

"Let them talk," he murmured.

I was about to lean up on my tiptoes and kiss him when I heard a voice break through.

"What the hell are you doing here? You stalking me, Harlow?"

Cam stiffened and turned. I looked past him, seeing my brother-in-law and my sister.

Fuck. I hadn't seen Sarah in so long. Hadn't heard from her. And here she was, alive and well, in the flesh in broad fucking daylight. Her hair was pulled back in a tight bun, a couple of lines crinkling around her eyes that hadn't been there the last time I'd seen her. She looked pale and tired and—*why* was she avoiding me?

"I was taking Haley to get some breakfast," Cam said, his voice cold. I could hear the temper simmering underneath the easygoing words. "Which, last time I checked, is in fact allowed, David."

"Don't talk to me like that," David sneered. "You're stalking me. I just know it. Fucking creep. Makes sense that you'd be with *her*."

Cam bristled next to me, his hands curling into fists. He took a step forward, but I pulled him back.

"Don't," I said.

I ignored David's insult, focusing on my sister.

"Sarah," I whispered, still staring at her. I took a step forward, reaching for her. Needing her now more than I ever had before. I could feel myself falling apart all over again, desperate to have my sister. Desperate to have the relationship we'd always had. "I haven't seen you in so long, and I need to talk—"

She took a step back, her lips pulling into a very tight line. She shook her head. "Not interested in what you have to say. I'm okay with you being around my sons if Honey is around, but I want nothing to do with you."

"That's right," David said, his arm going around her shoulders. The way she stiffened worried me. "Let's go, Sarah."

My breath left me. I felt Cam's arm loop around my waist, pulling me against him.

"Fucking hell. I'm so sorry," he said, watching them go.

I couldn't believe it. I went through everything I could in my mind around the time when we'd first stopped talking. It had been gradual at the beginning, and we'd had some arguments but nothing that justified being treated like dirt.

"I don't understand," I whispered.

I watched her and David get into a truck and leave.

"Something's wrong," Cam murmured. "I don't know what.

And I've tried to help. That's what started some of the blowouts with that fucking asshole. But I couldn't get through to her."

I felt myself deflating. Cam pulled me against him, planting a kiss on the top of my head.

"Let's get some food in you, sunshine. This place has the best breakfast in town."

CHAPTER TWELVE

Cameron

WE SLID into a booth against one of the big windows, settling in across from each other. Celosias grew in the window boxes, the downtown area of Citrus Cove crawling by. Haley leaned forward, taking in some of the subtle changes that had happened over the years.

She snorted.

"What?" I asked, leaning forward to follow her gaze.

"I've never seen anyone in the museum," she said, gesturing to the old spur museum.

"We used to tell ghost stories about that place in school. Everyone was convinced it was a portal to hell. They really do have all sorts of spurs in it. And the history of how boot spurs came to be."

She grinned, leaning back in my seat. Only in Citrus Cove would you find something so...small town. It was picturesque and familiar. *Home.*

The scent of pancakes and bacon made my stomach growl. I slid the menu over to Haley, already knowing what I was going to get. She picked up the yellow laminated paper, her lips pressing into a thin line.

I couldn't stand to see Haley in pain. The way that David had looked at her pissed me off too. I'd been worried about Sarah, but now I was just pissed at her. The way she'd treated Haley gave me a glimpse of the loneliness I could see trying to drag Haley down.

I wouldn't let it happen. Her sister might be letting her flounder, but I sure as hell wouldn't. Whatever happened, I wasn't leaving her side.

And fuck David. I hated him even more than before, which I hadn't thought was possible. Aside from the fact that he was a drunk, he was just a bastard. One that didn't deserve to even stand in the presence of either of the Bently ladies.

There had been many run-ins between the two of us over the years. I still remembered that first time in high school when he'd said something about my family. I'd been a lot more hot headed then. Hunter had pulled us apart, only to land one solid punch on the bastard that made him shut up for the rest of the year.

I couldn't do that now though.

Haley set the menu down, her head turning and gaze focusing on the outside. Her hands were clasped together, her shoulders tense.

"Hey," I said softly.

Haley looked up at me. There was a storm in those dark brown eyes, and I wanted to do everything I could to take it away. She was going through so much. More than anyone should have to go through.

"You're not alone," I said. "I know I'm not your sister, and I'm not who you'd probably like to be on your team right now, but I'm here."

Her cheeks flushed, her gaze turning glassy. "Thank you."

Amy, our waitress, bounced up to us, interrupting the moment.

"Hey, Cam," she said. "Been at least a week. You're starting to slack around here."

I grinned now. "Been busy. I'll take my usual."

Haley snorted, perking up some. "What's your usual?"

"Two sunny-side eggs, three pieces of bacon, a chocolate croissant, and one of their famous blueberry muffins. And a side of hash browns."

"Oh god," Haley laughed. The sound was music to my ears. She looked up at Amy. "I'll take a cup of coffee, an egg, some bacon, and the famous muffin he's talking about."

"You got it," she said, beaming as she left us.

Haley pulled a hair tie out of her pocket, raising a brow at me. I watched as she wrestled her blonde curls back, putting them in a bun. Sunshine streamed in, highlighting her. I felt like I was dining with an angel.

"You keep looking at me like you want to eat me," she teased.

God, that was closer to the truth than further. All I could think about was laying her back on my bed and tasting her, hearing her pretty voice get louder as she came. Fuck.

My cock throbbed against my zipper. I shifted in my seat, clearing my throat. "I have ideas."

"Mmhm," she chuckled. "I think I have a few myself."

Her words threw me off my game. There was a wicked tone there, one that I hadn't expected, one that made me feel weak. My heart beat a little faster. "I want to kiss you."

"I want to do more than kissing."

My ears were burning now. "Hal, you're going to drive me crazy."

"I plan on it." She smiled innocently, quieting as our waitress came back with our food. My gaze never left her as our plates were set down, Amy disappearing again.

I was hungry, but this food wasn't going to satiate my appetite. Only she would.

"What if after breakfast, I took you to get your car, and we went back to my place?" I asked before I had a moment to think things through. Fuck, I didn't even care. Maybe it was too forward. Maybe—

"Yes," she said, picking up her blueberry muffin. I watched as she bit into the top, letting out a soft moan. Brown sugar stuck to her soft lips, and she swiped the crystals away with her tongue. "It would be nice to get my mind off things, and... I want you."

Fuck. I was a goner. I blew out a breath and looked down at my food, finally digging in. The two of us ate in silence, but it was the comfortable kind. All I could think about was getting her home.

I'd never felt this way before about a woman. When I wasn't with her, I wanted to be with her. And when I was with her, I never wanted it to end. I never wanted her to leave.

There were a lot of things that I regretted. Being mean to her, teasing her, hurting her feelings. But I was grateful I had the chance to make things right. That she was letting me into her life.

"What's your favorite color?" she suddenly asked.

I raised a brow. "Are we doing first-date questions?"

She grinned. "Might as well. Unless you want to wait until the picnic."

"No, no. It's blue. Specifically, that blue you wore yesterday."

"Mm, that's a good color. Mine is peach."

"Is peach a color?" I teased.

She rolled her eyes. "You know what I mean."

"I do. What's your favorite food?"

"Enchiladas," she sighed happily. "And I haven't had any good ones since I moved out of Texas. Well, that's not entirely true. But I do miss getting good Mexican food all the time."

"Move back here for good and you won't ever have to miss it," I said.

She smiled. "Not sure about that, cowboy."

My chest squeezed a little. I didn't want her to leave again. Hell, I'd follow her this time if she let me. "My favorite food is my mom's fried chicken."

"Wholesome."

"It's true. She makes the best fried chicken. And her fried okra. When she gets home, I bet I could talk her into making some for us. You could come over."

Haley raised a brow. "You're trying real hard to keep me, aren't you?"

"Maybe." Yes. One hundred percent yes. "It's just an invitation. I see your grandma all the time."

She narrowed her eyes. "You know that's different, but I'll let it slide. Do you want kids?"

I damn near choked on my bite of bacon. Once I managed to get it down, I spoke. "With the right person, yes. I like the idea of having a family. Not because my mother hounds me to settle down, but because it feels right. Do you?"

"I think so. Sometimes I can picture myself being a mom; other times I think about all the traveling I've been able to do. All the things I've seen. I don't even have a pet right now—just my nephew dog, Donnie."

"And your real nephews," I chuckled. "Is Donnie Emma's dog?"

"Yeah. I forgot you talked to her on the phone."

"She threatened me." I couldn't help but grin. "She sounded very protective."

"Because she is. We've been friends for a decade. She's seen me through thick and thin. And when Sarah and I stopped talking, she became more of a sister to me. I love her."

I nodded, understanding that. It was how I felt about Colton. The two of us had seen it all together, and I wouldn't trade our friendship for anything. "I'm lucky to have Colton. I think he'd do anything for me."

"Yep. Knowing her was what made me realize that not all family is tied by blood. I love Honey. And I love Sarah, despite all of our problems. But Emma knows me and accepts me as I am. She doesn't try to change me. And she'll call me out on my bullshit, but she won't ever truly judge me for it."

"She sounds like a good friend," I said softly.

"She is," Haley sighed. She leaned forward, studying me. "I'd want to be married for a couple years and travel together before starting a family."

Now I was thinking about her being pregnant. About her having a family with me. Building a life. My cock throbbed, the thought of filling her with my cum making me shift in my seat again.

"I think that's smart," I finally said. "To be married for a while."

She smirked, as if knowing where my thoughts were. "Mmhm. What kind of things are you into in bed?"

"Fuck," I hissed, glancing around. "You've managed to shock me at least twice today."

"I don't have time for bullshit," she said, shrugging. "This is why I've been single the last few years. It's better to ask big questions up front before you end up with someone who is not right for you."

If I were a lesser man, I would have been intimidated. "So you want me to be honest, then."

"Yes," she said firmly.

I glanced around us, making sure no one was within earshot. Because the thing was—I had kinks. I had things that I enjoyed that would make half this town gasp and say prayers. And I didn't have any shame in it. I wanted what I wanted.

And she wanted to know.

"I love spanking. I love playing with things like blindfolds, handcuffs, any sort of restraint. And I've taken classes on how to do it properly so no one is harmed. I enjoy fucking outside. The idea of taking you tomorrow at our picnic is going to keep me up tonight. And I love eating pussy. I fucking love it. I'd die between a woman's thighs happily."

Her mouth fell open, her cheeks turning bright pink. "Fuck," she whispered. "I didn't think..."

"Think what? That a country boy could be kinky?"

"Yes. Exactly that."

I leaned back in the booth, studying her. "More than you can imagine, sunshine. I might be easygoing, but I'll put you on your knees and make you beg for my cock like a good girl any day of the week. But only if you want to."

"Cam," she rasped, turning her head to glance around us. She looked back at me, swallowing hard. "I don't think anyone I've ever met has shocked me this much."

I took a sip of my water, hiding my smile. I liked surprising her. In more ways than one. "What do you enjoy, sunshine? Anything in there I should know about?"

"Well." She cleared her throat. "I like being spanked. I like my hair being pulled." Fuck. My cock was hard now. "I've never done anything outdoors, but the thought of being caught..."

"Is part of the lure," I said. Because it was. I'd fuck her on my porch, knowing anyone could drive up, and that would turn me on. There was a thrill to it. "I haven't been caught yet. Scout's honor."

She shook her head. "I swear. You're crazy, Cam."

"Crazy about you. And ready to take you home."

"I'm finished if you are."

I pulled out my wallet and slid out of the booth, putting down cash. Her eyes widened.

"I can pay—"

"I know you can, but you're not. Come on, sunshine, before someone notices how fucking hard I am."

Her gaze fell down below my belt, that blush turning her whole face cherry red. She stood up, and I took her hand, leading her out of the cafe.

I led her to my truck and opened the door for her before she could do it. Her hand slid over my chest, her touch sending another spear of desire through me.

It was going to be the longest drive home known to man.

I went around to the driver's side and got in, starting the truck. I twisted in my seat, planting my hand on her headrest as I turned and backed up.

"How tinted are your windows?" she asked.

I let out a low growl. "As tinted as they can be legally."

"Can I touch you, Cam?"

Every part of my body screamed yes. "I'm all yours, baby girl."

CHAPTER THIRTEEN

I NEEDED TO TOUCH HIM. I needed to do something. I'd been squeezing my thighs together since the middle of our breakfast, my entire body wanting him more than anything else.

I needed to forget about what happened with my sister. I needed to get out of my head. But even if that wouldn't have happened, I would have wanted him.

I leaned over in my seat, running my fingertips over the outline of his cock, and his breath hitched as we hit Main Street. He bit back a curse as I gripped his belt buckle, undoing it and then the button of his pants.

"Haley," he moaned. "Fuck."

I pulled down his zipper and slid my hand into his pants, gripping his hard cock. The sound he made was low and possessive, his hands tightening around the steering wheel.

"I think we should go to my house, and then I'll take you for the car later. Also, Haley, I tested recently and was negative for anything."

"I agree," I said, licking my lips. "And thank you for telling me."

I pushed down his boxer briefs, his cock coming free. He was hard, the veins along his shaft pulsing. I leaned down, taking the head of his cock between my lips and sucking.

"Jesus fucking Christ," he huffed. "We're on Main Street, and you're sucking my cock."

I let out a soft moan. It had been too long since I'd done anything like this, and I was desperate. Desperate for his touch, for the taste of him. My heart beat faster, my cheeks flushing with heat.

"I can't wait to taste you," he growled. "God, I'm not going to make it home. Not if you keep touching me like this. I want to grab your hair and face fuck you." He let out a low hiss.

I took more of his cock, gripping the base. He adjusted in his seat, giving me space to do more. The truck's engine revved as he sped up, hitting one of the roads that would take us out of town.

"My house is like ten minutes from here, and I'm not gonna make it that far, sunshine."

I drew back, licking my lips as I looked up at him. His muscles were stiff, his eyes laser focused on the road. "Do you want me to stop?"

"No," he rasped. He drew in a steadying breath, glancing at me. My pussy throbbed from the intensity of his gaze. "No. But I'm going to pull over at a spot I know. Can you touch yourself for me?"

"Yes," I whispered. I leaned back in my seat for a moment, letting out a whimper as I undid my jeans and pulled them down. He stole a glance at me, his knuckles whitening on the steering wheel.

Had I worn a red lace thong wondering if something might

happen? Yes. Yes I had. And I was thanking past me for that decision now.

"Holy fuck," he whispered as I kicked the denim free. "I changed my mind. I think red is my favorite color."

I reached over and gripped his cock, pushing my other hand under the lace. I was wet, so wet for him.

"That's a good girl," he groaned. "We're only a couple minutes away from the spot."

All the tension between us was making every touch more intense. I whimpered as I touched my clit, pleasure electrifying every nerve ending in my body.

"I want to taste you," he whispered.

"Fuck," I groaned. "I'm so wet."

"I know, baby. Keep going, we're almost there."

My head tipped back, a gasp leaving me as he slowed the truck and took a sharp right down a country road. He sped down it, kicking up a cloud of pale dirt behind us.

"Fuck," he mumbled.

He pulled off the road behind three massive oak trees, putting the truck in park. I'd never seen someone get out of a truck so fast. Within a split second, my door was yanked open, a yelp leaving me.

He leaned in and cupped my face. I drank him in, searching his gaze, his searching mine.

"I want you," I whispered. "Please. I need you."

"I want you more than anything in this whole world."

I leaned forward, our lips crashing in a heated kiss. He unbuckled me as he kissed me, his hands running down to my hips and yanking me out of my seat.

I groaned against him, our kiss breaking as my head fell back. He kissed down my neck, sucking my throat gently. Pleasure rolled through me, spreading like a wildfire.

"Reach back and grab the blanket," he commanded softly.

"You were prepared for this?" I asked, raising a brow.

"I'm always prepared, sunshine."

I leaned back and found the blanket he spoke of, pulling it up front. He took it and threw it over his shoulder and then reached for me, picking me up and pulling me out of the truck. I gasped, my legs wrapping around his hips.

"Cam," I rasped, glancing at the road. There were a couple of massive oaks blocking us, but we weren't completely out of view. "Someone could drive by."

"No one will see us," he promised, his voice gruff.

He carried me to the back of the truck and flipped down the tailgate, putting down the blanket. Within a couple of moments, he sat me on the edge and pushed me back.

I gasped, my back arching as he pushed up my shirt and cupped my breasts. He trailed kisses down my stomach until he came to the red lace, pushing my thighs apart.

"You're fucking perfect," he whispered. "Do you want me to stop?"

"No," I gasped. "Please don't stop. I need you."

He nodded and pressed his face between my thighs. I gasped as he pulled the lace to the side, his tongue circling my clit. I arched up, gripping the blanket as I cried out.

"Cam," I moaned.

A hunger rolled through me, one that only he could satisfy. I ached for him, my body desperate for more.

"You taste so fucking sweet, sunshine," he rasped.

He continued, circling and sucking, teasing and driving me wild. His tongue dipped lower, pushing inside of me and lapping at my entrance.

"Cam," I rasped. "I'm so wet. I need more."

He grunted and gripped my hips, pulling me hard against him, burying his face in. The man wasn't a liar—he seemed happy to stay down there between my thighs until he made me see stars.

I gasped, waves of pleasure working through me. I wanted to feel his cock inside of me, but it felt so good to just be pleasured like this. I reached down and gripped his dark hair, letting out a sharp cry as an orgasm suddenly tore through me.

He didn't pull back until I finished. I melted against his truck, gasping through the lustful haze. He let out a soft hum, kissing back up my body.

"So. Fucking. Perfect," he huffed.

In one motion, I was lifted again, but this time, he climbed into the back of the truck. The tires bounced as he moved us up, spreading out the blanket.

"This is crazy," I said. But I felt the thrill, the wildness of being so close to a road where anyone could see us. My pussy throbbed still, the ache between my legs desperate for more.

Cam cupped my face and kissed me, pulling me on top of him to straddle his lap. He lifted my shirt and threw it to the side, letting out a low whistle, his gaze running over my body.

"This red lace is killing me," he said appreciatively, his gaze fixated on the matching bra I'd worn. "You're spoiling me, sunshine."

I grinned. I loved the way he looked at me. It had been a long time since someone looked at me like this, like I was everything they could possibly want in the world. Really, had anyone ever looked at me like this?

He reached around with one hand and undid my bra, drawing a gasp from me.

"Look at you," I teased him. "One-handed and everything."

"Keep teasing, sunshine. Soon, you'll be screaming my name so loud the heavens will hear you." He tossed my bra to the side and took a nipple between his lips.

I gasped as he sucked, my head falling back. I could feel his cock throbbing against me, his calloused hands running up and down my body, sending waves of need through me. I rocked against him, moaning as he moved to my other nipple and sucked.

"Fuck," I whispered. "*Cam*. I need you."

"You got me right here, baby. Right here."

I rocked my hips against him again in demand, gasping as pleasure kept rolling through me. The heat between us was magnetic, every sane thought short-circuited by the need for him. I ran my hands over his hard muscles, appreciating them. "Please," I rasped.

He let out a little growl and lifted me, pulling my panties free and lowering me back down on his lap. He paused, cursing under his breath. "Condoms. Glove box."

"I'm on birth control."

He looked up at me, his eyes searching me. "Are you sure? I don't want you to be uncomfortable."

"I want you to come inside me," I whispered. "But only if you also want that. If you don't, then we can grab the condoms."

"Fuck," he breathed out.

I started to pull back, wincing. "It's okay, we can grab them—"

"Sunshine, you have no idea how badly I want to shove my cock inside you and come." He bucked his hips up and kicked his jeans and boxer briefs off.

I looked down between us and gripped his cock, stroking up. Precum dripped from the tip. I licked my lips and leaned down, swiping it up. He cursed as I sucked, and then he gripped my bun, pulling me back.

I raised up, the head of his cock brushing against me. He kissed my throat as he lifted me, holding me in place before slowly sliding me down.

A raspy cry left me. I took him slowly, his cock easing inside, every inch making me moan.

"You're so tight," he whispered. "You feel so good."

I sank down all the way, his cock throbbing inside me. He kissed my throat again, his fingers digging into my thighs as he thrust up hard.

We both moaned. He pulled me up and then back down, the pleasure between us rolling into a storm of lust. I held on to him as we fell into a rhythm, a harsh one, a desperate one. I couldn't get enough of his touch, his kisses. I bounced up and down on his hard cock, my nails scraping his shoulders as I moaned.

He bit back another curse and suddenly pushed me onto my back, my legs wrapping around his hips as he pinned me beneath him and thrust into me harder. Deeper.

"Cam!" I cried, holding on to him.

He rutted into me harder, and I held on tighter, a release suddenly rolling through me. I arched against him with a cry as my orgasm took root, my vision blurring as I came. He didn't slow, didn't stop, just kept going, fucking me through the pure bliss.

"I'm so close," he rasped. "You feel so good."

"I want you to fill me," I whimpered.

"I am, sunshine. You're going to take every fucking drop."

He pumped into me harder until he let out a deep moan, giving one last thrust. I felt the heat of him as he came inside me, my legs tightening around him. He slowly relaxed, the two of us panting.

I met his gaze, and we both held on until I let out a laugh.

"We're crazy," I whispered.

"I'm crazy about you," he murmured, caressing my face. "More than I've ever been about anyone. I've never felt this way before."

I felt myself melt underneath him. I knew what he was feeling because I was feeling it too. And it made no sense, right? That the two of us would work this well together. But that had been some of the hottest sex I'd ever had, and he was sweet too.

The sound of an engine had both of our eyes widening. He lifted his head slightly and then snorted, hunkering back down. We tensed as a car rumbled down the road not that far away, but they never stopped.

The moment they were gone, I let out a low laugh. "You've turned me into a criminal, Cameron Harlow."

He chuckled and planted a kiss on me. He slowly began to pull out, leaning back and looking at his cum dripping out of me. He let out a soft moan, reaching between my legs.

I gasped as he pushed it back in. He had this look on his face, a possessive one. One I'd never seen before. The sun dappled his tan skin, his gaze searing me as he pushed more of his cum back inside of me.

Something shifted between us. I wasn't sure exactly what it was, but I knew there was no going back. Not after this. But I didn't want to go back.

"Cam," I whispered.

"I've wanted to be with you since the first day you came to Citrus Cove," he said, still looking at my pussy. "I've dreamed about you. Touched myself thinking about you. I've felt guilt over how fucking mean I was to you. How much of an idiot I was."

"Cam... I told you we can leave that in the past."

"You can," he said softly. "But now that I have a second chance, I'm going to spend every moment I can worshiping you. Making up for being such a damn fool."

My mouth fell open, a shiver working through me. I could spend all day with him. Hell, I *wanted* to spend all day with him.

He finally let out a soft moan, leaning back on his heels. "We've got to get dressed, and I need to get you to my bed, sunshine. I'm not done with you yet. Unless you have plans today."

The sun burned above us, a gentle breeze caressing my skin. I smirked, raising a brow.

Even if I did have plans, I'd be canceling all of them.

"I think all my plans are with you, Cam."

CHAPTER FOURTEEN

cameron

I WAS GOING to kill my older brother.

As I pulled up my driveway, I cursed, and Haley laughed. My cum was still inside her, and I planned on ripping off her jeans again and fucking her once we got inside, but all of my plans came to a halt as I parked next to Hunter's truck.

"He's been gone for a couple weeks, and today of all days, he shows back up," I muttered.

Hunter was sitting on my front porch, drinking a beer. He took a slow sip from the bottle, watching us.

"Well," Haley said, studying him. She grabbed her hair tie and began pulling her wild curls back, glancing at me. "I'm not sure if we were keeping things secret, but I think he's about to figure out what's going on."

I couldn't help but smile like a damn idiot. Her curls were mussed and her cheeks rosy from our activities. It wasn't too hot today, but we were both covered in a sheen of sweat. Yeah, there was no way in hell we'd sneak anything by him. But I didn't care. Fuck, I wanted the whole world to know that she was mine.

Mine. It was possessive. Maybe a little crazy. But now that I finally had her, I wasn't going to just let her go. That would make me an idiot, and I did my best not to be one.

"I don't know how to tell you this, but I'm pretty sure the whole town will know, considering we almost kissed at the cafe earlier," I said. And the way I looked at her. Anyone with eyes would know I wanted her.

"True. Well, we have to get out sometime."

I opened the truck door, going around to open Haley's before she could. I liked opening the door for her. I liked doing things for her.

Fuck. God damn it, Hunter. He was messing with my plans.

I glanced up at him as she got out of the truck and watched as he raised a dark brow, measuring the situation. He'd been the one to kick my ass all those years ago, and here I was with Haley Bently getting out of my pickup with my cum inside her.

Holy hell. That pleased me more than it should have. If I hadn't known before, it was clear now that I had a breeding kink. Or maybe Haley was my kink. Either way, I was satisfied knowing my cock would be filling her again soon.

Focus.

"You're home," I said to Hunter as I led her to the porch. Her hand slid into mine, and a wave of pride washed over me.

He rocked back and forth in the wooden chair, his gaze going from me to her and back again. "Haley Bently," he said, leaning forward. "I hope he's not being a pain in your ass."

"Far from it. Hi, Hunter," she greeted. "You look good."

"So do you," he said, his gaze rolling over her. Hot temper crept up my spine. He looked back at me. "I didn't realize I'd be interrupting something."

"Could have called," I quipped. "Or texted. Emailed even."

"You know I prefer snail mail." His teasing didn't amuse me.

My front door was already open, which wasn't a surprise. Sammy, Hunter, and Colt had keys to my house, I had keys to theirs, and we all had keys to Mom and Pops'. It's just the way it was.

"Was on a plane and then on I-35, which you know is always shit. They've been doing construction since before we were born." He stood up and gave Haley the warmest smile. "Want a hug, sweetheart?"

Fuck. I was a jealous bastard, it turned out. I glared at him as Haley gave him a brief side hug. I met his gaze over the top of her blonde ringlets, seeing a flicker of anger there.

Did he think I was going to hurt her?

"I'll see you later, and we'll catch up," Hunter said. "Mom and Pops are back. I think the plan was for us to have a family meeting over dinner tonight. You can come too, Haley."

"Oh, I don't want to intrude," she said.

"Nonsense," Hunter said. "I'm sure you'd be more than welcome. Besides, I have some questions. One of my best friends is an officer."

Fuck. I'd forgotten he was close with Alexa Davis, who was basically Bud's right-hand woman. Of course she'd called Hunter. Alexa and I had never been close, nor was she a favorite of mine. Probably because she'd stolen Jenny Hardy out from under me in tenth grade and left her with a broken heart. I could hold a grudge, that much was true.

Haley stiffened next to me. "I thought officers were supposed to keep things to themselves."

"Not in this small of a town," Hunter said, frowning. He took a swig of his beer, finishing off the bottle. "I won't pry right now. But are you okay?"

"Yes," she said, her voice becoming stoic. I stole a glance at her, feeling a bit of worry. Was she okay? Of course not. How could she be? "Maybe you can get them to actually do something helpful. Since she's your friend and privacy doesn't exist around here."

Hunter winced. "Sorry, Haley. I'll get out of y'alls hair. And hopefully see you later."

"The shower is upstairs," I said to Haley, opening the door for her. "I'll be up in a minute, sunshine."

"See you." She gave Hunter a wave and went inside.

I wanted to catch up with him just for a moment. Despite the flicker of jealousy and uneasiness, I loved my brother. Was I pissed that I'd been working my ass off over the last few weeks and got fucked by half the family? Yes. But now that they were all back, my work schedule would balance back out. Which meant I'd have more time for Haley.

I shut the door and turned and managed to step out of the way before Hunter landed his punch. He hit the wooden frame and cursed, shaking his hand as he drew it back.

"For fuck's sake."

"What the fuck are you doing?" he growled.

I pushed him back, letting out a low snarl. "What are *you* doing? We're too old to be fistfighting. You'll throw out your back, old man."

"Fuck off," he said, narrowing his gaze. "I'm only two years older than you."

"Your point? I see the grays."

Hunter looked a lot like me, except his hair was a little bit longer, and there were a couple of silver strands that sprouted near his temples.

"I blame our parents," he said. "I didn't know Haley Bently was back in town. And I sure as hell didn't know you were screwing her. And according to Alexa, she has been through hell and back. They called Baltimore and got the reports. So imagine my surprise when I got a call from her today and she asked me if I knew anything about the two of you and if I'd seen anything out of the ordinary."

I took a step closer to him, rage pumping through me. "First of all, watch your fucking mouth. This is more than some quick fuck or a one-night stand. Second, there is a lot going on. And you're right, she's been through hell. I'm hoping right now that demon didn't find anything out about her, or if he did, he just lets it go."

"Yeah, they're hoping that too." Hunter took a deep breath, shaking his head. "Is she really okay? She looks good. And before you growl at me like a fucking monster, the message is received loud and clear. She's off-limits."

"She is," I said, stiffening. "As far as okay—she's stronger than anyone I've ever known. And she's doing the best she can. She came here to forget what happened there, and now it seems like it's just going to follow her. All I can do is protect her."

"You can't protect everyone," Hunter warned.

Maybe he was right. Maybe he wasn't. I'd spent a lot of my time over the years doing what I could for people. Helping them, being a good neighbor, keeping Citrus Cove afloat. When I opened the winery, it had been partially because our sleepy town needed more tourists to thrive. And it worked.

"Maybe not everyone, but I can protect *her*."

We stared at each other for a couple of moments, and then he took a step back, holding up his hands. "You're grown. And not a dumbass most of the time."

"Thanks," I muttered, shaking my head. "I'll see you at dinner. I need to fill all of you in on some stuff too. Also, this is my formal notice that I'm taking off for a few days next week, considering I've worked nonstop since the three of you decided to go on vacation. Sammy and Colt have been working overtime. And I hired Haley to help with the bar." And to hopefully help her get through everything.

I wished that I could do more for her.

The thought of something happening to her sent a cold fear through me that bled into my bones. I'd seen those photos. I'd heard her story. I hated that Bud said there wasn't much he could do.

We didn't know the killer's name. Where he was from. Didn't know what info he had on Haley. None of it sat right with me, and there wasn't a damn thing I could do about it.

"I'll get more info from Alexa," Hunter said. "And I'd already planned on working the bar this weekend. You can relax. I'm not sorry for being gone though. We all need a break sometime." His so-called "break" had come after a fight with Pops. One I still wasn't one hundred percent privy to.

I decided to pry a little. "You and Pops okay?"

Hunter's eyes glistened with a hint of anger. "Do you want to talk about that, or do you want to go be with Haley?"

He had a point. Family problems could come later. There was a naked woman waiting for me upstairs. "I'll see you," I sighed. "And thank you."

He winked and then went down the steps to his truck.

I went inside and locked the door behind me, my shoulders slumping.

Small towns. Word traveled too damn fast. And the gossip that had blown in with Haley's arrival would be too much for Citrus Cove to withstand. They'd be talking about her, talking about us.

Maybe it was a good thing. We protected our own here. If someone felt out of place, people would scrutinize them. It was a curse and a blessing.

I heard the water running upstairs. My house was two

stories and decorated by my mom. I didn't have a sense of style when it came to homes.

It was too big for one man. I kicked off my shoes, thinking about Haley.

There was a very real part of me that wondered if she'd ever share this home with me.

Or would she leave?

I started up the staircase and went to my bedroom. Steam billowed in my room, her voice a soft hum. A song. I smiled.

Haley sang in the shower.

That was cute. And hot.

I stripped off my clothes, put my worries out of my mind, and opened my shower door, thankful that I'd invested in the kind that I could have fun in.

"Hey," I said.

She turned, hot water running down her naked body. I let out a low whistle, looking at her unabashedly, feasting on how knock-down-dead gorgeous she was.

"Hey," she said.

"Mind if I join you?" I was already reaching for her, pulling her against me. She leaned up, wrapping her arms around my neck, my cock pressing against her.

"I was waiting for you to," she said.

Fuck. She was the end of me. I couldn't get enough of her.

I backed her against the stone wall, the water beating on my shoulders as I kissed her. My hands ran over her smooth skin, touching and cupping and squeezing. She moaned against my mouth as I slipped two fingers between her soft thighs, circling her clit.

"Oh," she rasped, arching against me.

She'd come twice for me, but I wanted more. I wanted to watch her face, to feel her on my hand as she cried out. Steam swirled around us, her eyelashes dark against her cheeks as she closed her eyes.

Fuck. She had a beautiful voice. Perfect for singing and for moaning. I kept teasing her clit, rubbing her faster as I leaned down and sucked her nipples.

More soft noises, cries and gasps, all growing more urgent as I continued. I watched her, enchanted by her. Touching her this way was a gift.

"Cam," she moaned. "Fuck. You're doing something to me."

I smiled as hot water rolled over my body, never easing up. She thrust against my hand, grinding against me as I circled her faster, egging her on.

She gripped my shoulders, her nails scratching me again. The pain made my cock hard. I wanted her to leave her marks on me.

"That's my girl," I rasped. "You're so close, sunshine."

She responded with a sharper cry.

"Are you going to come for me, baby?"

"Yes," she gasped. "*Fuck.*"

I fought back a chuckle as she suddenly yelped, every muscle in her body tensing as she came on my hand. I held her, kept her from falling, all while feeling her orgasm.

Fuck. She was gorgeous. She was everything I could ever dream of and more.

She collapsed against the shower wall, her eyes finally opening as if she were floating back down to earth. I lifted my fingers to my lips and sucked, the taste of her making me moan.

Her eyes widened.

"Can't get enough of you," I whispered, licking them clean.

"You keep shocking the hell out of me."

And I liked that. I chuckled and kissed her, pulling her against me. I reached for the soap on the rack and lathered it up, washing the two of us. I took my time, rubbing her muscles, feeling every part of her.

That familiar silence settled over us. It was sweet, like pulling on a favorite sweatshirt. How could it be like this with her? Years passed like no time at all. As if we'd always known each other.

I kissed the curve of her neck as the last of the soap went down the drain.

She turned, looking up at me and smiling. "You're good at this."

"Thanks," I said, kissing her again. Again and again. I couldn't stop myself.

Haley was a drug made just for me. I'd never been a man of faith, but seeing how perfect she was for me made me start to question.

"I propose that we order pizza and snuggle," I said.

"I think that's perfect."

CHAPTER FIFTEEN

I'D BEEN SMILING for days. Smiling so much that my cheeks were starting to hurt.

Not really, but I wouldn't be surprised if they started.

I sat in the kitchen across from Honey, the two of us drinking our coffee and reading. She read her newspaper, and I scrolled my phone mindlessly, thinking about Cam.

The last few days had been perfect. We'd yet to get to the picnic, although the plan was for this week, because we'd been in bed what felt like the whole time. We'd found a nice rhythm too.

Wake up, have breakfast, make love, have lunch, make love, work at the bar for a few hours, and come back to his place and make love until we passed out. I had to make a point to come by Honey's today and grab my laptop and pack a bag—and to also have breakfast with her instead of Cam.

"You might as well be whistling," Honey teased, eyeing me over the edge of the paper. She took a sip of her coffee.

"I'm not that bad," I hissed.

"Thou doth protest too much, sweetie. You got that look. I felt that way about your grandfather."

I looked up at her, surprised to hear her mention him. There were only a few things that she never talked about, but he was one of them. I'd never known him. He'd passed in a car wreck before I was born. I had a suspicion that my mom started struggling around the time he went.

"You never talk about him," I said softly.

She swallowed hard, her shoulders sinking some. "I've been thinking about him more recently. About how proud he would have been of you. Of Sarah. I think seeing Mr. Johnson has got me in my feels. But your grandfather was the light of my life. I loved him more than anyone else in the whole world. And he was a good dad too."

"It makes me happy to hear about him," I said.

"It makes me happy to talk about him. A little sad, still, but mostly happy. He would have liked Cam."

"You think?" I asked.

"I know," she said, beaming. "I like him. He's good. And hopefully that means you're staying here for good."

I blew out a breath. I wasn't sure about that. In fact, I'd done my best not to think about it.

"We'll see," I said.

She pursed her lips but didn't say anything else, going back to her paper. I studied her for a few moments and then finally asked something that had been bugging me for almost a week.

"Why is Sarah refusing to see me? To speak to me? I saw her at a cafe last week, and she refused to talk to me. I get that it has become tense between us, but I never did anything to her. And I'm concerned about her and David." All of it came spilling out, but Honey never interrupted.

"I don't know exactly when things changed," she said, putting down her newspaper. "Quite frankly, I blame that man. He doesn't seem to hit them. No physical abuse. But I worry about her, and I worry about the boys. Everyone in this town knows that he drinks. Cam would know, certainly, since he's banned him from his place."

"So is it David, then?" I asked. "Are you sure she's okay?"

"No. But she claims she is. I barely know her anymore."

Fuck. I glared at Honey and then shook my head. "Why didn't you call me? Why didn't you tell me about any of this? She's my sister."

"And I raised her as my daughter. This has been a tough situation. And I didn't want to burden you."

"Burden me?" I asked, setting my phone down. "This is a big deal. I saw the way he spoke to her, Honey. It's not right. Something ain't right."

"I agree," she said, exasperated.

"Then why isn't anyone doing anything?" My voice was a little louder than I'd intended, and I quieted back down, leaning back in my seat.

"Sweetie. I love you. But you haven't been home in a long, long time. Things have changed around here. I've done my best to be here for her, but you can only do so much. And I love those boys, so I'm not going to rock the boat with David."

Rock the boat. I hadn't heard that phrase in so long, but it infuriated me. There had been so many times growing up that I'd been told to quiet down. To be placid. To not cause any trouble.

Asking valid questions and seeking answers was not looking for trouble. If my sister was being harmed, then someone had to hold the person doing the harm accountable.

This was why I'd left. Things like this. The only parts of me that I shed when I moved were the toxic habits ingrained so deep into families that it was a pollution in the roots.

"I know this sort of thing upsets you, but I think you should focus on yourself. On you and Cam. And on forgetting what happened in Baltimore. That was a nightmare, and you've already had enough of those in your life."

I took a deep breath. Counted to three. And made myself let it go. Because I wasn't going to get anywhere with her.

But I needed to get my sister alone. Maybe then she'd talk to me.

"What's her address?" I asked.

"Haley." I heard the warning in her voice and ignored it.

"What is her address, Honey? If you don't tell me, I'll just find out from someone else in this hellhole."

Her eyes glimmered, but she caved. "1210 Honeydew Lane. If a blue car is in the drive, that's David's, and you'd be smart to move on."

I was so frustrated. So fucking frustrated. I stood up and went to the foyer. I slipped on my tennis shoes and grabbed my bag, keys, and a ball cap.

As I went out the door, I could have sworn I heard her whisper that she was sorry.

It hurt. It hurt knowing that Sarah could be hurting. And it hurt knowing that Honey let it happen. But I couldn't put that on her entirely.

My phone buzzed in my pocket as I walked out to my Corvette. I pulled it out and sighed.

He called me sunshine, but in truth—Cam was the rainbow through my storm.

Cam: *Hey pretty lady. How about some lunch? I know you miss Honey but she can't keep you all to herself...*

I snorted.

Me: *It's funny, she said something similar earlier.*

I hesitated but decided to tell him where I was going.

Me: *I'm going by Sarah's.*

Cam: *Everything okay?*

No. Yes. It was hard to tell.

Me: *I'll tell you later. I'll meet you at the cafe after?*

Cam: *How about we finally do our picnic instead?*

Me: *Yes. I'll come once I'm done*

Cam: *Preferably while I'm inside you*

I hissed through my teeth, my cheeks flaming. This man drove me wild in ways I didn't know were possible.

I sent him some kissing emojis and then got in my car, cranking it on.

I decided to stop by the gas station on the way there to fill up and grab a couple of Pepsis. When Sarah and I had gone rounds when we were younger, that had always been our truce beverage.

Maybe it would pull her out of her shell.

I hopped out to pump the gas and then went inside to pay. The hair on the back of my neck stood up as I went to one of the coolers. I glanced up, seeing the reflection of David standing there.

I spun around, my heart skipping a beat. He'd already turned around so I didn't see his face.

Maybe he had a lookalike? The clothing he wore was different from anything I'd expect to see David Connor in. I snatched my Pepsis up, my gaze following the man as he went outside to his car.

I breathed out. Definitely not David. He was driving a small electric car.

I took my sodas to the counter and paid for everything, shaking off the jump scare as I went back out to my car.

Within a few minutes, I was easing down Honeydew Lane. I slowed as I passed her house, staring at the driveway. It was empty, aside from a small Honda. Her old Honda.

"Jesus Christ," I muttered.

That thing didn't have AC when we were teens, and I

somehow doubted it had any now. The fact that she was still driving that made me feel bad. I went to the cul-de-sac at the end of the street and turned back around, pulling up to her drive and parking.

She was going to be pissed, and I braced myself as I went to the front door and knocked, holding the soda out as an offering.

It took a few moments, but the door pulled open.

"I told you I don't want to talk," she growled, but her voice held no bite.

"I know when you're lying, Sarah," I whispered. "It doesn't matter that I haven't talked to you in so long. I *know* you."

Her cheeks flared red, her gaze sliding down to the drink. One moment, two, three... And then her eyes filled with tears. "You can't be here, Hal. You can't. You can't come in."

"Then come with me," I pressed. "I'll drive you out of town. We'll take a day trip. We'll go talk somewhere safe." I needed to get her out of here. Cam would understand.

She shook her head. "No. I have to be here. And I have a shift later tonight. You can't come in."

Pain. Rage. Sadness. All of those emotions whirled inside me, but through it all, I felt worry. A deep-rooted worry that my sister wasn't okay.

"Sarah," I said. "I'll meet you at your work tonight. Okay? I'll be in the back. We'll be sneaky like we used to."

She crossed her arms, but she nodded. "Okay."

"Okay," I breathed out. "Is he hitting you?"

"He doesn't hit," she said.

Somehow, that didn't make me feel better.

"What time do you work?"

"Meet me at 10:00 p.m.," she said, her voice sounding a little stronger. "But you need to go. Everyone knows your car, Hal. And he doesn't like visitors here."

That fucking bastard.

"I love you," I said, my voice soft. Softer than I'd meant to be. I shoved the soda at her and she took it reluctantly.

"I love you too." She shut the door.

I stood still for a moment. How had things become so fucked-up? I felt tears in my eyes, and I fought their harsh sting as I went back to my car.

Everything was falling apart. My life. My career. My family.

I started the car and felt my phone buzz again. I sighed and pulled it out, expecting Cam.

Unknown: *You're next*

CHAPTER SIXTEEN

MY BREATHING BECAME SHALLOW. My hand began to shake, my entire body trembling. I looked around, expecting to see someone. A monster, a shadow, a man with a mask and a gun. Something.

But there were no signs of movement in the quiet Citrus Cove neighborhood.

"Fuck," I whispered, my voice shaking.

It had been easy to forget there was a killer out there, hunting me down.

My phone rang again.

Unknown: ...

A photo came through. I refused to look at it. Not until I was home to Cam.

Not until I was safe.

I felt like I was going to vomit as I floored it, speeding as much as I could without actually getting a ticket. It took about fifteen minutes before I got to Cam's.

I parked abruptly, throwing my door open. He was on the front porch in his rocking chair, grinning.

But then he saw me, and his grin fell.

He was up and moving. I stumbled forward, and he caught me, the weight of everything bringing me to my knees.

I let out a loose sob, holding on to him.

"What happened? What happened? Are you okay? Baby." He held me, his arms tight.

I saw her face again. The blood. The life leaving her. The knife. The man in the mask who'd promised I was next. It replayed in my mind over and over again.

Cam lifted me, holding me tight to him. Within a few moments, he settled into his rocking chair, holding me in his lap, cradling me as it rocked back and forth.

The nausea settled, the shaking stopping.

I realized that he was singing.

Tears filled my eyes as I listened to his voice. Soft and sweet, his touch gentle and firm. I buried my face against him, breathing in his scent as his chest reverberated with his song.

And I realized he was singing "You Are My Sunshine."

I let out a soft laugh, but it was mixed with a sob. If I could go back in time and tell my sixteen-year-old self that one day, Cameron Harlow would be rocking me on his front porch, singing me a lullaby, I would have told myself I was crazy.

But I wouldn't have it any other way.

"I think I can talk now," I whispered. Fuck, I was a mess. I sounded like one too.

"You don't have to," he said gently, nuzzling the top of my head. "Not yet. We can just sit here for a few minutes. I could hold you forever. And I'll protect you from whoever put that look in your eyes."

I melted against him, staring out at his yard. He owned the perfect country house, surrounded by oak trees and flowers. The only things missing were pets and kids.

I blinked, startled by that thought.

That I could grow old like this.

He kept humming and rocking until I felt a calmness I hadn't felt in ages. I took a deep breath again and looked at him, cupping his face. He'd trimmed his beard today, keeping it nice and neat. He gave me a gentle smile, even though I could see the worry.

To think that the man who'd made me come last night while he bent me over the couch and pulled my hair was the same man holding and singing to me was a mystery and a miracle.

"You are my sunshine?" I asked.

He chuckled, still rocking us. "My grandma used to sing it all the time. It was her favorite lullaby. And it always calmed me. She passed away a few years ago."

I softened even more. "I'm sorry."

"She lived a long life," he said. "She was ninety-eight and surrounded by six sons and daughters and eighteen grandchildren. Some great-grandchildren too."

"Your family amazes me."

"I still need to show you our family tree," he said. "Her initials are up there next to my grandpa's. Been there for a long, long time."

I grinned at him.

"There she is," he whispered, cupping my face, running his thumb over my dimple.

I leaned in and kissed him, sinking into the feeling of him until I really could talk about what happened. "I saw Sarah. I'm meeting her after work tonight, and we're going to talk. I'm worried about her."

He frowned, his brows drawing together. "I can come with you."

"No," I said. "Well, maybe." After the text message, I wasn't so sure I wanted to be out at night alone. I was brave, but I wasn't stupid. "After I spoke to her, I got into my car and got a text message. There's still one I haven't looked at yet."

He stiffened. "Where's your phone?"

"In the car."

"Fuck," he mumbled. He lifted me, deposited me back in the chair, and then went down to my car.

I pulled my legs to my chest, watching as he grabbed my phone. I knew the moment he saw the messages because his entire body stiffened, and I heard him curse.

He came back to the porch, his eyes the color of flint. "Can I call my brother? He can help."

"Hunter?" I asked.

"Yes," he said, his voice firm. "He has friends. Friends who run in different circles than me. We're going to figure this out."

I nodded, swallowing hard. "What was the other message?"

Cam pressed his lips in a thin line. His reluctance made my heart beat a little faster. He handed me my phone, and my stomach dropped.

The photo that the number sent was of us. Of me and Cam, together at the cafe in town. We were laughing, oblivious to the fact that someone was watching us.

I felt light-headed.

Cam leaned down in front of me, making me meet his gaze. "I'm going to handle this. Okay? No one is gonna hurt you. No one is going to touch you. I'm going to call Hunter, and we're going to figure this out."

"Honey" was all I could whisper.

"We'll make sure she's okay. I'm going to step away, but I'll be right here. Okay?"

"Okay." Tears welled in my eyes. "I'm sorry. This isn't even your problem, and you don't have to do anything."

"Haley," he said, his voice more serious than I'd ever heard it. "I need you to hear me when I say this. Any problem of yours is a problem of mine. And if tomorrow, you decided you didn't want me, I'd still do everything I could to help you. You've been through enough. You've shouldered a lot alone. And you don't need me to handle your problems, but I'm here to help because I want to."

"Why?" I knew why. He knew why. But neither of us said it.

He just squeezed my hand, and that said more than any words possibly could. He rose and went down the porch steps, out onto the drive. "I'll be right here if you need me."

CHAPTER SEVENTEEN

cameron

HUNTER, Colt, Haley, Sammy, Emma via a video calling app, and I all stood around my kitchen table with papers spread out. I'd done my best to cover any gruesome photos with sticky notes, but it hadn't been as thorough as I would have liked.

"Alexa is breaking laws by doing this," Hunter said tightly. "If this ever leaves this house, I'm burying all of you except Haley. She's been through enough."

"Can't bury me," Emma quipped through the mic. She was just a blank screen, set up on Sammy's laptop. Her camera was turned off because she'd claimed she "hadn't slept a wink since her dear best friend abandoned her." I was torn between being amused and annoyed, but I knew beyond a shadow of a doubt she was the person I had to win over in Haley's life.

Hunter snorted. "A corrupt cop for justice. You know Bud isn't going to do shit. And Alexa can't really do anything. So it's up to us to try and figure this out."

I shot him a wary look but didn't disagree. It made me wonder just how often Hunter got involved in things like this. He kept a lot of secrets.

"We won't tell anyone," Colt said for the thousandth time, raking his hands through his hair. He was furious.

We all were.

When I'd called the three of them, it wasn't five minutes later that two trucks and a Jeep barreled down my road. Haley called Emma and filled her in, and Emma demanded to be part of the team.

"I still need to meet Sarah later," Haley reminded me. "At the cafe."

I glanced at the clock. It was 5:00 p.m. The hours had already flown by.

"I know, sunshine," I said gently. "We'll meet her."

"I can go alone," she said. "I'm not helpless." I could hear the frustration in her voice, but it was Emma who spoke up.

"Haley. This is how girls die in the movies, babe. You're going to let Harlow go with you, unless you want me to fly my ass down with Donnie."

"Who's Donnie?" Hunter asked.

Haley fought off a smile. "Her dog."

"He's a ten-year-old Chinese crested," Emma explained.

The four of us guys exchanged glances.

"Is that one of those hairless dogs?" Sammy asked.

"Yes. He wears sunscreen."

Hunter made a face. "Can we get back to business?"

"You're an older child, aren't you?" Emma asked. "I can hear it in your voice."

Hunter glowered at the laptop. "And you must be the youngest."

"Hey," Sammy quipped.

"Children," Colt groaned. "For fuck's sake."

Haley leaned into me as our group argued. I snaked my arm around her, pulling her tight against me. I pressed my face against her curls, breathing in her scent. Jasmine and honeysuckle and a hint of my soap. It made me happy in a way that shot straight to my core.

I was so fucking angry. The photo of us sitting in the cafe had shaken me in a way I never had been before. Someone was stalking us, watching us. Watching her.

It scared me. I'd already shopped online and bought cameras for the property and was planning on making an entire system around Honey's house and mine. The moment they arrived, I'd be installing them. But I wasn't sure what else I could do.

Thunder rolled in the distance, and I raised a brow. Everyone paused. Maybe it was a Texan thing, but getting rain was a good thing. A great thing. Unless it was going to be a flash flood and potentially hurt the farm.

"Check the radar," Sammy told Hunter.

"Already on it," he grumbled.

"What the hell is happening?" Emma asked.

"Just some thunder," Haley snorted. "Probably a storm rolling through." She turned and went to the front door, opening and shutting the screen. The sky was dark, a heavy lull before the rain.

"Not bad," Hunter said. "Farm will be fine. Mom will text us if needed."

Sammy glanced at our brother, giving him the same curious but wary expression that I'd given him before. We'd both noticed he hadn't mentioned Dad.

I gathered that it had to do with who was taking over the Harlow farm. Out of the three of us, I was the only one that ever enjoyed the work our family did, but even I had branched out and created a winery.

"Awesome, so can we get back to finding this maniac?" Emma asked.

"We don't have much," Colton muttered, leaning over the table.

Even with an officer breaking the law and handing over all the info, it didn't look good. They hadn't been able to narrow down who the killer was. Didn't have a name. He hadn't left fingerprints or hair or anything that could be traced back to him.

Hunter had reached out to another friend of his who tracked missing people, but we hadn't been able to trace the phone number. So there was also that.

Haley moved toward me, and I pulled her close. Over the last few days, anytime she wasn't at my side, I found myself feeling like I was missing part of my heart.

"So, I think the best thing that can be done for now is that Haley never be left alone," Hunter finally said. "And maybe keep your gun on you, Cam."

"Do you just carry a gun around?" Emma's voice echoed.

All of us snorted.

"You never know," Hunter said, his jaw set. He clearly wasn't a fan of Emma.

We spent the next hour talking through everything and finally ended the call as the rain began to pour. Hunter and Sammy gave me a hug before leaving, Colt not far behind.

Ultimately, we'd all decided that our only plan at the moment was to be on the lookout. None of it sat right with me, but there wasn't much else we could do.

We stepped out on the front porch as their cars disappeared down the drive. Thunder rumbled, a flash of lightning streaking across the sky. I pulled her close to me, listening to the rain. The scent of it was calming.

"We can sit out if you want," I said. "We still have some time before we go to meet Sarah. No one will find us here." It felt fucked-up that I even had to say that.

"Let's do that," she said.

"Let's go to the porch swing." I offered my hand, and she took it.

I led her around my porch. It wrapped around the entire house, taking us to the back. There was a wooden porch swing waiting for us. I sat down in the center and pulled her against me, my hands settling on her hips.

She let out a sultry laugh, cupping my face. "You're insatiable."

"I haven't been able to take you today," I said, my cock already hardening in my pants. "We've been busy."

She was wearing a long dress. She hiked up the skirt and straddled my lap, her hands bracing my shoulders.

"You're so hard already," she breathed out.

I reached up and undid her bun, watching as her golden curls fell free. Her eyes lit up like the sky behind her, thunder rolling the same way she did her hips. Need struck me fast and hard.

"Haley," I whispered hoarsely.

"I *want* you," she said.

I would never get tired of giving her what she wanted.

CHAPTER EIGHTEEN

I NEEDED him more now than ever. I needed to forget today, to let everything fall away, at least for a bit.

He kissed my throat, lifting my dress over my hips. The rain grew louder as I reached between us, undoing his belt and button. He groaned, cursing under his breath.

"I can't get enough of you." His voice was low, his need raw. He knotted his fingers in my hair and yanked me down, our mouths closing in on each other.

I groaned as we kissed, drinking him in. My body felt like a live wire, the tension of need growing stronger with every touch. He scraped his teeth along my bottom lip, a low moan leaving him.

"I want you to be rough," I gasped.

I needed it. I needed to give in, to be taken in a way that would make my brain stop working.

His grip tightened in my hair, and he paused, his gaze searching mine. "You'll have to tell me what you mean, sunshine. You know the things that I like. And you've told me what you like. But today is not a day we should cross any lines. Ask me what you need, and I will give it to you."

My eyes teared up. I'd never been with anyone that was like him. "I want you to spank me. Restrain me. Blindfold me. I want you to make me come so hard I feel like I'm dying. I want you to use me over and over again, Cam. I *need* you."

He ran his thumb over my cheek, stroking my skin. His eyes reflected the storm around us, his cock throbbing against me. "You want to be my good girl?" he whispered.

A silent thrill ran through me. "Yes. More than anything."

"And if anything is too much, you'll say 'red.'"

"Yes," I promised.

"And you know how much I care for you, right, sunshine?"

"Yes," I said. "I know." Because I did. I knew it more than anything else in the world right now.

He held my gaze and slid me off his lap. "Good. I want you to bend over the porch swing. Use the back to hold on to, and spread your legs for me. And push your ass out."

My pussy pulsed, his demand spreading through me. I turned over and took the position he asked for. I glanced over my shoulder, watching as he leaned forward and grabbed the hem of my dress.

And ripped it.

"Cam," I gasped.

"I'll buy you another one," he promised, tearing it again.

I gasped as he made a strip of fabric and stepped up behind me, pulling it around my head. I gripped the smooth wood of the porch swing, feeling it sway slightly as he leaned against it. He tied the fabric over my eyes, using it as a blindfold.

His fingers curled into my hair, and he yanked hard, drawing a laugh from me. A *laugh*. My entire body lit up, the slight pain turning me on in a way I didn't know was possible.

"You're so needy, sunshine," he whispered, brushing his

lips against the side of my neck. A chill ran through me as he tightened his grip, the butterfly kisses drawing subtle gasps from me.

I shivered. He wasn't even fucking me yet, but every nerve ending was alive. Just the kisses along my neck were making me desperate.

"Cam," I rasped.

He bit my earlobe, drawing a sudden yelp from me.

"Fuck," I cried.

"Spread your legs a little wider, baby. Push that pretty ass back against me."

I gripped the swing, moaning as I arched my back and pushed back against him. Being blindfolded made all of my other senses more intense. He gripped the ends of my curls and tugged, winding them around his fist. I heard the sound of his buckle being undone, his pants being unzipped, and then felt the slap of his cock against my ass cheek.

I gasped, my nipples hardening. He looped a finger around my panties and tugged them down, exposing me completely.

"You're already so wet for me, sunshine," he said. "You look so fucking good like this."

His hand was broad and rough. He gripped my ass cheek and squeezed, drawing a helpless moan from me.

"You're so perfect," he huffed. He squeezed my other ass cheek and then slapped it.

I groaned, arching more as the impact reverberated through my body. "*Cam.*"

He rubbed the other cheek, his hand warming the skin. The anticipation, not knowing when he might spank me, set me on edge. I gripped the back of the swing, my eyes closed. He pulled on my hair as he spanked me, drawing a throaty cry from me.

Being spanked by a hot man wasn't a replacement for therapy, but it damn sure felt like it at the moment.

He grunted and spanked me again, alternating between each ass cheek. I gasped as my muscles became hotter, each impact stinging more.

Right when I expected him to spank me again, his hand slid down, two fingers pushing inside me with ease.

I gasped, cursing. "Fuck."

"You're so wet for me, aren't you, darlin'? You like being spanked and having your hair pulled. If there is a god, they made you just for me."

His words sent a spike of pleasure through me as his fingers began to thrust in and out, slow and teasing. I trembled, my muscles coiling with tension as he leaned down and kissed my spine, his lips soft and beard slightly rough. The sensations came in waves, and my body responded.

The sound of him finger fucking me turned me on.

"Such a dirty girl," he chuckled.

I whimpered, pushing back against him, eager for more. "I need you inside me," I moaned.

"Soon, sunshine."

I gasped as he kept pushing them in and out, his hand smacking my ass. The sound split around us at the same moment thunder rumbled, a low groan leaving Cam.

Pleasure rushed through me until I let out a throaty cry, an orgasm crashing through me. He pulled my head back, making me yell through the wave, my entire body breaking apart just for him.

I sank against the porch swing, feeling it sway slightly. He slowly pulled his fingers free, and then I felt the head of his cock rubbing against me.

He leaned down, his voice like a whisky shot straight to my core. "I'm not done with you, baby."

I whimpered, still catching my breath as he gripped my hips. The porch swing creaked as he thrust forward. I yelped as I took the first few inches and then eased the rest of the way in slowly.

His cock throbbed inside of me. He stayed still, making sure that I was adjusted to his size. I sucked in a breath, craving what was next. Craving to feel him let loose.

"Cam," I whispered.

He hummed to himself, his grip turning gentle for a moment. He slowly pulled back and then thrust forward. I moaned as he did so again and again, setting a rhythm that had my cries echoing out into the stormy evening.

I yelled his name and tossed my head back as he fucked me. It was hot and primal and everything I'd ever needed, especially right now. A shiver ran through me, and I gripped the wood of the swing, groaning as I felt the edge of another orgasm flooding in.

"Cam," I rasped. His name might as well have been god with the way I kept repeating it. *"Cam."*

"Come for me again. I want to feel you squeeze my cock as I come inside you."

I gasped, my back arching as he slammed into me again. Pleasure curled through me, tightening and tightening until I felt it burst, one that rocked me to my very core. I let out a sharp cry as I came, squeezing Cam's cock as he groaned. His grip on me tightened, his breaths hard as he came.

The heat of him filled me, and I felt like I was floating back down from the heavens, my breaths hard.

Finally, he let out the softest chuckle. "You're too good for me, sunshine," he murmured.

I was breathless as he leaned down and kissed my back. His beard tickling my skin, his cock still pulsing inside me.

He reached around me, his arms circling my body. I gasped

as he lifted me, swiftly moving and seating himself on the porch swing, bringing me with him. His cock was still inside me, my back against his chest as he pulled me back.

His hand slid across my thigh, pulling them wide apart.

"Fuck," I whispered.

"I'll never be done with you," he murmured, kissing my neck. He breathed in my scent, his fingers sliding across my clit. His touch was a lightning bolt straight to my pussy. I squeezed him as I gasped, my head falling back on his shoulder.

He was getting hard again.

"I've had years to dream about this," he whispered, slowly circling my clit. "Years, sunshine. To dream about holding you just like this. To have my cock buried in your pretty cunt."

"I can't believe you ever wanted me," I whispered.

His lips were soft against my neck, sending pleasurable waves of lust through me. I let out a short breath, the sensations almost overwhelming. I never realized how sensitive my neck was until now.

"I've wanted you since I laid eyes on you," he rasped. "There's something about you. The day we met, you carved your name into my heart, and ever since then, I haven't been able to let go. Even when you left. There was a part of me that hoped and prayed you might come back again."

His fingers began to circle faster. I tensed against him, my body buzzing with carnal delight.

"I'm yours," he huffed, his hips giving a thrust. "I'm all yours, Haley."

His words were sweet, his touch beyond wicked. I cried out as his free arm wrapped around my waist, holding on to me tight as he began to fuck me again. I bounced up and down on his cock, his fingers still circling my clit. It was like a roller coaster, a never-ending one.

"Fuck," he growled, giving one more thrust.

He came inside me again, his cum shooting in hot ropes. I gasped, another orgasm curling through me, a slow and delicious one. I shivered, my eyes fluttering.

Finally, the two of us melted against each other.

"Holy hell," I whispered.

There were no words. None that could possibly come to mind.

"I have an idea," he said.

"I like your ideas."

"How about we go take a shower, get dressed, and snuggle before we go see your sister?"

I nodded, feeling a smile take over. I couldn't stop myself. "Sure. I think that sounds like a plan."

CHAPTER NINETEEN

I ENDED up falling asleep for an hour or so, which was probably for the best. It gave me the rest I needed before facing Sarah.

By the time Cam pulled us into the diner's parking lot, my nerves were eating me alive.

His hand gripped my thigh as he pulled into a spot at the back of the cafe. It was within eyesight of where Sarah asked for us to meet. He glanced around us, eyeing the other cars.

"He's not here," he confirmed. "And we're right on time."

I glanced at the clock. 9:59.

Nerves and worry rolled through me. Having to meet my sister in secret like this told me that she wasn't safe, and neither were the kids. It infuriated me that no one had done anything.

"Hey," Cam said softly. "It's going to be okay. She's your sister. That much hasn't changed."

She was my sister, but she hardly felt like it.

We sat in silence for a couple of minutes. He squeezed my thigh gently. "I'll be right here," he murmured. "Nothing will happen. Okay?"

I nodded. I swallowed hard as the back door of the diner swung open. The worst of the storm had passed, and now it was just raining. I grabbed my umbrella, leaned over and kissed Cam's cheek, and then got out of his truck.

I popped the umbrella open and walked over to Sarah. She glanced up at me, leaning against the brick wall as she lit a cigarette.

"Hey," I said, giving her a soft smile.

She blew out smoke and put the cigarette out. Our gazes locked, her eyes filling with tears.

"Sarah," I whispered. "Fuck, you've got me so worried."

"I know," she said and then threw her arms around me. I stumbled back slightly but found my footing, holding on to her.

Tears filled my eyes. "I've missed you," I croaked. Her hug was like a knife to the chest, my heart squeezing. I'd missed her so damn much and had done everything I could to forget it. But now, standing here with her, I felt every emotion.

The feeling like we'd abandoned each other.

That she'd stopped caring for me.

There had been many moments over the years, but I'd always shoved them back. Always told myself that we were just busy. She had her kids, and I had my career.

Different lives.

"I've missed you more than you know," she whispered. "I'm sorry I stopped calling. I'm sorry I ignored your messages and calls."

Fuck. Tears started to stream down my cheeks. I didn't let her go, holding her tight, the umbrella protecting us from the rain. Over the last ten years, I'd convinced myself that she'd stopped loving me, but I knew that wasn't true.

She pulled back, cupping my face. "I'm really proud of you. You got out. You made a career and a life for yourself. You followed your dreams, and you do whatever you want. I've never had it in me to do that."

"Yes, you do," I said. "Sarah, you can do whatever you want. And I can help. I can help you get away from him."

Her eyes widened and then softened. "It's impossible to," she whispered, her voice barely audible. "He's never hit one of us. But he breaks things. He yells. He controls everything, Hal. He has all of our finances wrapped up. All of my paychecks go to him. Jake and David do their best to stay away from him."

My stomach twisted, rage rolling through me. "How did it end up like this?"

"It was slow," she said. "At first, he was good. And then we had the boys, and after that, things changed. I don't think he ever loved me to begin with. And I've tried fighting. You know I have a temper and a backbone. But it's not about me anymore."

"It's about the kids," I whispered.

She nodded, swallowing hard.

"You can leave him," I said. "You can. We'll start a new bank account. I'll do whatever I can to help. You can move in with Honey, or I can buy a house here for you and the boys."

"I couldn't let you do that," Sarah said, her shoulders stiffening. "I can't take your money. It's not fair to you. None of this is even your problem."

"You're my sister. And you can take money from me," I insisted. "Especially if it means getting you away from that monster. I had no idea. It seems like everyone else in this fucking town does though."

She snorted, her eyes flickering over to where Cam was parked. She raised a brow, and briefly, I saw a glimpse of the Sarah I knew. The mischievous one. The one that was fun and smart and kind. That didn't have a care in the world.

"You and Cameron? He used to bully you. You hated him."

"Yeah," I said. "I did hate him. And now I think I'm falling in love with him."

"Shit," she whispered. "He's a good guy. Was an idiot in high school. But he's tried to help me, which was what led to him and David having problems."

"I heard." I was glad he fought for her. That he saw what everyone else turned a blind eye to. "What can I do, Sarah? We can move Jake and David first. Send them to Honey. Then I can come to help you move out."

"They're his sons," Sarah said, shaking her head. She let go of me and leaned back against the wall, her shoulders slumping. "He will have the right to visit them. I can't just get rid of him."

I pressed my lips together. She had a point. "You're telling the truth when you say he hasn't hit you?" I felt rage flood through my veins that I even had to ask. "I'd bury him if we weren't in the twenty-first century."

"Haley," she hissed, but she let out a helpless laugh. "But yes, I'm being honest. There's just... something wrong with him. I look back and feel like an idiot. I never saw how broken he was. And it was a slow decline. By the time I realized what kind of man he was, it was too late. I was in too deep. And alone. So fucking alone. I wanted to run away, but I couldn't. I have my kids, and I love them more than anything else in the world." Her words were fiercer when she spoke of Jake and David.

"I always thought you and Colton would end up together," I said.

"Me too," she whispered.

We were silent for a couple of moments. She finally drew in a breath, steadying herself. "He's forbidden me to see you. If we get caught, I don't know what will happen. I've never gone against him."

He was at the very top of my shit list, even above the serial killer that was after me. I hesitated, unsure if I should tell her about everything. About the murder and about how I was being hunted.

But I could see how tired she was. I could see the exhaustion tearing at her soul, and I refused to give her more to worry about.

I reached out, gripping her hand in mine. "We're going to figure this out. You're going to make it out of this. I'm going to make sure you're safe. Do you still have access to my phone number?"

"He checks my phone."

This fucking bastard. "I'll get you a burner phone. I'll talk to Cam. We will figure this out." I felt like I'd said that a million times now, and maybe I was trying to convince myself of it too.

"I need to go," she said sadly. She pulled me into a hug, holding me tight until finally letting go. "I'll talk to you soon. Let's do this again Monday night. I have the late shift again."

"Okay," I said. "Please be safe."

"I will be."

I watched as she went to her car and got in. She turned it on, the engine sputtering to life.

I watched her go, my thoughts churning. My sister had been through hell alone. I felt guilty for it, but then I felt the streak of rage that she'd let herself be pulled into this kind of mess. That she didn't see how she deserved so much better from the start.

But I knew it was hard once you were in that type of relationship to get out. I'd seen Emma go through her own toxic partners, the difference being that she didn't have children involved. It was easier to walk away from someone when you hadn't built a life together, but that didn't mean it was actually *easy*.

Cam's truck lights flashed at me, and I finally snapped

myself back to the moment. I lifted my head and walked over to him, fighting off a snort as he leaned across the seat and opened the door for me before I could.

"Always the gentleman," I teased him, pulling the umbrella closed and getting in.

"I am," he said. "How did that go?"

I sank against the seat, sighing. "Well. Everyone wants to kill me, and all I can think about is murdering David Connor."

CHAPTER TWENTY

cameron

I DECIDED that despite everything happening, if I didn't whisk Haley off for the picnic I'd been promising her, it would never happen.

It had been a couple of days since the text message from her stalker. Nothing else happened since then, and it almost gave me a false sense of security. A hope that maybe he'd decided to move on.

Even if he hadn't moved on, we couldn't let our world simply stop. We had to keep living.

My foot eased on the brakes as I pulled up to Haley's house, eyeing her red Corvette in the driveway next to Honey's old beat-up truck. I smiled, glancing at the picnic basket in the back seat before sliding out and going to the front door.

I knocked and waited.

After a few moments, the door opened, and I was met with her grandmother.

"Mrs. Hamilton," I greeted.

She narrowed her crystal-blue eyes. I suddenly felt like a kid again, ready to be scolded. "You know you can call me

Honey, Cameron Harlow. I'm assuming you're here for my granddaughter and not me."

"I could be here for you too," I said. "I can arrange a nice date for the two of us. Wine and a steak dinner."

She laughed, stepping to the side. "I've got Mr. Johnson for that. Didn't you hear?"

Yep. Haley told me all about her grandmother dating Mr. Johnson. "I may have heard a thing or two..."

She snorted. "Come on in, Cam."

I stepped inside. I'd always loved Honey's house. It reminded me of my own grandmother.

"This is a surprise." Haley's voice drew my gaze to the top of the staircase. She cocked her head. "I thought you said we were meeting up tonight."

"Well," I said, "if you're free, I'd like to steal you for our picnic."

Honey chuckled. "He offered to take me on a date. I think he's a keeper, Haley."

She grinned at her grandmother. "I think he is too."

"You kids have fun." She left us alone, heading toward the back porch.

Haley broke out into a broad smile and came down the steps. I met her on the bottom one, unable to stop myself from bringing her into a kiss. She was freshly showered, her curls damp. Her arms wrapped around my neck, her touch going straight to my cock.

We both pulled back, a soft curse leaving me. I wished that she lived with me because then I'd be able to take her upstairs and taste her before our date.

"Are you sure going out is okay?" she whispered.

I cupped her face. "Yes. No one will find us where I'm taking us, and we can't hide, sunshine. Part of me hopes that the bastard has moved on."

"I wish," she sighed. "I really wish. But you're right. We can't simply sit around and wait."

"I've been promising you a picnic for a week now," I said. "We'll be safe. And I'll finally get to spoil you some..."

She kissed me again, chuckling. "You do like that, don't you?"

"More than you know. If I could buy you the moon, I would."

"What if I don't want the moon?"

"Then the stars," I said. "Or whatever you desire."

"What if I just want you?"

"You've got me."

She pressed her forehead to mine. "Let me get dressed," she whispered, her cheeks blushing. "I'll be back in a few, and then we can go."

"Perfect."

* * *

The drive out to my parents' place went by fast. I'd told them not to disturb us because I didn't want her to be over-whelmed with pleasantries and nosy questions, but I could still see my mom's face in the window as she stole a glance at us.

I was honestly impressed that she was giving us privacy. But she also knew everything that was going on.

Haley grinned at me as we got out of the truck, the picnic basket and blanket secure in my arms.

"Should we go say hi?" Haley asked.

"Nope."

"Do you need help carrying anything?"

"Nope."

"Where are we going?" she asked.

"Just come with me, sunshine," I chuckled.

She rolled her eyes but followed me. I led her back through my mother's garden and then down a path to the vineyard.

"It's not too far of a walk, but if it's too much, I can always carry you," I said.

I heard her snort. "I can walk by myself, Cam."

A smile tugged my lips as I kept treading on. The rain had ushered in cooler weather, and even if it was brief, it was nice. A breeze ruffled us as the path led us on, winding through the rows of grapes until we came to the apple orchard.

I slowed, glancing over my shoulder at Haley. She was beautiful, wearing a pastel-yellow dress that gleamed in the dappled sunlight. She winked at me, and I felt lust curl through me, taunting me.

After another couple of minutes, we finally came to an open field with an oak tree at the center. It was massive, the branches winding up toward the blue sky. I huffed as I sat our basket beneath it, spreading the blanket over the dirt.

"Is this the famous oak tree?" Haley asked.

I took a step back and looked up at it. "Yes, it is," I said proudly. "The Harlow family oak tree."

From here, I could see the different carvings. Initials with hearts, our own ancestry carved into the wood of it. It had weathered storms, the hottest of summers, fires, and much more —just like ours.

"It's amazing," Haley said. "It's even better than I imagined."

I beamed, my heart beating a little faster.

I dreamed of us, one day, carving our names there.

Of her initials next to mine.

Haley's arms suddenly circled around my waist, her face pressing against my back. I closed my eyes, her touch soothing me. We stood like that, soaking up each other's presence, basking in being together.

I'd always wanted this.

I turned around, cupping her face. Gold eyeshadow glittered, drawing out the shades of brown in her eyes. The sun dried her curls, her cheeks rosy from the walk. I wanted to kiss every freckle that dusted across her nose.

"You are stunning," I whispered. "I—" I cut myself off, the words almost tumbling out of my mouth. *I love you.*

Her eyes widened. "Cam..." she whispered.

"I was just going to say that you're so beautiful. I have no words."

My recovery was lame, but she arched a brow and then smiled. She leaned up on her tiptoes, her mouth brushing against mine. "I have a hard time believing that the boy who gave me so much trouble growing up is the sweet-talking man in front of me right now."

I ran my thumb over her cheek, humming. "I've learned a lot from being an idiot. Grown a lot."

Her hands slid over my chest, drifting lower. "You have *grown* a lot."

I swallowed hard, my cock hardening against her. She smirked, a wicked look in her eyes turning me on.

"I wanted to eat first," I said. "And drink. I had it in my mind that I would romance you first and then devour you."

"At your family oak tree?" she teased.

"Right in front of god and my ancestors."

She laughed, her voice music to my ears. "Is that so?"

"Yes." I drew in a deep breath and forced myself to take a step back. There were reasons why I wanted to have our picnic first. "That's what we're going to do."

"You're such a tease," she rasped, shaking her head.

"I am," I said, although it was just as cruel to me. My cock strained against my jeans, protesting at my decision for us to eat first. But it would be worth it.

I moved past her and knelt on the plaid blanket, opening up the basket. She kicked off her shoes and joined me, sitting next to me as I drew out bottles of wine, two glasses, and a plate of cheese and fruit with crackers.

"This is lovely," she gasped. "You made all this?"

"I did," I said. "When I first decided to open a tap house, I visited several in the area. I ended up taking some classes on what pairs nicely with what. I'm a fan of making boards like this."

She reached into the basket, her eyes widening as she pulled out edible flowers and fresh bread.

"Oh my." She bit her bottom lip as I took the items from her. "Bread is my weakness."

"You and me both."

"It looks fresh."

"Mhmm. Picked it up from the bakery this morning. Fresh loaf of rosemary sourdough."

"You're the devil. And by devil, I mean angel. This is amazing, Cam."

I chuckled as I spread everything out. It was lovely, just like her. Just like today. For once, everything had gone to plan.

"I'll open the wine," she said. She poured us two glasses. "I don't know how you kept everything cold," she chuckled.

"Magic and ice packs," I said. "That is a plum wine. It's refreshing and not as sweet as other fruit wines. It's one of my favorites. I also brought a reserve bottle of my favorite cider and a bottle of white wine."

And one of my plans was to lick it right off her body.

I scooted closer to her, lifting a bunch of grapes. She parted her soft lips, taking one into her mouth. I loved watching her; the intimacy of feeding her like this amazed me.

Her cheeks turned red as she swallowed. "This is..."

"A surprise?" I murmured. "There's something... deliciously hedonistic about being fed while being pleasured. And that's what I'd like to do to you."

"I'd like that too," she said.

Her pleasure brought me pleasure. I smiled as I lifted her glass of wine, offering her a sip. I tipped too far, and she made a noise of surprise as it dripped down her chin, streaming down to her breasts.

She swallowed and gasped as I licked it up.

"Oh. This is something I never knew I needed until now." Her voice was filled with lust.

The neckline of her dress dipped down, her breasts pushing against the fabric. I pressed my face between them, biting her softly before drawing back.

"I'm so turned on right now," she whispered. "You're driving me crazy."

"We're just getting started," I murmured.

I set the wineglass down, reaching for the grapes again and watching as she pulled one off, enjoying her blush. I chuckled as I leaned away, reaching for the cheese and bread.

"Drink your wine while I make these," I said. "And open the others if you'd like."

"I feel like a princess."

"You are a princess."

Her silence made me frown, so I looked up at her. Tears glistened in her eyes. I reached for her, cupping her face. "Well, this wasn't how I wanted to make you cry."

"It's just really kind," she whispered, sniffling. She blinked back tears and then laughed. "I don't know how I can be this turned on and teary-eyed at the same time. It's just that no one has ever done this sort of thing for me before."

"Get used to it," I murmured, stealing a kiss.

I spent the next couple of minutes making other snacks for us, slices of cheese on bread, strawberries, grapes, and other fruits spread out on a board I'd brought. She finished her wine and reached for the bottle of cider, uncorking it.

"How did you get into this?" she asked. "Is it just because of the farm, or...?"

"Well. I always wanted something that was my own," I said. "And I love my family, truly, but I needed it to be something that was apart from them. It's still connected, of course. But I just fell in love with it. I like the atmosphere of my place, seeing friends and loved ones come in and spend their time there. And then we get the tourists who are always surprised by the charm of Citrus Cove. It's hard to find places now to live where people take care of their own, but I feel like we do here. And I wouldn't trade that for anything else." I cleared my throat, giving her an apologetic look. "Sorry, that was lengthy."

"Don't be. I love listening to you talk. Especially when it's something you're clearly passionate about."

"I am," I said. "It's stressful sometimes. I work more than I should. But it fulfills me."

She leaned against me, her head on my shoulder. "That's how I feel about my articles. And traveling. I do love to travel— I don't think anything will ever change that. But I think it's mostly that I just love discovering those places that are hidden gems. When Katie and Anna told me they planned their honeymoon around places I recommended, that fulfilled me. That I helped them live their dreams with just my words."

"You're amazing," I said, kissing the top of her head.

I felt the ache return. I would never stand in the way of what she loved. But perhaps there was a middle ground we could find, one that would make us both happy.

I wanted her to stay more than anything else in the world.

"I swore I would never come back here," she whispered. "But lately, it has started to feel like home again."

"That makes me happy," I murmured.

"I'm sure," she chuckled, leaning back to look up at me.

I was drawn into her all over again, and this time, I couldn't resist. I slid my hand behind her neck, fisting her hair. Her breath hitched, her eyes fluttering.

"I thought the plan was to eat."

"It was." My grip tightened. I leaned down, my voice a soft growl in her ear. "But now, I think I'm going to drink our wine off your body and then fuck you so hard you beg me to stop." Her breath hitched, her body pressing against me. "How does that sound, sunshine?"

"Please," she whispered. Her gaze locked with mine, our lips almost touching. "Make me beg, Cameron."

My fingers tightened. I felt a part of me, the part that I did my best to keep at bay, rise up—a primal hunger to take her. To fuck her, to make love to her in a way that could only happen with her.

"When you spanked me, I wished that your handprint would have stayed," she whispered. "I wanted to wake up with your mark on me. To know that you used me. To remember how much pleasure you gave me. Is that wrong?"

"No," I murmured, my cock now fully hard. I ran my hand down her body, cupping her breasts as I kissed her neck. "I want that too. I want every part of you. I want to hear you cry out my name and beg me to fuck you."

She reached out, grabbing the bottle of wine. She held my gaze, her lips pulling into a wicked smile as she tipped it over herself, the drink running down her breasts, soaking into her dress.

"Another dress ruined," she whispered.

"I'll buy you another," I promised.

"I was smart and packed another one in my bag."

"That *was* smart."

I shoved her back onto the blanket, moving on top of her. I parted her thighs with my knee, admiring her.

She gasped as I kissed her chest, licking up the wine. It was sweet on my tongue but not as sweet as the sound of her moans. I grunted and bit her nipple through her dress, biting down until she cried out.

"Oh, Cam," she gasped.

I reached down between us and gripped the bodice of her dress, ripping. The fabric tore, her breasts spilling free. She moaned as I leaned down, licking up the trail of wine that ran all the way down her soft stomach.

"Fucking perfect," I rasped.

She raised up for a moment and unclasped her bra. I pulled it free, immediately taking one of her nipples between my teeth. She cried out as I bit her, a growl leaving me as she arched against my body, her fingers gripping my hair.

I sucked the bite mark, moving to the other breast and doing the same. Biting and sucking, I slowly worked my way down to her pussy.

The noises she made were perfect. The soft gasps of surprise, the whimpers. I pulled the rest of her dress free, her lace panties all that was left.

"How come I'm almost naked, and you're still dressed?"

"Because that's how I want it right now," I teased. "Turn over," I rasped, my voice husky.

She obeyed me, turning over onto all fours. I moved closer and pushed her torso down, her ass up in the air.

"How do you feel about being spanked with a belt?"

Her body stiffened, but her breath hitched. She looked at me over her shoulder. "Are you going to spank me with your belt, cowboy?"

Fuck. The taunt went straight to my cock. I strained against my jeans, needing to fill her. To fuck her.

But not yet.

Patience was a virtue, and I was doing my best to be virtuous today.

"Is that a yes, sunshine?"

"Yes," she said.

I chuckled and leaned back. I started to unbutton my shirt and tossed it to the side and then stood, unbuckling my belt and jeans. Her ass gleamed in the sunshine, the white lace bright against her skin.

I pulled the belt free, the sound of the buckle making her tense again. It turned me on.

All of my clothes ended up in a pile on the ground, my cock hard and ready. I placed the belt to the side of her as I knelt right behind her.

She moaned as I gripped her ass cheeks, giving them each a light tap. I reached down, tugging on her hair before letting go.

I slid my hand between her thighs, feeling how wet she was, even through the lace. I pulled it free and pushed her thighs further apart, admiring her gleaming pussy.

Soon, my cum would be dripping from her.

I kept her thighs spread and leaned down, running my tongue over her dripping cunt.

She gasped, the taste of her hitting my tongue, musky and sweet and what I wanted to drown myself in. I licked her, lapping at her until I drew back, rubbing her ass cheeks with my palm.

"Please," she whimpered. "Please. I want more."

"You're so needy," I said. "You really want me to spank and fuck you that bad?"

"*Please.* More than anything else."

"Beg me."

My words were met with a gasp. She looked back at me, her lips parting.

"Please. Please fuck me. Please spank me."

I rubbed her ass cheeks, chuckling. "I think you can do better than that, my love."

Her words were filled with a raw, aching need. "Cameron Harlow, I need you to fuck my pussy and breed me like I'm your own personal slut. I want you to spank me so that when I sit at Honey's table in the morning, I know that ache is because of you. I need you to fuck me, Cam."

CHAPTER TWENTY-ONE

I'D NEVER BEGGED anyone like this before. I listened to the way his breath hitched, his touch becoming rougher.

"As you wish, princess," he huffed.

He slapped my ass cheek hard, repeating the motion over and over, working up the intensity as I writhed beneath him. I moaned as he spanked each side, my skin becoming hot.

I heard the sound of the belt, the tinkle of the metal.

My pussy was dripping for him.

"Cam," I breathed. "*Please.*"

The leather belt slapped over me, hitting both sides at the same time. I cried out as I felt the zap of pain, followed by a wave of euphoric pleasure. I gripped the blanket beneath me, curling my fingers into it as he spanked me again.

The sound of the leather on my skin reminded me of a crack of lightning. It was loud and sudden and sent shock waves through my entire body.

Fuck.

The way I needed this. The way I needed him right now. It

was primal and deep, a type of connection that I'd never shared with another.

"Good girl," he praised. "You're taking this so well, sweetheart."

"Thank you," I moaned.

What was this feeling? This lust was uncontrollable, swallowing me whole. I felt better than I ever had before, my blood singing with delight.

He spanked me again, harder than before. The pain took my breath away. I groaned as he did so again and again, each time feeling more intense than the last.

The pause threw me off. I expected another strike but was instead met with two of his fingers running over my clit.

"Oh fuck," I groaned.

His touch sent need straight to my core.

"So wet. Do you want to taste yourself? See what I've done to you, sunshine?"

"Yes," I rasped.

He slid a finger inside of me slowly. I arched, my body trembling as he pulled it free before leaning over me and sliding his finger into my mouth. I sucked, closing my eyes as I did so.

"Good girl," he said softly.

Tasting myself was something I'd never done before either.

He kissed my ass cheeks, his touch reminding me of the marks the belt left. The pain made me moan, all while I sucked my juices off his finger.

"I'm going to fuck you," he whispered. "Keep sucking."

The anticipation was killing me. I kept sucking as he moved closer behind me, his cock slapping against my pussy.

He pulled his finger free and gripped my hips. "Are you ready, baby girl?"

"Yes," I whimpered.

The head of his cock pressed against me. He slowly began to ease forward, filling me inch by inch.

"You feel so fucking good," he huffed. "Fuck."

He thrust forward, filling me completely. He held me like that, my body adjusting to the size of his cock. I groaned, my cunt clenching him. Pleasure bolted through me, need and lust working together.

Cam pulled back before pumping into me again. He began to fuck me, holding on to me as he thrust in and out, over and over. I cried out, closing my eyes as bliss rushed through me.

I felt his thumb press against my other hole. I gasped, looking at him over my shoulder. "Cam," I moaned.

"Have you been fucked here?"

"No."

"Do you want to be?"

I felt excitement roll through me. Nerves. Desire. "Yes," I whispered.

He paused in his thrust and leaned over, pulling out a bottle of lube from the picnic basket.

This bastard had packed a bottle of lube.

In our picnic basket.

That turned me on.

"You're prepared for everything," I huffed.

His cock pulsed inside me. He gave me a devilish smile. "Well. It doesn't hurt to be prepared, does it?"

"Not at all," I whispered.

The anticipation was killing me.

He thrust back inside me, drawing another cry from me. He fell back into a rhythm, this one slower and harder, as he opened the bottle.

I felt the lube fall onto my ass. He rubbed the hole, circling it with his finger as he fucked me.

I shivered, my voice growing louder as he fucked me harder. "Cam!"

"Relax," he commanded. "Close your eyes and relax, princess."

I did as he asked, drawing in a breath. My muscles melted, my cunt still squeezing him as he fucked me, every movement measured.

I felt his finger slowly push, stretching my ass as he kept fucking me. I moaned, my breath hitching. I'd never felt so full before, not like this.

"You're so fucking tight," he whispered.

He was gentle, teasing me until he was able to push one finger further inside. I moaned as I stretched around him, adjusting to him slowly.

This was so different. So *new* to me.

I fucking loved it.

"You're taking me so well, baby," he murmured. "Soon, you'll be taking my cock here too. I should get us a toy to use."

I shivered, pleasure rolling through me. "I'm so close," I rasped.

"I know, sunshine. I can feel you milking my cock, my desperate little whore."

I moaned with need.

He began to thrust harder, his cock spearing me. My eyes fluttered, a cry leaving me as the edge of an orgasm cut through me. I came hard, squeezing his cock.

"Fuck," he groaned.

I was breathless as I melted under him, waves of euphoria rolling through me. He suddenly cried out, and I felt his hot cum shoot inside me, his body pressing against mine.

He slowly pulled out, rolling to the side and pulling me against him. Our breaths were ragged. I grinned, letting out a satisfied laugh as I laid my head on his chest.

183

"I'll never stop wanting you," he murmured, kissing the top of my head.

"I can't believe you just fucked me in front of this tree."

He snorted. "This, of course, means you have to marry me."

"Oh yeah?" I asked, turning over to look at him. He was grinning, wearing the look of someone thoroughly satisfied. "Is this how you're proposing to me, Cameron Harlow?"

"Yes. No." He chuckled. "You'll know when I'm proposing to you, Hal. There won't be any question about it."

My stomach erupted in butterflies. I smirked and sank back against him. The idea didn't scare me the way I thought it might. Sunlight was scattered by the massive branches above us. I drew in a breath, reveling in the moment, enjoying being with him like this.

"I think it's safe to say that you're always welcome to take me on a picnic," I said.

"Excellent. Maybe next time, I'll eat fruit off your nipples."

I laughed, swatting his chest. "You're ridiculous."

"I'm a man of many ideas. Some might call me a genius."

"Uh-huh, I can think of many things some might call you."

"Hot. Sexy. Smart."

"Sweet and thoughtful," I countered. "Surprisingly, into ripping all of my dresses apart."

"It's true, I do enjoy that."

"You're full of many surprises."

Many more than I could have ever imagined. If someone told me a few weeks ago that I'd be naked and in Cameron Harlow's arms out underneath a tree, I would have told them they'd lost their mind.

Now, I couldn't think of any other way to spend my Saturday.

Fuck. I was falling in love with him. I was already in love with him.

I let the feeling settle in, ignoring the wave of panic I felt with it.

"Hey," he murmured, kissing the top of my head again. "How do you feel? Are you okay? We did a lot. I brought some chocolate, and that might be good right now, if you'd like."

"Chocolate sounds good," I whispered.

"I'll be right back," he said, sitting up. "I also brought body wipes since it'll be a walk back..."

I raised my head, the panic disappearing. "You literally thought of everything."

"I did," he said, reaching into the picnic basket.

"That thing must have weighed fifty pounds. Are you sure there's not an alternate dimension in there too?"

"There might be," he teased.

He pulled out body wipes, sanitizing wipes, a bag of milk and dark chocolate, and two water bottles. I was amused as he wiped his hands and then came over to me, bringing all of the goodies.

"I'm going to start calling you Mary Poppins," I teased.

He opened a piece of chocolate and knelt next to me. "Spoonful of sugar, darlin'."

I bit the chocolate and let out a soft moan, closing my eyes. He had been right to bring it.

We settled next to each other, him feeding me chocolate while we looked around. The sun was high now, and it was warm, but not too much so.

Really, everything was perfect.

I swallowed hard, trying to chase the demons from my mind. To forget that there was someone out there wanting to hurt me. That my sister was in trouble.

All of those things could wait. They had to wait. This moment was for me and Cam.

Cam rubbed my shoulder, kissing my cheek. "How are you feeling?"

"Good," I said. "More than good."

"Good," he chuckled. "I wanted to ask... if degrading you was okay. We should have talked about that before."

"Yes," I answered. "I enjoyed it way more than I thought I would. Secretly, I'd like to—" I cut myself off. Was I really going to say this?

"What is it? You can tell me."

"Well. Have you heard of CNC? Consensual nonconsent."

"I have." He let out a soft hum. "Is that something you're interested in trying?"

"Yes," I answered, feeling my heart beat a little faster.

"We can try that. I like the idea of hearing you beg me to stop."

My pussy throbbed despite the orgasms I'd already had. I relaxed against him. "I love that I'm discovering things with you. New things. Hot things."

"Me too," he said. "I love that you're comfortable enough to share what you want. It's hot. And that you trust me enough to try that with me."

"I trust you all the way."

His hand slid into mine. "I trust you all the way too, sunshine."

We let our words sit for a few minutes, enjoying each other's presence.

That was the other thing I loved about him. Sometimes, we could just sit in each other's silence, and it was a conversation all of its own.

"How about we go to the tap house tonight?" Cam asked.

"Do they need a hand?"

"No," he chuckled. "I'm technically supposed to be off. We

could go get drinks though... maybe enjoy the space. Maybe run home first and relax."

I let out a happy sigh. "Sure. I can't think of why not. I might work on an article if that's okay."

"That's fine by me," he said, smirking. "What are you writing about?"

His winery. I wasn't going to give that away though. Not yet anyways.

"It's top secret," I told him.

My plan was to publish it once we got back.

He let out a soft chuckle. "I suppose I can accept that."

CHAPTER TWENTY-TWO

I PULLED my Corvette into the Citrus Cove Wine & Ciders parking lot and let out a low whistle. Cam chuckled next to me as I fought to find a parking spot.

"Just pull off into the grass," he said. "The owner will allow it."

"Aw, tell him thank you," I teased, unbuckling. "Give him a kiss for me too."

"I think you can give him a kiss if you want."

I grinned and leaned over, kissing his cheek. I then reached for my purse on the floorboard and grabbed it, fishing out my lipstick. Cam watched me intently as I applied the sultry red, letting out a low moan.

"I want you to suck my cock while wearing that."

"Cam," I hissed. "We're in public."

"And? No one can hear us, sunshine." His hand slid up my thigh, giving me a squeeze that made me shiver with want.

After our picnic, we managed to make it back to his place, where we showered and got dressed again. I'd ended up publishing my article on the winery and couldn't help but wonder if I'd made a little influence on how packed it was. My phone had been going off since I submitted it.

Of course, I'd promised sexy bartenders and great ciders and wine—all in a sweet Southern town.

I was wearing the extra dress I'd packed, a soft black cotton with a sweetheart neckline. I'd pulled my hair back into a bun, but a couple of curls loosened to frame my face.

"You're the most beautiful woman I've ever seen," he said.

I blushed and swatted at his chest, meeting the hard muscle there. "Alright, cowboy, enough flirting, or else we won't make it inside."

"Maybe that's my goal."

I shook my head and let out a phony dramatic sigh. We both got out of the car, and I glanced around. "It's *packed*."

"Yeah," he said, his smile disappearing for a moment. "Fuck."

"If we need to hop in to help tonight, we can," I said. "I wouldn't mind."

"I'm supposed to be off." He grimaced. "And this is supposed to be a date."

"I'm still running on the high of our picnic, Cam. It wouldn't be a big deal. Who's working tonight?"

"Hunter and Colt, but I can already tell this is too much. Fuck, I need to hire more people. It's hard sometimes in a town this small."

"Right. Well, I'm not saying this is my fault. But it might be my fault? My article was about your winery. I couldn't think of anything else to write and needed to put something out. But I also wanted to push it. It's a great date destination."

Cam's brows shot up, and he stepped closer, pulling me tight. "You mean to tell me you wrote about my little winery?"

"I did," I said, smiling.

"You didn't have to do that."

"I know," I said. "It's not like you asked. This is also why I feel inclined to help out the guys tonight. I didn't actually think it would be packed. And even if the article did nothing, we can still jump in."

His eyes softened. "Have I told you that you're the best? And that you mean everything to me?"

I leaned up on my tiptoes and kissed him, basking in the warmth of him. I slung my bag over my shoulder and pulled back. "Let's go."

"Yes, ma'am," he said, following me.

The two of us made our way to the front doors and squeezed past the line. It was packed inside, with people waiting at the bar while others waited at tables. I felt a gaze on me and turned around, scowling. I could have sworn I saw David, but maybe it was that guy who looked like him.

There were so many people here. I glanced out at the patio and shook my head, raising my voice to talk over the hum of the crowd. "This is wild."

Cam agreed as we both slid behind the bar. Hunter was standing there, working as efficiently as possible. He wore a black T-shirt, a line of sweat down the back and a bar towel slung over his shoulder. He glanced up at us and then shook his head.

"I don't know why you're here, but I'm glad you are. Maybe prayers do get answered."

"You should have texted me," Cam said, clapping him on the shoulder. "We'll jump in. This is madness."

"Someone said there was an article written about us," Hunter said, glancing at me. "Don't suppose you know anything about that?"

I winced. I had no idea that it would do this, but I felt a flare of pride that it had.

Cam shook his head. "Baby, I knew people read your travel articles; I didn't know it would be like this."

"It's... a little something."

"This isn't a little something." Hunter barked out a laugh. "Get to work, please, before our customers drown us. And send Sammy back to the stage. We need entertainment."

Cam went to Sammy, and I moved down to the other end of the bar, where Colt was working his ass off. He was wearing a backward ball cap and gave me an easygoing smile.

"I've never been happier to see you," he said as he poured two glasses of wine.

"I think this is my fault, so the least I can do is help," I said. "Where do you want me?"

"Focus on that group at the very end. They've got ten people with them and want several flights of ciders. The flight is our six flavors and the serving boards."

"Got it."

We got into a good rhythm, one that was nice and easy despite the many people we had. I felt autopilot kick in, which was the best place to be mentally when working. Music began to roll through the winery again, Sammy's voice a sultry Southern melody over the chatter.

An hour later, Cam ended up next to me, our hips bumping. We'd made it through the rush, both of us gleaming with sweat. I stole a look at him, thinking about how damn hot he was. His sleeves were pushed up his forearms, his gaze raking over me and leaving a trail of heat.

He leaned down, whispering in my ear. "If you keep looking at me like that, we'll have to go to the office."

"Oh yeah?" I laughed. "Am I in trouble, boss?"

"You will be," he teased.

"No flirting while working," Hunter called. "You'll scare everyone off."

I laughed as I poured wine, shaking my head.

"Y'all are together?"

The unfamiliar voice threw me off. I glanced up and frowned, recognizing the man I'd dealt with my first night here. Andy, the creepy jeweler.

Cam was already down the bar again, helping a couple that finally picked out the wine they wanted.

"Yes," I said, holding his gaze. "Did you want a drink?"

"I want your number," he returned, giving me a smarmy smile.

"Well, that's not on the menu." I raised a brow. "Drink or no drink?"

His eyes blazed, his face contorting. "You're such a stuck-up whore. I don't know why you'd go for someone like that when you could be with me."

My heart skipped a beat, but I felt a wave of rage creep up. "Either pick a fucking drink or leave me alone, Andy."

"Oh, you remember my name," he said, leaning over the bar. "Just give me your number. I promise I can show you a good time. I'd fuck you so hard you'd never remember his name. I bet you sound good when you scream."

A fist came out of nowhere. I gasped as I took a step back. Cameron hopped up onto the bar top with ease and punched Andy again.

"Cam!" I yelled.

It happened fast, but Colt and Hunter were over the bar, too, like fucking cowboy acrobats, pulling the two of them apart.

Cam rose, holding Andy by the front of his shirt. "If you ever speak to her, look at her, or think about her again, I will fucking end you." He shoved Andy away, his hands curling into fists. "Get the fuck out of my bar."

Andy put his hands up, blood gushing from his nose and

down his shirt. "I was just being nice to her. She doesn't even deserve it. She's just some city whore. I've been reading all of her articles I could find and she's not even a good writer."

Hunter shoved Andy back, the three of them surrounding him. His eyes widened as he realized he'd just poked the bear.

"Get the fuck out. *Now*," Cam snarled.

Colt and Hunter both crossed their arms, and Andy finally got the hint. I swallowed hard as he looked past them, glaring at me before finally making his way out. People let him by, murmuring as he went through the front door.

A pretty woman who was sitting on one of the stools shook her head, giving me a knowing smile. "Think you have a keeper, honey."

I nodded, my eyes fixed on Cam as he turned. I felt a wave of emotion rush through me, part shock and part fear. I'd never done anything to Andy, but the way he looked at me was like he hated me.

What if he was the killer?

The thought made my breath hitch, my heart pounding. Cam looked at me, his face and expression finally relaxing. "Are you okay, sunshine?"

"Yeah," I lied. His eyes narrowed on me. "You didn't have to do that."

"Oh, but I wanted to," he said, his voice deadly serious.

Hunter and Colt both looked at me and then back at Cam.

"Alright," I said, trying to keep my voice from wavering. "Back to work."

"You two take a break," Hunter said. "It's chilled out some. We don't need the help."

"Yeah," Colt agreed. "Go."

I was already going. I went through the back doorway and down the hall, going straight to Cam's office. He was right behind me. The moment he closed the door behind us, I turned, only to be swept up into his arms and pinned against the wall.

"Cam," I rasped. "Fuck."

My legs wrapped around his waist, feeling his cock pushing against me through the fabric of our clothes. His expression was still murderous, his adrenaline clearly still riding high.

"I wanted to fucking kill him for what he said to you," Cam breathed out.

"Hey," I said, grabbing his face, trying to reassure him. "He didn't hurt me."

"I only heard the tail end of what he said and saw red. Are you really okay? I should have kicked him out the first night he spoke to you."

"I'm okay," I whispered. "I just... He hated me. I could see in his eyes how much he hated me. I never did anything to him. I don't even know him. And part of me that wonders..."

Cam's eyes widened, his jaw stiffening. "If he's the killer."

CHAPTER TWENTY-THREE

HE'D VOICED my deepest fear.

I didn't know Andy. I wasn't sure anyone did. But the way he looked at me, the venomous hatred...

Cam started to put me down, but I tightened my legs around his hips. "No," I whispered. "No. I don't want you going after him. He's already gone. I want you here right now. With me. Okay? Please don't go."

Cam exhaled, pressing my back against the wall. "Fuck." He closed his eyes, his jaw ticking. "Sunshine, I have to keep you safe," he whispered. "You're more important to me than you know. I can't let anything happen to you. I wouldn't be able to live with myself."

"I'm okay," I said. "You kept me safe. Is your hand okay?"

He chuckled, his gaze burning into mine. "Baby, I've been in many bar fights. My hand is fine."

"Promise?" I whispered, pressing my forehead to his.

"Promise," he murmured.

He breathed in deeply, his hand cupping the back of my

neck. I felt his cock against me, the heat between us turning into an inferno.

"Hal," he whispered, his voice breaking.

Our lips crashed against each other, desperate and hungry. He devoured me, groaning as his tongue met mine. I held on to him, needing him so badly that it was hard to breathe.

He broke away and set me down, turning me around and pushing me back against the wall. I gasped as his cock pressed against my ass, one hand pinning my wrists above my head.

"I need you, Hal," he whispered, his voice almost a plea. "I need you now."

"Take me," I rasped.

"Are you sure?" he murmured. "I won't be gentle right now, Hal. I can't..."

"If I need you to stop, I'll say 'red.' I want..." I drifted off, my heart beating faster. I knew exactly what I wanted. I wanted him to fuck me, even if I begged him to stop. I wanted him to take my control, to force me. I wanted to give in to him in a way that I never had before.

That's what I needed right now.

And I knew with him I would be safe. I knew that with him, no one would hurt me.

"Swear to me that you'll say red if it's too much," he murmured.

"I swear."

He kissed my neck, his touch turning gentle for a moment. He undid his buckle and jeans with one hand. I felt his cock come free, slapping against me, his touch still soft, his kisses almost soothing.

But then I felt the change.

"Don't fuck me," I suddenly gasped, but I didn't mean a damn word.

And he knew it.

"I'm going to fuck you whether you want me to or not," he growled.

I whimpered, my breath hitching as he kicked his clothing away, still keeping me against the wall, his grip tight on my wrists.

He hiked up my dress and yanked down my panties. I shoved against the wall, trying to pull out of his grip and escape. He slammed me hard against it, fighting to hold me in place as his fingers sought out my clit. I cried out as he circled me quickly, his touch driving me to the edge, rough and demanding.

"Let me go!" I cried. "Please! Let me go, you bastard!"

"No," he growled.

I cried out, arching against him as he drove me straight into an orgasm. His hand gripped my wrists, holding me there, forcing me to take the pleasure.

He pulled his fingers away and dragged me over to his desk. My mind whirled as he shoved everything off and lifted me, sitting me on top. I pushed him hard, glaring. "I hate you," I said. "You're such a fucking bully."

Cam's eyes darkened, a low laugh leaving him. He gripped my jaw, drawing a whine from me as he forced my lips apart.

He *spat*. I was shocked as his saliva hit my tongue, the action something that I never would have thought would turn me on the way it did.

"Swallow," he demanded.

But I wasn't in the mood to obey. I wanted him to make me. I wanted him to work for my submission, to pull it out of me as I fought tooth and nail.

So I spat back at him. It hit his face, and I saw the momentary shock there. Just a split moment, followed by the fire I'd just dumped gasoline on.

"Fuck. You."

"Oh, now you've done it," he whispered. "Nothing is going to help you now."

He grabbed my bun and pulled. I gasped as he turned me around, shoving me down onto the desk, holding me there. He pushed up the skirt of my dress, my ass bare to the cold office air, and brought his hand down. Hard.

I yelped, the pain shocking me. He spanked me again, harder and harder, until tears filled my eyes.

"Stop," I cried.

But he didn't. He didn't. And it felt too fucking good to beg.

"Please! Please stop!"

Slap. Slap. Slap.

My ass cheeks burned. I pushed back, trying to escape him, but he was too strong. He kept me there, spanking me until I started to cry.

He pulled my head up, looking at my face with a dark chuckle. Tears rolled down my cheeks.

"Let's see how wet you are," he whispered.

His fingers ran over my pussy, dipping inside of me. I gasped at the intrusion, realizing just how fucking wet I was.

"I knew it," he said. "I knew this pussy would be dripping for me."

Fuck. I let out a helpless groan as he shifted behind me, the head of his cock replacing his fingers.

"No," I rasped. "No."

He leaned down, kissing my shoulder as he thrust forward. I yelled as I took every hard inch of his cock, gripping the edge of the desk with a moan.

"That's a good girl," he whispered. "You're squeezing me so tight with your perfect little cunt, sunshine."

He began to fuck me, every movement hard and powerful. I

groaned as he took me, pumping in and out, his cock burying as deep as possible with each movement.

"You're so fucking tight," he groaned. "Fuck."

I gasped, holding on to the desk as I felt another orgasm rush through me. I groaned as I came on his cock, my entire body coiling with pleasure.

He cursed under his breath as he fucked me through it, finally letting out a growl. His cum shot inside me, his hands holding on to my hips as he filled me.

He melted against me, his touch returning to gentle. I panted beneath him. He kissed down my back.

"How do you feel, sunshine?"

"Good," I whispered. "Fuck. That was intense but... everything I needed."

"I needed that too. But I hope you know how much I cherish you."

"I do," I said, smiling.

"Good." He slowly pulled out, his cum dripping down my thighs.

We spent the next few minutes cleaning up and putting ourselves back together again. Cam cupped my face and kissed me before we headed to the office door, stepping out into the hallway.

Cam paused, listening. "It's quiet out there now. Want to go home?"

"Yes, so long as we stop and get something to eat," I laughed.

"Deal. I'll meet you out at the car?"

"Yep," I said, leaning up to kiss his cheek.

We went back out to the bar, and I grabbed my bag and waved at Colt and Hunter as I went to the front doors.

I stepped out into the warm night air. The sun was set, the

moon shining bright. I looked at it for a few moments, still smiling like an idiot.

When I was with Cam, everything felt right.

I crossed the parking lot, heading toward the very back, where I'd parked. I reached into my bag, fishing out my keys as I came to my Corvette.

And froze.

Whore. Bitch. You're Next. Slut.

Glass glimmered in the grass, all of my windows broken in. The words were carved into the cherry-red paint, the side mirrors broken off.

But that wasn't what made me scream.

The woman sitting in the front seat, blood dripping from her slit throat, was what did.

My blood turned cold, my whole world falling apart all over again.

CHAPTER TWENTY-FOUR

cameron

I HEARD Haley scream right as I walked out the doors and took off running. My heart pounded as I sprinted across the parking lot, reaching for her as I made it to her car.

Fuck.

She screamed the moment I touched her, but I turned her around, gripping her shoulders. "It's me, Hal. It's me."

Every muscle in her body was tense. She threw herself into my arms, burying her face against my chest. My gaze fell on her cherry Corvette and on the damage that someone had inflicted.

And the body in the front seat.

"Fuck," I breathed, shock settling in. Haley clung to me, a broken sob leaving her.

"She was at the bar," Haley cried. "She was at the bar. She told me you were a keeper. Now she's dead. Why is she in my car?"

I drew in a breath, forcing myself to stay calm. Someone had been murdered right here in my parking lot, their body shoved in my girlfriend's car. This was a nightmare.

"Everything alright?" a stranger called.

I glanced over my shoulder at them. "Go inside and get Hunter if you can."

The man nodded and jogged toward the winery. I held on to Hal as I pulled my phone out of my pocket, calling the police station. My eyes never left the body in the front seat. It was dark in this part of the parking lot, but I could still see her expression, lifeless but frozen in terror.

That could have been Hal.

My blood chilled.

"Are you calling the police?" Haley whispered.

"Yes," I said.

She nodded, her sniffles quieting.

The line answered, a familiar voice. "Police Department—"

"Alexa," I said. "We have a problem at the winery."

"First of all, Harlow, you should call me Officer—"

"Someone's dead."

"Fuck," she growled. "God damn it. My night was looking like it was going to be easy, but nope. I'll grab the sheriff and call others in. Don't touch them. Don't move anything. We'll be right there."

The call ended, and I shook my head. I sometimes questioned the benefits of being in a small town, but at least I knew that the entire department would be here within a few minutes.

"Hey!"

I glanced over my shoulder as Hunter and Colt ran up.

"Y'all okay?" Colt asked, grabbing my shoulder. Haley peeled away from me, her expression pained. Colt's eyes flashed to the car and then to the woman. "Holy fuck," he breathed out, paling.

Hunter slowed to a stop next to us, his expression becoming unreadable. "That's Darlene Abbott. She's a teacher at the elementary school. Fuck."

A solemn silence settled over our group.

It wasn't supposed to be like this. Not in a place like Citrus Cove. Nothing like this ever happened here before.

Haley shook her head, tears streaming down her cheeks. I pulled her close again, not wanting to let her go.

Not wanting the killer to get to her.

Her arms wrapped around my waist. I closed my eyes, breathing in. Breathing out. Steadying myself. I needed to be strong for her right now.

"We'll shut down the bar," Hunter said, "Sammy is wrapping up a few things and can help. While y'all were busy earlier, it died down quite a bit, so it should be quick."

I nodded. "I think that's for the best."

"Do you want me to stay with y'all?" Colt asked.

"No," I said. "We'll be right here. Go ahead and help get everyone out."

Colt nodded. He and Hunter both jogged back toward the doors. Like Hunter said, most of the parking lot had cleared out now. There wasn't anyone parked near where we stood.

"I can't believe this," Haley whispered.

"I know, baby. I can't either."

"He's haunting me. Someone's dead now because of me."

"No," I said, grabbing her shoulders. I made her look up at me, holding her teary gaze. "This is not your fault. None of this is your fault. You're just as much a victim as she is. Okay?"

"He's watching me. I knew that, but I still came out tonight and... what if he hurts someone else? What about you? What about your family? What about Honey and Sarah and the kids? If something happened to any of you, I would never forgive myself."

"Nothing will happen to us."

"You don't know that," she whispered. Her brows drew together, her head shaking. "You can't promise that. Something could happen to any of us."

The sound of her phone receiving a text interrupted what I wanted to say. I felt a chill up my spine as she fell silent.

"Let me see your phone," I said.

She reached into her bag and pulled it out. I took it, looking at the screen.

Unknown: *Do you like my gift? It should have been you.*

Every part of me wanted to respond. To tell them to fuck off. To tell them I would stop them.

"It's him, isn't it?" Haley whispered.

"Yes."

"Let me see."

She snatched the phone away before I could tighten my grip. I watched as she read the message, her expression becoming unreadable.

I hated this. I hated seeing the way her shoulders slumped as she looked back at her car. I hated knowing that I couldn't do anything to make it better at the moment.

It couldn't keep going like this. Somehow, we had to catch the killer. I couldn't let anything happen to her. I couldn't let her end up like this woman.

My stomach twisted, fear rolling through me.

She was the woman of my dreams, and yet she was living a nightmare. A nightmare that I couldn't stop.

The sound of shoes on gravel drew my attention. I looked back to see Hunter locking up the front doors. Colt and Sammy were already running toward us. The last few people straggled to their cars, getting in to leave.

"Hey," Sammy said as he joined us. "Fuck." His expression fell when he saw Darlene.

"We'll need to look at the cameras," Colt said. "Maybe they caught something. A face or car. License plate, maybe. We could at least see what happened with Darlene, maybe."

"Maybe," I said.

What I didn't say was that I already knew the cameras didn't reach this far, especially at night. In fact, this part of the parking lot was darker than I would have liked.

If the killer murdered her right here, more than likely, we would have nothing. No clues. No footage to find the criminal.

"We need more lights," I said, glancing at Sammy.

Not like it mattered now.

Sammy grimaced. "This is terrible. Maybe we should go inside until the police get here. And where the fuck are they?"

"Alexa probably called the whole damn squad," I sighed.

The four of us were silent for a moment, staring at the car.

Hunter joined us. "Everyone's gone. I locked the front doors for now."

"Thank you," I whispered.

"Haley," Hunter said. "How are you holding up?"

We all focused on her. She slipped her phone into her purse and pressed her lips together. "First, my apartment is ruined, and now my Corvette." Haley sighed. "He's taking everything from me. Soon, I'll have nothing left. I feel like all of this is my fault. She didn't deserve to die."

The flicker of fear in her words enraged me.

"This isn't your fault, Haley," Colt said. "Do you want me to call anyone? Honey? Sarah?"

"No," she sighed. "I'll call Emma later. I don't want to worry Honey. It's late. And Sarah... can't talk to me."

Colt's expression turned icy. "Right."

Red and blue lights flashed down the road leading to us.

"About damn time," I muttered, glaring.

We watched as a cruiser pulled in, skidding to a halt and kicking up dust. Several others pulled in behind them, and as I'd guessed, the entire department was here, along with an ambulance.

Bud got out of the car, regarding me over the top. "I should have known you'd be involved, Harlow."

I resented that. It wasn't like I was an actual troublemaker. At least not anymore. The only person in this town that I truly had it out for was David Connor.

Well. And now Andy. Andy had put himself on my shit list as of tonight.

"There's a killer on the loose, Bud," I returned, keeping my voice light and friendly despite the seriousness of what I said.

"Keep your voice down, god damn it," Bud hissed, glancing back at the parking lot. The last car was already leaving but driving slowly.

"Rubberneck," Hunter muttered.

"The whole town will know something's going on by tomorrow morning," I said. It was just the way it was.

Alexa got out of the cruiser with another officer, the two of them coming over to us. Our group took a step back to let the cops do what they needed to.

I took one last glance at Darlene and then slipped my arm around Haley. "I think we should move a little further away."

"Why?" she whispered. "She's still dead, even if she's not in our sight."

I winced.

I heard Bud cuss as he went to the Corvette, checking the body. "She's dead."

"No fucking shit," Hunter hissed.

"Hey," Alexa snapped, giving him a sharp look.

Hunter shrugged, his expression tense.

Bud came back over to us as other officers began to work. He stopped in front of Haley and me. "This your car?" Bud asked her.

"Yes," Haley said, pulling away from me. "It is."

"Any idea who could have done it?"

"Really, Bud?" I bit out. I didn't fight to keep the edge from my voice. I was frustrated, and sheriff or not, I was going to make sure he knew that.

"Well, I'm asking because we got a call from someone saying you beat the shit out of them, Harlow."

I ground my teeth, trying to keep my temper at bay. "Andy," I growled. I hated that guy.

"This wasn't him," Haley interjected. Her voice had become eerily calm and strong, not a single word wavering. "It says 'you're next,' which is exactly what the killer has said to me before. He must have done this to my car and then killed the woman. Or the other way around. Andy was rude to me earlier, but I don't think he would have killed Darlene."

I glanced at Hunter and Colt, the three of us wary.

"You don't know for sure," I said.

"Andy didn't do this," Haley insisted.

"We have to explore all the options," Bud said, but he didn't sound convinced.

The fact was Citrus Cove was currently home to a killer. And we didn't know who they were or how to find them.

CHAPTER TWENTY-FIVE

cameron

WE SPENT the next hour answering questions. Endless fucking questions. In that time, they moved Darlene's body, called her family, and cleared out everything they could.

Haley ended up showing Bud and Alexa the text message, which they requested to get copies of. Ultimately, we decided to leave the Corvette overnight and go home, everyone exhausted.

As I guessed, the cameras gave us no info. The Corvette was just out of view, and whoever was responsible for the damage made sure they stayed out of view too. It appeared that Andy had wandered that way, but he'd left a few moments later.

Killing Darlene and wrecking Haley's car had taken longer than that.

"I want to go home," Haley whispered.

We were sitting in my truck. I looked over at her, reaching for her hand. She took mine, the two of us gripping each other. It was already 2:00 a.m., and tomorrow, we'd go up to the station to answer any other questions.

I hated the haunted look in her eyes. Finding Darlene had been heartbreaking. Frightening. Her lifeless face was still in my mind, and all I could think about was how it could have been Haley.

"I'll stay the night," I offered, squeezing her hand.

She nodded, leaning back in her seat. "Let's do that. And then tomorrow, I need to tell Honey what else has been happening. And maybe I can convince her and Sarah to go on vacation with the kids. I'll pay for it. I'll send them somewhere safe. Or I could just leave. Go back to Baltimore. Even better, maybe I'll leave the fucking country."

"You're not leaving," I said firmly. "You're safer here than anywhere else."

"But no one else is. A woman died tonight, Cam. Another woman. In Citrus Cove, of all fucking places. I'm being stalked. No, I'm being *hunted*. And I worry that everyone I care about is no longer safe."

"Sunshine," I whispered, squeezing her hand.

"All I could see tonight was her," Haley whispered. "All I could see was me holding a woman as she died. She bled out on me. I tried so fucking hard to help her. I called 911 and stayed on the phone as I undid the ropes that bound her. And I watched her life turn to nothing. It's selfish, but all I can think about now is how if that happened to you, to Sarah, to Honey... to one of the boys... I would never recover. I would never forgive myself."

"That's not going to happen," I said. "I swear it, Haley. They're going to catch him. Whoever is doing this is going to be caught and never see the light of day again."

"You don't know that. He's already gone this far."

"There is a high chance that he fucked up somewhere. Whether he left evidence in your car or his fingerprints. They will catch him. They will find him. We're going to be okay."

"Darlene wasn't okay."

I leaned my head back, letting out a slow breath, trying to let my tension unravel. She was silent. We sat like that for a couple of minutes.

"Cam," she murmured. "I'm not going to leave."

"Good." I wouldn't have let her anyways.

I sighed and turned on my truck, pulling out of the parking lot. The drive to Honey's house wasn't long, and the two of us winced as I pulled in and we saw every light on in the house.

"Fuck," I mumbled. "I didn't call her. Did you?"

"No," Haley said. "Damn it."

"I don't know how she would have known."

"Well," Haley sighed. "Word travels fast. I'm sure someone called her."

We got out of the truck and went to the porch. Haley reached for the door right as it opened, Honey standing on the other side.

"Oh boy," I whispered.

I'd only seen this woman furious once in my life. Her eyes were like lightning, and she was holding a rolling pin of all things.

"Honey," Haley said, her eyes tearing up.

Honey shook her head and waved the pin. "I got a call from Alexa's mamma, saying there was a dead body found in a red Corvette. There's *one* red Corvette in this town. *One*, Haley Marie Bently. You didn't answer my texts. Didn't answer my calls. *You* didn't either," she said, pointing and passing her glare to me.

I winced. "I'm sorry, Honey. Tonight was a nightmare. We didn't think to call anyone."

Haley let out a defeated breath. "We were talking to the police."

"I'd like to think I'm more important than *Bud*," she bit out.

Finally, she let out a sigh, her face softening. "You *scared* me, baby."

"I'm so sorry," Haley said, stepping into her arms. They hugged, Honey visibly relaxing.

"I know it's 2:00 a.m., but I cook when I'm stressed, so I hope you're hungry."

"What did you make?" Haley asked.

"Everything but the kitchen sink."

CHAPTER TWENTY-SIX

BY THE TIME Cam and I crawled into my bed, it was 3:00 a.m., and I was exhausted. Emotionally, mentally, physically. Honey had been furious, and then after we explained everything, she'd been worried.

I *worried* about her worrying. I hated that she'd stayed up tonight thinking that I might be dead.

After talking to Honey, I'd sent a message to Emma, telling her everything that happened. She'd promised to call tomorrow morning.

Through it all though, Cam stayed by my side.

His arm looped around my waist, tugging me close. He spooned me, the bed creaking with any movement we made.

Fourteen years ago, I'd sat in this same bed and cried over him. Hating him, cursing him, wishing that he'd never speak to me again.

Cameron's voice cut through the darkness. "I..."

He trailed off. My heart hammered faster with what I thought he was going to say.

"I'm here for you, sunshine."

I swallowed hard, my heart squeezing. "Thank you."

Secretly, I'd wanted to hear him say I love you.

I'd fallen for him, harder than I could have ever imagined. Eventually, I'd have the guts to tell him.

His breathing softened as he slowly fell asleep, his body warm against mine.

I closed my eyes, knowing I was safe with him.

* * *

Since Saturday night, Cam and I had been in and out of the police station. We'd ended up skipping Sunday dinner with his parents, shutting down the winery until further notice, and hardly left each other's side until today.

It was Wednesday, and the investigation had turned up nothing, only more questions. The footage hadn't shown much —just Andy leaving, followed by Darlene.

"We'll let you know if we have any more updates, Haley," Alexa clipped, giving me a stressed smile.

"Thanks," I murmured, giving her a wave.

I left her office and stepped out into the morning sun, only to be met by Colt.

I raised a brow. "Are you on Haley duty today?"

Colt winced, giving me a guilty smile. "I am. Cam asked me to meet you here. Said Alexa called you again to ask about Andy."

"Yeah," I sighed, adjusting my purse. "She and Bud are trying. They're working on this case, but whoever killed Darlene did it well. No fingerprints or hair." At some point, I'd become numb to talking about this.

"And Andy?"

"Still gone."

Andy had been missing since Saturday, which meant that he was a suspect. I wasn't convinced, but I wasn't an officer.

Alexa and Bud suspected that it was him, or at the very least, that he might've seen something.

I'd learned more about that guy than I would have cared to. He owned a jewelry store that had gone bankrupt and seemed to be spending whatever money he had left on drinking.

Hardly the killer type, in my opinion, which I'd said multiple times.

Cam had dropped me off this morning before heading to the winery. He'd spent the rest of the day installing new lights in the parking lot with Hunter, who—to no one's surprise—had a friend who was an electrician.

"How 'bout we get breakfast?" Colt offered. "We can walk to the Citrus Cove Cafe. Stretch our legs some, get some sunshine."

I hesitated but nodded. I hadn't talked to Sarah since last week, but she should be working the late shift tonight.

Fuck, I'd forgotten about meeting her.

"A bit of normal would be nice."

Colt smiled, offering me his arm. "My lady."

I laughed as I hooked my arm in his, falling into step next to him. He was tall and lanky, just like he was in high school, but all of the boyish awkwardness was washed out by the looks of a roguish golden man.

It was humid out, but flowers bloomed everywhere there wasn't concrete. Citrus Cove was sleepy for a Wednesday morning, cars creeping down Main Street.

Colt slowed his pace to match mine, his legs infinitely longer than my own. He led us to the crosswalk, his demeanor easygoing.

Part of me wondered how he was even able to meet me this early in the middle of the week.

"What do you do, Colt?" I wondered out loud.

"Like for a job?"

"Yeah," I said. "I'm being nosy. I know you work at the winery, but you do other stuff too."

He snorted as we crossed the street. The cafe diner sat on the corner. I smiled at the bright blue building, admiring the owner's choice to make it stick out.

"I'm the vintner for the winery. Technically, I work for Cam, but I'm also one of the owners, so... I guess I work for myself? I went to college for a couple years and got a degree in viticulture and food science. I don't actually drink anymore, even though this is my job."

I raised a brow as we went through the front doors. "I literally saw you drink a beer at the party at your place."

"They're non-alcoholic."

"Oh. So...you one hundred percent planned for me to run into Cam that day you first stopped by."

He laughed. "Maybe. I'm a little devious sometimes. I know your history is rocky, but I want what's best for my friend, and well..."

I shook my head. "You're a rat."

He grinned. "Table for two," he told the waitress. He looked down at me, clearly amused. "It worked out though, right? Even though I thought you were going to kill him that first night."

"I thought about it," I said. "It's not like our past was warm and cozy. I think he started to win me over when I dumped the beer on him."

Colt grinned again and shrugged. "That's just like him, though. He's obviously changed a lot since high school. We both have."

We were seated quickly, sliding into a booth.

"Coffee?" the waitress asked.

"Yes, please," I said.

"Might as well bring us a whole pot, angel," Colt teased.

She blushed and practically ran off.

"God, between you and Cam, I don't know how you're not married already with the way you flirt. Especially in this small of a town."

"It's in our blood," Colt teased. "I think he learned a thing or two from me. Although he's straight, and I'm most definitely not."

"Oh. I can't say I'm surprised."

He chuckled. "Cam said the same thing when I told him. I'm bi," he said. "It's not like I advertise it. I mean, I of course dated girls in high school but then realized a lot more about my sexuality. I was dating a guy in Austin for a while last year, but it didn't work out. Nothing ever works out."

I frowned, following his gaze. My eyes widened as I saw Sarah darting back and forth between tables.

"I didn't know she was working this early," I whispered.

How much did she work? Once again, I felt a flash of worry for my sister. For her and the boys and their lives. All she did was work and take care of them. What the hell did David even do?

"She works doubles on Wednesdays," Colt answered, his voice somewhat cold.

I scowled, looking back at him. I knew I shouldn't pry, but I couldn't help it any longer. The two of them had been so golden years ago, but now? The tension was unsettling. "What happened between you two?"

Colt shook his head. "I don't want to talk about it, Hal. Sorry."

Damn. "It's okay," I said, grimacing. "I just hate... David."

"You and me both."

I thought about the bastard, and then decided to ask Colt something that had been bothering me. "Hey. Is there another man here that looks exactly like David?"

Colt scowled. "What do you mean?"

"Like a doppelgänger or something. A brother?"

"Not that I've seen."

Sarah's gaze flitted over to us and then she looked away. I sighed and looked at Colt, alarmed by the way he watched her.

Damn it, I was turning into a small towner again. Trying to get into people's business I had no place in.

"I'm sorry," I said, deciding to pretend like nothing happened. "Dating sucks. Honestly, Cam is the first person I've seriously dated in... god, I can't even remember. Maybe forever? I've been so focused on traveling and my career."

"I have to admit, I was surprised the two of you have ended up working it out. Even with me meddling somewhat. I love him, but he was an ass to you growing up."

I took a sip of coffee, letting out a low hum. It was the jolt I needed after a morning that had already gone on too long. "He was. He's not the same, though. And he's pretty good at apologizing for things."

"Good at groveling, too, I hope?" Colt chuckled.

"He is," I said, smirking.

"Good. I've never seen him this happy before, even with everything happening," Colt said. "He deserves it. You deserve it too. So does that mean you're staying in Citrus Cove?"

My stomach twisted.

We hadn't said the L-word Saturday night, but I'd felt the shift. The change between us. It hadn't been said aloud, but something was different.

Did that mean I'd stay here forever? With Cam?

The waitress brought back our coffee, offering us a grin. "Y'all know what you'd like?"

"Just some toast and eggs and..." I said. I decided I wanted their muffin as well. "The muffin, please." It was too damn good not to get.

"You got it." Her gaze fixed on Colt. "And you, darlin'?"

"Will you pick for me?" he asked, his dimples flashing. "I like being surprised and would love to know what you choose."

She blushed again. "Sure. I-I can do that."

I gave him a flat look as she left. "You're terrible!"

He grinned now, leaning back against his seat. He had that ease about him again, like nothing in the world could ruin his day. "I'd like to think that I'm absolutely amazing."

I was about to retort when I saw a familiar truck pull into the diner parking lot. My words failed, my lips pressing as I watched my brother-in-law get out, stalking toward the doors.

I really didn't want to see him right now. I had half a mind to run up to him and kick him in the balls, but that would just land us all in trouble.

Colt turned, cursing under his breath. "Motherfucker."

"Why do they even let him in here?" I whispered.

The way he walked was more of a stagger. It was clear that he'd been drinking. My spine straightened as he came through the doors.

"Just ignore him," Colt muttered.

That might have worked. But then, David looked up, his gaze meeting mine. I could see the rage, the hatred, all of it cross his ugly face.

"Too late," I said.

David stalked toward us. He stopped in front of our table, glowering.

"Can I help you?" I asked flatly.

He snorted, looking at me and then Colt. "Shoulda known you'd be sleeping with this one too."

Colt's jaw ticked. "Walk the fuck away, David."

"Or what? You'll try and sleep with my wife? She's a whore too. You know, I heard what happened Saturday night. Bet that woman was supposed to be you, wasn't it?"

218

My blood ran cold.

David sneered. "Bet you would have fucked him too, huh?"

Colt pushed out of the booth and grabbed David. I barely had a moment to register his movement before he was slamming David down on the tabletop, holding his head there even as he tried to fight against him.

"You're drunk," Colt said, his voice eerily calm. "And you don't deserve to even be alive. I'm going to let you go, and if you don't leave this place, I will call the police. Do you understand?"

David glared at me, his eyes burning with hate. Pure fucking hatred. My heart pounded, my body frozen in place.

"This is all your fault," he whispered, his voice clear. Not a single word was slurred.

Colt let him go, which was a mistake. I yelped as David grabbed me by the hair, yanking me out of the booth. I hit the floor hard, the back of my head smashing against the tiles. Even as the pain flared, I tried to pull away. Everything was happening too fast, and I felt his boots collide with my ribs, knocking the breath out of me.

There was an explosion of movement and shouting, but not before he kicked me hard one more time. Pain burst through my side, and I curled into myself.

"*Leave her alone!*"

I blinked a few times, trying to focus on what was happening. I watched in shock as Sarah and Colt grabbed David, the two of them taking him down to the floor. Tables toppled, chairs screeching out of the way. Colt pinned him down to the ground.

I closed my eyes, my head spinning. Why couldn't I have one normal day? Just one. That's all I wanted. No crazy brother-in-law or killer. I wanted no drama.

I felt a set of hands touch me gently, my sister's voice breaking through the pain.

"I'm right here, Hal," she whispered. "Fuck, I'm so sorry."

"Not your fault," I wheezed.

"I'm so sorry," she said again.

I grabbed her hand, giving it a squeeze. "We're buying a house tomorrow. Okay?"

"How can you even say that?" she cried. "How can you even think of me right now?"

"Because you're my sister, and I love you," I said.

"I think you have a concussion."

"Probably..." My eyes were already closing.

I felt myself fall into the sweet darkness.

CHAPTER TWENTY-SEVEN

cameron

"I'M GOING to fucking murder him," I snarled.

Colt pulled me back before I rushed down the hall to where David Connor was. He was sitting in the hospital waiting room, three officers standing with him. He was cuffed to the chair, which meant he'd have to just sit there and take the beating I wanted to give him.

"Stop," Colt growled. "I already got him once. And Hal needs you, Cam."

It wasn't enough. It wasn't enough that Colt already punched him.

David's gaze lifted, meeting my own. My stomach twisted as he slowly smiled.

That son of a bitch.

I was seething. I was panicked. I'd gotten the call from Colt that Haley was being taken to the emergency room, and I'd felt my world turn upside down.

I should have never left her alone.

Guilt pumped through me. I hadn't been there to protect

CLIO EVANS

her. Hadn't been able to stop something terrible from happening.

"Cam."

I turned, spotting Sarah. She walked over to Colt and me, her eyes red from crying.

"She's okay. She has a concussion and a couple of bruised ribs. Some bad bruises. He kicked her so hard." Her voice was a pained whisper. She paused to take a breath, but her voice broke as she spoke. "I'm so sorry. I don't know why he hates her so much. I can't do this anymore."

"You don't have to," Colt reassured her. "We'll help you, Sarah. All of us will help you get away from him. And after this type of situation, it'll be easier for you to get custody of the kids. They shouldn't be around someone like him."

I glanced at my friend, wary of his words. I could see the want on his face, the desire to take care of her.

There was a part of me that hated that. Even after all this time, he'd never let go of the Sarah Bently he once loved.

But how could I blame him? I'd never let go of Haley.

Sarah nodded, her expression falling. "She's getting checkout instructions. Honey is in the room with her, but I think she'd like you there too."

I didn't say a word as I turned and went down the hall.

I went to the room she was in and poked my head in. Haley was sitting in a chair, Honey next to her.

Tears sprang to my eyes, and I rushed to her, falling to my knees in front of her. She grabbed my face, planting a kiss on me before I could say anything.

"Don't let her move too much," Honey said. "Her left side is pretty busted up. I'm gonna kill that son of a bitch."

"*Honey*," Haley rasped.

I couldn't say I'd really heard Honey curse before, but there was a first time for everything.

I drew back gently. "Sorry. Fuck. I'm so fucking sorry I wasn't with you. He would have never—"

"He would have," Haley said, her eyes darkening. There was a bruise on her cheek from where his boot had clipped her. Rage rolled through me. "It wouldn't have mattered who was sitting there, Cam. He was determined to hurt me. Something's wrong with him."

I cupped her face gently, swallowing hard.

"You don't happen to know of any houses for sale, do you?" Haley whispered.

"You can move in with me," I said bluntly.

"No," she said, letting out a soft laugh. She winced, clutching her ribs. "Fuck. That hurt. Don't make me laugh."

"I wasn't trying to."

"Trying to steal my roommate, I see," Honey chuckled, standing up. She gave my shoulder a pat, heading for the door. "I'll be with Sarah and Colt if they're still waiting."

"We'll be there in a few, Honey," Haley said.

She left us alone, shutting the door softly.

Haley slowly leaned back, her expression clearly one of pain.

"What can I do?" I whispered. "What can I do to help? I'll do anything, sunshine. Anything that'll keep me out of jail right now."

She sighed. "He'll get what he deserves. Right now, I need to get Sarah and the kids somewhere safe. I have enough money to buy a house. I'll break my lease with my apartment, which, considering everything that has happened, I don't think will be a problem."

"Do you really think buying her a house is the answer? Sarah's an adult," I said.

"She is. But she needs my help. The rage he had, Cam. If he ever turned that on her or the boys... They're my family."

"She could move in with Honey. You could move in with me."

She raised a brow. "You really want me moving in, huh?"

"Yes," I whispered. "I want you to stay. I want you to be with me. I want to build a life with you, whatever that means for us. But you know what? Even if you left tomorrow, I'd pack up my bags and go with you, Hal."

"You want me," she murmured.

"I *want* want you, sunshine."

She grinned. And it was the brightest smile, despite the hell she was living through right now.

A knock on the door interrupted us.

"Come in," Haley called.

It opened, a nurse poking her head in. "We're ready to get you checked out, Haley, if you're ready. You must be Cam."

"Yes, ma'am, that's me," I answered.

"I talked about you," Haley admitted. "I might have put you down as the one helping care for me..."

"Which was the right thing to do," I said proudly, standing. "You're not leaving my sight, sunshine."

The nurse got us checked out, giving me a packet of instructions on how to care for Haley. Ultimately, nothing was broken, but we'd be icing her side and giving her medicine to numb the pain for at least a week.

By the time we stepped outside of the hospital, my temper was boiling again. I hated David. Hated him so much that I wished he'd just disappear.

"I'm going to take Sarah, and we're going to go get the kids," Honey said. "They're gonna be staying at my house until we get everything figured out."

I nodded, giving her shoulder a soft squeeze. "Let me know if you need anything, Honey. We're going to go back to my place. I know that Hunter has some houses for sale in Citrus Cove, so I will get everything figured out."

"You better take good care of my girl, Cam," Honey said, her voice mildly threatening. It was the tone of a Southern grandmother, a politeness that carried an undercurrent of violence.

We said our goodbyes to everyone, and I promised Colt that we would reconvene later. I wanted to get Haley home and in my bed, away from everything else that was happening. I walked her out to my truck, and before she could protest, I gently lifted her and put her in the passenger seat.

"Thanks," she whispered, kissing my cheek as I buckled her in.

I paused, turning my head and kissing her deeply. I needed to taste her, needed to feel her.

I needed to know that she was safe.

I savored the moment, my touch as gentle as possible. Finally, I drew back and shut her door.

I went around to the driver's side and happened to look up right as David walked out of the hospital. Alexa and Bud followed him, but he was no longer in cuffs. Bud glanced up at me and winced.

"Cam," Haley warned.

But I was already moving. I crossed over to them.

"Harlow," Alexa said, holding up her hand. "We got this."

"Really? Why isn't he in cuffs?"

"Haley didn't press charges," Bud explained, his gaze flickering over to the truck. His bushy brows drew together. "Per Sarah's request."

I was about to see red. My gaze met David's, and he smirked, his lips tugging just enough.

"You motherfucker," I whispered.

"Back off, Cameron," Alexa said. "*Now.*"

I looked at her, and if I hadn't seen how pissed she was too, I would have tackled David.

"It's because she knows she got what she deserved," David said.

"That's fucking enough," Alexa snarled. Before I could lunge for David, she grabbed my shirt and pushed me back, surprising me with her strength, given she was half my size. "Get your girl home, Cam."

"This isn't over," I whispered.

David only smiled.

I had to take a breath and walk away. I marched back to the truck, fuming.

I got in, cranked the engine on, and peeled out of the parking lot.

Haley was silent on the drive back to my house. When we hit the gravel road, I slowed significantly, trying to dodge any bumps that would jar her. I was pissed, so fucking pissed.

I finally pulled to a stop and looked over at her, trying to understand why she didn't press charges. "Why?" I whispered.

"Because I'm hoping that he'll just leave us alone."

I didn't understand that. If she pressed charges, then we would've been able to do a restraining order. But now, this wouldn't even go on his record. At least we lived in a small town where no one would forget what happened. But I was furious that he had simply just been able to walk away today.

"Listen," Haley said. "I know that you're pissed. And I know that you're probably feeling guilty. But he would've attacked me today regardless of who was there with me. He had this look in his eyes, Cam. He hates me so much. And I can't help but wonder if that's why Sarah hasn't been able to talk to me. I just don't know what I did. I haven't been around. I haven't done anything to him. Hell, I barely even remember him from high school."

"He's a son of a bitch. And Sarah should've never married him," I growled.

Haley nodded, reaching over and grabbing my hand. "I agree with you. I really do. But after everything that has happened the last few weeks, I'm just trying to do my best to keep things from blowing up even more."

I leaned back against the headrest and sighed.

If something worse were to have happened to her today, I never would have forgiven myself. And David would be in an early grave. There was a part of me that still wanted to go find him, track him down, and beat the shit out of him.

It wouldn't have been the first time we'd gone rounds together.

But I understood what Haley was saying. And I wouldn't do anything that would make things worse for her.

"Tomorrow, we will get everything straightened out with Sarah. I'll send Hunter a text and ask him to look into housing. But for the time being, I think that you should move in with me. My house is big enough for both of us, and if you didn't want to share a bed with me, you could even have the spare room."

"Oh, I think I like the idea of sharing a bed with you, Cam," Haley teased. "Are you sure... that's what you want?"

"More than anything. I know it's just temporary." Fuck, I didn't want it to be. I almost said so. I almost told her I wanted her to move in forever. Instead, I took a deep breath and continued. "For now, I think it's the best thing. You'll be with me until things settle down and you go back to Baltimore."

She hesitated for a moment. My stomach twisted, but then I looked over at her and saw a little smile.

"Fine," she said, finally looking at me. "You've won me over, Cameron Harlow. I'll move in with you."

My heart skipped a beat, excitement swelling through me despite how today had gone. "Really?" I asked.

"Yes," Haley whispered. "I'll move in."

I grinned like an idiot, unable to stop myself. All I could do now was hope that one day it would be permanent.

"Excellent," I said. "I'm going to carry you inside the house, get you in my bed, and treat you like the goddamn princess that you are."

She chuckled at me as I got out of my truck, glancing at the storm that was starting to roll in. We were finally about to get that rain we'd all been hoping for.

Perfect. We'd get settled, watch a show, and listen to the rain.

I went around to her side and then opened her door. Haley looped her arms around my neck, holding on to me as I lifted her out of the truck. I managed to grab her bag with everything we needed inside of it, and then I carried her to the front porch.

"You'd be a good dad," Haley murmured.

My brows raised as I balanced holding on to her while fishing my keys out of my pocket.

"What makes you say that, sunshine?"

"The fact that you've managed to hold me like a princess, grab my bag, and still open the door without any help," she laughed.

She pressed her face against the crook in my neck as I opened the front door, stepping into the cool air. I kicked it shut behind us, feeling myself relax.

"We're home," I said.

"We are," she whispered.

"How are you feeling?"

"My body hurts, but other than that, good."

I let out a soft hum as I carried her up the staircase, taking her to my bedroom. Our bedroom. I laid her down on the blankets, planting both hands on either side of her.

Her breath hitched, her lips close to mine. "I want you right now," she whispered.

"There's not a chance in hell that we can do anything right now, sunshine," I murmured. "You're injured."

"*I* can't do anything," she said, her voice holding a hint of mischief. "But you can."

"What's the fun in that?" I asked.

"The fun is that I get to lie here and watch you come for me."

Her words went straight to my cock. I gasped, taken aback by her words, by her assertiveness. Her eyes dance to a need, pleading for me to do as she asked.

"Is that what you want right now, princess?" I asked.

"Yes," she whispered. "I want to lie here and watch you come for me. Since I can't do anything."

I let out a little whistle, leaning back. But who was I to tell her no? Especially after the day she'd had. I would do anything to please her, even if it meant stepping outside the normal role that I filled in the bedroom.

I slid off the bed, went to the corner of the room, and grabbed the chair that sat there. I picked it up and dragged it all the way over to the bedside. She raised a brow, smirking at me.

"I can't believe you're making me do this," I huffed. "Do you really just want to watch me come?"

"Yes," she whispered eagerly.

I let out a dark growl, taking a step back from her. My hands felt for my belt buckle, and I slowly unlatched it, metal clinking against metal. My eyes locked with hers, unable to leave her as I slowly slid it off and then unbuckled my jeans, dropping them to the floor.

The way she watched me made me hard. My cock throbbed, eager to be buried inside of her, but having her watch me come for her would be good enough.

"Tell me what to do, sunshine," I whispered.

"I want you to unbutton your shirt slowly."

I did as she asked, popping every button with purpose.

Her eyes widened as if she was discovering the power she had over me.

A power that she'd had from the moment she met me all those years ago.

"Do you like telling me what to do?"

She let out a soft, helpless moan. "Maybe."

She did. I raised a brow. "Is this what you need right now, sunshine?"

"More than anything else."

Then I'd give her whatever she wanted.

CHAPTER TWENTY-EIGHT

I NEEDED THIS RIGHT NOW, I realized.

I need to feel the control. To know that he was here for me and to be able to give in to my desires. No one else was in control of my life.

Not David.

Not a serial killer.

Not anyone else.

And having this moment with Cam was helping give me that power.

Cam's breath hitched, his eyes never leaving me. He pulled his shirt off, tossing it to the floor. He stood completely naked in front of me, his body perfect. I wanted more than anything to touch him, to explore his hard muscles with my hands.

But the fact was, my body still hurt, and I couldn't move without feeling pain. Fucking bruised ribs would do that. For now, he would have to touch himself for me.

That turned me on in a way that I never expected.

"You're so hot," I whispered. "I love it when you look at me like this."

"Like what?" he asked, his voice slow and sultry. He knew exactly what.

I bit my bottom lip, watching as he slid his hand down to his hard cock.

"I wish I could touch you right now," I whispered. "I wish that I could suck your cock. I wish I could be on my knees, pleasing you." Fuck, I would do anything for that.

I moved ever so slightly on the bed, fighting off a wince as pain ran up my side.

"Haley," he rasped. "Baby, I don't know if I should be teasing you right now..."

"I'm the one teasing you," I said, raising a brow. "Or have you forgotten that?"

His eyes darkened, his mouth tugging into a helpless smile. "No, ma'am, haven't forgotten that at all."

I was shocking myself right now, but the feeling was the highlight of the day. "You'd like that though, right? Me on my knees for you." My own cheeks flushed, my words surprising me. "Wouldn't you like for me to suck you off? You could hold my head while you fucked me."

"*Sunshine.*"

He stepped closer, reaching down to grip my chin. His hand was gentle yet firm. He leaned down, his lips hovering a breath away from mine.

"The moment you feel better, I promise that we're going to do every fucking thing that you can think of. Including me fucking your throat until you can't breathe and you beg for me to stop."

"Is that a promise?" I asked.

Cam chuckled and straightened, stroking his cock only a few inches from my face. "Yes, baby, it's a promise. Now, spit on it."

I spit on his cock, watching as he used it to lube his entire

232

throbbing shaft. He let out a soft whimper, a noise I never expected to hear from Cameron Harlow.

He took a step back and then sat in his chair, his eyes fixed on me as he worked his cock up and down.

A shiver of need worked through me.

"Does that feel good, baby?" I asked, my voice husky.

"More than you know," he huffed.

His cheeks were flushed, his lips parting with every pant. He let out a soft groan.

"Hand me a pillow," he whispered. "If you can."

I slowly reached back, grabbing a pillow and tossing it at him. He caught it, bending it so that he could thrust his cock into it. I sucked in a breath as I watched him, realizing that this was one of the most erotic things I'd ever seen in my entire life.

He was fucking a pillow, his eyes still fixated on me, never leaving me as he groaned, over and over. He cursed under his breath, his head falling back.

"Are you imagining that's me?" I asked.

"Yes," he rasped.

My pussy throbbed in response. I still couldn't do anything about it, but watching him still brought me a sort of pleasure I'd never experienced before.

"Are you imagining filling me up? Giving me every drop of your cum?"

"I'm imagining bending you over this bed and fucking your ass. I'm imagining taking you over and over again. I'm imagining spanking you as I fuck you. And I'm imagining giving you every fucking drop of my cum and getting you pregnant."

"Fuck," I whispered. "Is that what you want? To get me pregnant..."

"More than you know, sunshine," he grunted.

He kept fucking the pillow, thrusting into it, until he tossed it to the side. He let out a guttural growl, stroking his cock until he finally came. I watched his cum shoot out, landing on his thigh and dripping down his hand.

"Good boy," I whispered. I blushed again, excited by saying such a thing.

He moaned softly, relaxing into his seat. I watched as he lifted his hand to his lips, his tongue licking up his own cum.

"Cam," I breathed out.

"What?" He smirked. "Isn't that what you would do?"

"Yes. I would..."

"Then open your mouth," he said.

My eyes widened, but I did as he said. I parted my lips for him as he licked up the rest of his cum, but he didn't swallow. Instead, he stood and walked to the edge of the bed, leaning over me. He gripped the headboard behind me, his face hovering right above mine.

And then he spat his cum on my tongue.

"Swallow," he instructed. "This is what you do to me, sunshine. This is what you made me do."

I swallowed, shivering beneath him. I'd never been this turned on in my life, and there wasn't a goddamned thing I could do.

"Good girl," he whispered. "I promise when you're better that I'll make it up to you. Maybe you can call me a good boy again."

"Please," I whispered.

His lips pressed against mine, the two of us sharing a depraved kiss. I moaned against him, my mind whirling. He always wound me up in a way no one else had ever done.

He slowly pulled back, kissing my forehead. "How are you feeling?"

"Horny and like I could kick David in the nuts."

"Get in line," he growled. "I'm going to make some food and then get in bed with you. And give you your meds."

"Thank you, Doctor," I chuckled.

He winked at me and then reached for a T-shirt and a fresh pair of boxers from his dresser. I watched as he got dressed and disappeared down the stairs, leaving me alone for a few minutes. I closed my eyes, sinking into his bed.

Our bed.

Fuck, I was moving in with this man. I was going to build a life with him.

I knew it. Every part of my heart and soul knew it.

I had always sworn up and down that I would never stay in Citrus Cove. That I could never call this place home. But with Cam in my life, it was the only home I could imagine.

I thought about it. Thought about leaving tomorrow, packing everything up, and putting all of the things that had happened behind me. I could just move around the world, staying in hotels and Airbnbs as I traveled. Hell, I'd done it for most of my twenties.

It wasn't impossible. But it didn't feel right anymore.

The longer I knew Cam, the harder it was to envision a future without him.

If only they could catch the serial killer hunting me.

I sighed, thinking back to David. To the way he lunged for me, the hatred burning in his eyes.

I thought about Andy. The way he'd looked at me too.

Both of them hated me so fucking much, and I'd never done anything to them. It confused me, infuriated me, made me feel guilty for no reason. Like it was my fault that they'd decided to be psychotic.

What had David been like all those years ago? How in the hell had Sarah chosen him over Colt? Colt was who I would've sworn she'd marry. They'd been together in high school, always side by side unless she was with me or he was with Cam.

I'd never known why they stopped dating. Sarah never told

me. I regretted not asking. The way Colt looked every time my sister's name came up pained me.

After all this time, there was still a wound there. Maybe it was David.

David was older than me. Perhaps that's why I didn't remember him.

Andy was just a mystery entirely.

My phone's text message alert sounded through the room. I opened my eyes and grabbed it off the dresser, dreading whatever had come through.

I breathed out a sigh of relief when I saw Emma's name.

Emma: *Bitch, if you don't call me and update me on what's going on, I'll fly down there tomorrow.*

I rolled my eyes and hit the call button, putting her on speakerphone.

Emma picked up. "What is going on? Hunter texted me."

"Hunter did?" I asked, shocked.

"Yeah. I have the gun squad's numbers now, remember? That was part of the protection plan that has apparently failed miserably."

"It's not like that." I sighed. "But yeah, today has been a shit day. Sarah's husband attacked me."

"Do you have a psycho magnet implanted somewhere that I don't know about?"

I giggled and then winced. "Noo, don't make me laugh. I have bruised ribs. My whole body hurts."

"Jesus Christ," Emma breathed out. "Babe, I'm really worried about you out there."

"I'm staying," I whispered.

Emma was quiet, followed by a soft hum. "I knew the moment you told me about Cam this would happen. It was how you said his name. Something's different. And now I have to move."

236

"You know you don't have to move."

She scoffed. "And be away from you?"

"Yeah... I miss you. And I think you'd like it here..."

"You really think they could handle me? Big-city girl in a town the size of my street growing up. Don't you dare laugh at that."

I snorted. "I think you'd like it. We can get you some cowgirl boots and bedazzle them."

"Deal."

I grinned. "So this means I have the perfect boyfriend, the perfect town, and the perfect best friend."

"Yeah, we just need to catch the serial killer, throw your brother-in-law in jail, and oh—find this infamous murder-weasel named Andy."

I giggled despite the flare of pain, exhaling slowly. My eyes were starting to droop, my muscles relaxed entirely. "I miss you," I sighed.

"I miss you too. I'm glad you're okay though. Well, relatively speaking."

"Me too."

"Have you told Cam you're staying yet?" Emma asked.

"No," I whispered. "I will soon. I mean, he asked me to move in, and I said yes. We just didn't clarify if that meant forever or not. There's just been so much going on. And it's fast, you know? The way we both feel. But it's right. I think once you know, you know sometimes."

"I think so too. I'm sure he'll be happy."

"I hope so."

"If he's not, we can run away together."

I let out another laugh and then groaned from the pain.

"I think that's my cue to let you get some rest. You'll call me tomorrow? Or at least text and let me know you're alive? I'm tired of harassing the squad."

"Yes," I promised. "Also, they're really not bad. Sammy is a sweetheart, Colt is a good guy, and Hunter is—"

"Sorry, nothing you say will make me like Hunter."

I raised a brow. Once Emma made up her mind, it was no use trying to change it.

"He's not that bad," I said.

"We'll see. Get some rest. I love you."

"I love you too."

I hung up right as Cameron came back, holding a plate with a bowl of soup and crackers. If he'd eaves dropped on me, he didn't show it. I thought about telling him now I was going to stay, but decided to wait a little longer.

"Hey," I said, smiling at him.

"I'm going to feed you, and then you'll sleep," he said.

"Yes, Doctor," I chuckled.

CHAPTER TWENTY-NINE

cameron

THE SUN HAD YET to rise over Citrus Cove when I sent out a 'family meeting' blast text to my parents and brothers. I left Haley sleeping with a note on the pillow and snuck out of the house, driving in silence to the Harlow house.

With everything going on, I wanted to keep them in the loop. But, beyond that, I wanted them to know something else too.

I was in love with Haley.

I wasn't sure exactly when it happened. It was quick, like a viper striking me, stealing my heart. Maybe it was everything going on that was making me think about our own mortality, but I loved her. I'd almost whispered it to her in the dark Saturday night, but I'd worried I'd scare her off.

But..

I wanted my family to know I loved her. Eventually I'd tell her, sooner rather than later. But, I wanted them to know I was going to build my life with her, even if it meant I left Citrus Cove and the winery all behind.

I'd do it to be with her. I'd leave it all. My home, my business, even my family. I hoped she'd stay here, but in case she didn't want to...I needed them to know I'd go with her.

I pulled down the dirt road and wasn't surprised to see Hunter and Sammy beat me here. I stepped out into the cool morning, the sky brightening slowly but surely. Lights were already on inside the house, and the kitchen. I walked through the back door.

"You better kick off your shoes!" Mom called.

I snorted, but kicked them off right as Benny came to greet me. I knelt down and ruffled his head, giving him a good scratch before heading to the kitchen.

I wasn't surprised when I walked in to see that the coffee was going, biscuits and bacon were being made, and Hunter and Sam were already there at the table. Hunter gave me a long look over the top of his mug.

"It's early, brother," he grumbled.

"Well, I didn't think you'd already be here..."

He rolled his eyes. He knew that was bullshit, and so did I. None of us ever called a meeting unless it was serious. Except for that one time in fifth grade where Sammy had called a meeting to announce his discovery that the tooth fairy was a fake, and that our parents were tricking us.

Pops had laughed so hard he'd started crying, while Mom had done her best to take his accusations very seriously.

"Morning," I said.

"Morning." Mom gave me a worried look and I went up to her, giving her a hug.

"It's okay. I just need to talk with y'all."

She let out a breath, her shoulders still tense. She pulled another row of bacon out of the pan and spread them out on paper towels to soak up the grease. "How's Haley? You could have brought her with you. I don't like the idea of her being alone. Pops will be down soon, too."

I kissed the top of my mom's head. "She's all good. She's still asleep at the house. She's a trooper."

My voice was calm, but everyone knew underneath it I was raging. Hell, we all were. Seeing Haley hurt was something I never wanted to see again. I hated that I hadn't been there, but was grateful Colt was.

"Need help with anything?" I asked.

"Get some orange juice out and set the table. If y'all want veggies, one of you better start cooking them. Biscuits will be done in a few and bacon is almost ready."

Sammy leapt up. "I got it."

I snuck a piece of bacon and crammed in my mouth before she could swat at me, and then grabbed out plates. Within fifteen minutes, the table was set with food, Pops finally came downstairs, and the Harlow family was seated. I took note of the way Hunter and Pops sat apart from each other, their gazes never meeting even if they passed food to each other.

"Where's Colt?" Pops asked.

"I'll talk to him later," I said.

He raised a brow at me, because I never excluded Colt. But, I wanted to talk to him alone.

"You gonna keep us hanging?" Hunter asked as he piled bacon on his biscuits. "Is everything alright?"

"Yes and no? There's been a lot that's happened, as you all know. But, between it all, I've met a woman I'd do anything for. And I wanted to call this meeting to tell all of you that I plan on marrying Haley Bently, if she'll have me. I love her."

Mom grinned at me and then teared up, fanning at her face.

"Aw, don't cry," I pleaded.

Pops smiled too, his hand sliding over to hers like it always did when he was happy.

Sammy leaned over and clapped me on the shoulder, giving me a firm shake. "She's amazing," he said. "I'm happy for you."

"Thanks," I said.

"I'm happy for you too," Hunter said. "I don't know if you deserve her, but shoot for the stars, right?"

I laughed. "Right. Fingers crossed she loves me back."

"You haven't told her yet?" Sammy hissed.

"Not yet. I will," I said. "There's just been... God, she's been through so much."

"All the more reason to tell her," Mom said softly.

Hunter nodded. "Agreed."

"Does this mean Haley is moving here?" Sammy asked. "If and when things happen."

I winced. "I don't know. That's also why I wanted to talk. If she decides to keep me, I won't make her move here. If she doesn't want to stay, especially after all that's happened, I wouldn't blame her."

"You'd go with her," Mom said softly.

I nodded. The dining table was quiet for a moment, but then Pops spoke. "Cam, if that's what happens, we'll support you. I hope you'll both stay, but...we can let you go so long as y'all come back for holidays."

"We'll figure it out," I chuckled. Hopefully. This was all hoping that she loved me back. I kept wanting to tell her, but I wanted it to be the right moment. But how would I know?

"And the winery?" Hunter asked.

"I'm not sure," I said. "But, if we leave, we'll figure it out. Colt could always take over."

Hunter nodded, although he didn't look as convinced. It was hard to imagine a world where Colt and I didn't live down the road from each other.

"It'll be fine," Sammy said, glancing at our older brother.

"Besides, Cam can distract our mother from hounding us about getting married and having kids now."

"Hey," she laughed, although she narrowed her gaze on me.

"We aren't even married yet. Hell, I haven't even told her I love her. What if she kicks me to the curb?"

The whole table burst out laughing and I shook my head, taking a sip of my coffee and leaning back.

Everything was going to be alright.

"You got a ring yet?" Dad asked.

"I'll get one," I said.

"You better take me with you when you do," Mom said. She gave me a very stern look, pointing at me. "You better, Cameron Harlow."

"If I take you with me, I'll end up spending half my savings."

"Honey, you'd end up spending *all* your savings. Haley Bently deserves a damn fine ring after all this shit she's gone through."

"Alright, alright," I chuckled. "If and when, I'll take you with me."

She nodded, her eyes glistening as she took a sip of coffee. I gave her another smile and then we all settled into small talk and catching up like normal.

After breakfast, I helped clean up and then made my way back out to my truck. I texted Haley good morning just as I heard boots behind me.

I turned as Sammy came up to me. "Heading back?" he asked.

"Yeah," I said. "I'm gonna swing by Colt's and then back to Haley."

"Good. Hey...what's going on with Pops and Hunter?"

I frowned and leaned against my truck, keeping my voice

low. "I don't know. Hunter didn't tell me and you know how Pops can be. Why?"

Sammy sighed, glancing up at the house. "I don't know. Their fights don't usually last this long."

"Yeah." He had a point. "I haven't really had the ability to worry about them with everything."

"I know," he said. "I just thought I'd ask. But, I guess I shouldn't worry. They're adults."

"Sort of," I chuckled. "We definitely get some of our stubbornness from Pops. And Hunter and him are alike in so many ways, it's a problem."

Sammy nodded. "Yep. Alright, well. I'll see you later. Shout if anything happens."

I gave him a hug and then got in my truck, cranking it on and peeling down the road.

Within a few minutes, I was pulling up Colt's drive and parking next to him. There was another car here, but that wasn't going to stop me from popping inside. The general rule between us was if there was a guest, just don't go to the bedroom.

My phone beeped in my pocket and I pulled it out. Haley's photo came up of her in bed, her expression sleepy and nipples hard and...

"Fucking hell," I growled, swallowing hard.

Haley: See you later, cowboy ;)

How in the hell did I respond to a woman who could make my mind stop working with just a picture? What was I supposed to say to a goddess?

Me: Damn, sunshine. I have no words. I'll be home soon

I blew out a breath and slipped my phone back in my pocket. I adjusted my pants and then got out, going up to Colt's door. I picked out his house key and slid it in, stepping inside.

"Colt," I called. "Better put some boxers on."

I heard a grunt and then a whisper and raised a brow. The living room had all the signs of a tussle, and I knew Colt definitely wasn't alone. Good for him. Maybe it would keep him from pinning so damn hard over Sarah. I snorted and went to the kitchen right as a man I hadn't met before darted towards the front door.

"Rude," I mumbled as he left.

Colt came to the kitchen wearing nothing but a pair of jeans. He looked hungover and exhausted, which worried me since he didn't drink anymore. "You scared off my one night stand, man."

"Did he think I was your husband?" I teased.

"Maybe," Colt snickered. "What are you doing here so early? You rarely drop by like this. Start up the coffee, will you?"

I glanced at his coffee pot and the thin layer of mold growing there. "How about you put on a shirt and shoes and we go get breakfast?"

"Are you okay? Has something happened?" Colt asked as he slid onto a barstool. It was clear he didn't want to get out of the house quite yet.

I'd braved washing the coffee pot. I sighed as I picked it up and took it to the sink, blasting the hot water. "I'm in love with Haley," I said, glancing back at him.

"Yeah?"

"Yeah."

"I knew that already."

"I mean like *love* love."

"Have you told her?"

How this fucker knew me so well was beyond me sometimes. "Not yet."

"You better tell her," Colt said. "I'm sure she loves you too. It's cute the way she talks about you."

My stomach did a little flip. I was quiet for a couple minutes as I finished cleaning out the coffee pot. I dumped the portafilter, washed it, put a fresh filter down and filled it with Folgers. Added water, turned it on, and sighed once it finally started percolating.

"Cam," he sighed. "She loves you. You love her. Why else are you here?"

"What if I end up moving?" I asked.

I joined him at the bar and took a seat.

Colt raised a brow and then ran his fingers through his hair. "I'm a little too hungover for this, man. But what do you mean? Like you leaving Citrus Cove?"

"Yeah. What if I say I love you to Hal, she says it back, we get married and she doesn't want to stay here."

I saw a prickle of hurt flash in his eyes. But then he relaxed, studying me. "Are you worried about me or the winery?"

"Both?"

"Well, I'd be fine. I'd miss you. Hell, I'd probably miss Hal too. She's already become a part of everything again. But I'm not going to stop you. As for the winery, you could either transfer the entire ownership to me, or stay in it in case y'all ever move back. It's not the end of the world."

He had that business tone right now, the one that always surprised me. But he was right. I felt myself relax once again.

"I called a family meeting this morning but I wanted to talk to you alone," I said. "I love Hunter and Sammy, but you're different. We've been through thick and thin. You've seen me at my worst."

"I have," he chuckled. "Let me know when you get better?"

"Hey," I snorted. "Dick."

I got up and found two mugs and poured us each a cup. I was already buzzing from the two cups I'd downed earlier, but I didn't care.

"When are you telling her?"

"I have no idea," I sighed. "When it's right? When I feel like I won't scare her off? When things calm down?"

"You should leave and go tell her now," he said. "Just get it over with. Rip that bandaid off. Profess your undying love and then ride off into the Texas sunset in a big ass truck."

"Fuck off," I laughed.

It was a stupid image, but enough to pull me out of my mood and worries. I took a sip of coffee and thoughts about Haley, while also trying not to think too hard about her because then that sexy photo came to mind.

"When are we moving Sarah and the boys out of the house?"

That sobered me up quickly. "Soon," I said. "Hopefully next week. We'll get them out."

"I worry about the boys," he said.

I worried about them too, but not in the way Colt did. Not in the way he always had since everyone started noticing problems with David Connor.

I bit my tongue. I wanted to ask when he was going to tell Sarah he loved her and flip the whole thing back on him. But he wouldn't take that well.

So, instead, I sat there drinking coffee—keeping my fingers crossed that all of us caught the break we desperately needed.

It was probably too ambitious, but I stared at Colt for a moment, a thought crossing my mind.

I hadn't even told Haley I loved her...

And yet...

"Hey," I said. "Mom would have to tag along but... Do you want to go ring shopping?"

Colt split into a wide grin. "Hell fucking yeah I do. We can pick up Mama Harlow. Make it an event?"

"Yes," I chuckled. "Fine. She did want to help. I'm not going to have any money left."

"That's fine," Colt chuckled. "I can loan you some."

I rolled my eyes and took the last sip of coffee, waiting for him to down his too. I snatched up our mugs, took them to the sink, and flipped off the coffee maker.

"Go get some clothes on unless you want everyone talking about you," I teased.

"Yeah, yeah." He slid off the bar stool and rolled his shoulder. "Five minutes. Let's go get your girl a ring."

CHAPTER THIRTY

cameron

"THAT'S THE LAST OF IT," I said. "Well, I think there's one more."

Colt shoved the final box into his truck. I glanced at Sarah's house, knowing that at any point, David could come home. In theory, he was out of town again, but I didn't trust it.

The good news was that they were out of there.

I knew there was a lot Haley's sister was holding back. When I looked at Jake or Davy, I worried. I wondered what happened behind closed doors, what they wouldn't say.

Haley adjusted her ball cap, her lips pressed in a thin line. I didn't like that she'd come here for this, but I knew better than to argue with her. The trade-off was that she wasn't allowed to lift a damn finger.

To no surprise, she was very good at giving us instructions.

"Let's get out of here," Colt said, "before that bastard arrives."

Haley nodded and checked her phone. "Sarah made it to the house. The boys are doing okay."

It had been a week already since David attacked Haley. In

that time frame, Hunter helped Haley find a house that Sarah and the boys could live in.

Haley was still living with me, for now, which made me happy. I rather her be with me than anywhere else.

"I'll grab the last box," I said, turning for the house.

"I'll meet you at Sarah's," Colt said, hopping into his truck.

Haley squinted at me. "I'll be waiting here since I can't lift one finger."

"Damn right," I said, raising a brow.

I went back through the front door and through the living room. The house felt empty now, eerie. Sarah decided to leave most of the furniture. Most of the boxes belonged to the boys.

I went down the hall, walking into the room they shared and grabbing the final box. I lifted it, taking a deep breath.

The air was musty here. There was a foul edge to it, faint but still noticeable.

"What the fuck is that smell?" I muttered.

I carried the box down the hall, following the scent. There was a staircase that led down to the door to the basement. I stood at the top, staring down.

"Cam?"

I startled, nearly dropping the box.

"Coming," I called back to Haley.

I went back outside, shutting the front door behind me. Haley was sitting on the tailgate of my truck.

"All good?"

"Yeah," I said. "It smells like something died in there. Did Sarah mention anything about rodents? I know one time, a bat got stuck in the walls at the barn. Smelled for days."

Haley wrinkled her nose. "She didn't say anything about that. If it's been dead for a while though, maybe they stopped noticing it..."

I winced. "God, I hope not. Colt or I would have helped."

Haley raised a brow as I slid the box in behind her. She parted her thighs for me, drawing me close.

"Hey," I murmured, chuckling as I tucked a rogue curl behind her ear.

It was moments like this that I knew I wanted to be with her forever. Her dark brown eyes shone in the sunlight. She was wearing my T-shirt, one she'd stolen.

I liked seeing her wear what was mine.

"I love that you're concerned," she said, pulling me closer. "I'm sure it's nothing though. Maybe a mouse or something..."

"Right."

It wasn't that, but I had no inclination to investigate. It was probably some sort of rodent, but that could be David's deal. I sure as hell wasn't going to do him any favors.

I leaned down, cupping her face as I planted a kiss on her soft lips.

"Fuck," she murmured, pulling back. "Maybe we should make a quick run home..."

"Haley Marie. You have been injured."

"Yeah, but that doesn't mean I've stopped wanting you to rail me."

I feigned a gasp, lifting her up and pulling her legs around my waist. She laughed as she held on to me. I shut the tailgate and carried her around to the passenger's seat, opening the door and putting her in.

"I see," she mused. "I see how it is."

"We have to go meet up with the rest of them," I said.

But I couldn't hide my smile as I shut her door and went around to the driver's side. I got in and cranked the engine, giving her a look.

"Are you going to behave?"

"Nope."

I pulled out of the quiet driveway, my gaze lingering on the house as we left.

She blew out a breath. "We did it."

"He's not going to take this well." My stomach twisted. "Not to mention, that might have been a violation of our restraining orders?"

"Well, none of us saw you there. And no, he won't take it well, but it'll take some time before he figures out where they moved. And we already have a lawyer lined up for her."

I glanced over at her. Her voice sounded so strong. After everything she'd gone through, she still hadn't broken. I wasn't sure I'd ever be as strong as her.

"Have I told you how much of a badass you are?" I asked.

Haley chuckled. "Well, when I want something, I get it."

"I see," I said. "Haley..."

Tell her you love her. Tell her now.

Every time I was about to tell her, I choked. I worried it was too much. Too soon. Or maybe I wasn't good enough for her. I wanted her to have the whole world, and I worried that I couldn't be the one to give it to her.

Her hand slid over, touching my thigh.

"*Haley*," I growled.

"It's been at least a week. I'm dying. I'm certain that if you don't touch me or fuck me soon, I'll turn into a puddle. Like the Wicked Witch of the West."

My cock was already responding to her touch. "We've had a lot going on. And you've been healing. I don't want to hurt you."

"I'm healed."

"Baby, I don't think—"

She unzipped my jeans, her nimble fingers slipping through the fabric and gripping my cock.

"Fuck."

Every sane thought went out the window.

"Can you keep your eyes on the road?" she purred.

This woman. This woman was the end of me. "Yes. When we get home tonight, I'm going to fuck you as hard as I can without your ribs hurting for this."

"Oh, so a reward," she chuckled, her voice seductive.

Fuuuuck. I moaned as I turned onto Main Street, thanking the gods that my windows were tinted. I slowed to the stoplight right as her lips closed around the head of my cock.

"Fuck. *Baby.*"

My hips thrust up, my body reacting to her instantly. Needing her. She sucked, her tongue swirling over the head before she took me deeper.

I cursed again, every thought evaporating except for how much I wanted her and how much I loved her. I looked down at her, moaning as she sucked me, only for her to stop.

"Eyes on the road, cowboy."

Fuck me. I forced my gaze up right as the red light turned green. She started sucking my cock again, stroking it in a way that would make me come at any moment.

I sped up a little down the quiet street. I turned off onto a neighborhood road and slowed since no one was behind me. I was already on the edge.

"You're killing me," I grunted. "Fucking hell."

She let out a feminine chuckle, stroking me a little faster.

"I'm going to come," I rasped.

I was so close. So fucking close. I gripped the steering wheel as she tore an orgasm out of me, my hips bucking as I came in her mouth, filling her throat with my cum.

She swallowed every drop, waiting until I was completely finished before she slowly pulled off.

She readjusted my pants, zipped the zipper, and sat back

like nothing had happened. The wicked smile she wore made me want to get on my knees for her.

"Are we almost there?"

I breathed out, narrowing my eyes at her. "Later. You and me, sunshine."

She grinned as she turned her head. "Sounds like a date."

* * *

The house Haley bought was perfect. It was also just enough out of the way that we were certain David wouldn't immediately find it and hoped that he wouldn't even try. Sarah met with the lawyer, the papers were filed, and if things got nasty she would go to the police.

Everyone in this town knew how nasty a drunk David could be. Knowing him, if he bothered us, he'd do something stupid that would land him in trouble.

Part of me wanted that. The other part of me just wanted him to leave everyone the hell alone. He clearly didn't care about the boys or Sarah. So why go after them?

The house was also only a few blocks from Honey, which was also good. Haley made sure of that, even if she'd never said it aloud to her sister.

By the time we got Sarah and the boys settled in, it was late. Colt decided to stay the night on the couch, claiming he wanted to be around in case anything happened.

Would David really be that stupid?

We were finally back at my house. *Our house.*

Haley and I got out of my truck and went to our front porch. She reached for my hand, tugging me toward the rocking chair. I sat down, pulling her into my lap.

Her arms wrapped around me, her head resting on my shoulder.

"Are you comfortable like this?" I whispered.

"More than," she said. "When will this all be over? When will they catch Andy? And when will they catch the killer?"

"Maybe they're the same person," I said softly.

"Maybe," she breathed out. "It's possible."

I swallowed hard, holding her a little tighter. "One day, we'll look back on this and be amazed that we came together in the midst of a storm."

"I hope so."

I rocked in the chair, easing us back and forth. The sound of cicadas rattled through the night, the wind rustling the trees. I hummed softly, breathing in her scent.

She shifted in my lap, her hand sliding down my chest.

I raised a brow.

"How tired are you?"

"Not tired at all," I lied.

She snorted. "I know you're tired. You've been helping out my family all day. I was surprised Colt stayed..."

"I'm not," I muttered. "I just... I worry about him."

"Yeah. I can see why." Her hand slid down lower, settling on my belt buckle.

"Sunshine," I said softly. "How about you run upstairs and get naked for me?"

She looked at me, her eyes lighting up. "Yeah?"

"Yeah."

She slid off my lap and stood, looking down at me as she tied her hair back.

"I want you on our bed with your thighs spread. I want you to get the lube and work it into your pussy and ass for me. I have a surprise for you."

One that I'd ordered the other day and had finally arrived.

Her eyes lit up. "Okay," she breathed out.

"Go," I urged.

I watched as she ran inside. I rocked back and forth in my

chair, giving her a few minutes to do exactly as I asked. As I waited, my cock began to harden, knowing she was getting herself ready for me.

I finally stood and went inside, closing and locking the door behind me. I'd already opened the toys, cleaned them, and hidden them in the bathroom downstairs.

I retrieved them—a glass rose butt plug and a vibrator that I was going to make her scream with. I went up the staircase, slowing as I came to our bedroom.

Haley was lying at the center, her legs spread and lube glistening on her pussy and ass. Her fingers were inside herself, her cheeks rosy.

"Good girl," I praised softly, my cock now straining against my pants.

She was so goddamn gorgeous.

I couldn't wait to make her beg.

I came to the edge of the bed. "Turn over for me on all fours. And don't look."

She did as I asked, her breath hitching as she rolled onto all fours, her pretty little ass facing me. I got onto the bed behind her, sucking in a breath as I sat the toys down, taking a moment to squeeze each cheek.

"How are your ribs feeling?"

"They're fine, Cam," she groaned. "I swear. If I need you to stop or if they start hurting, I'll say red."

"You promise?"

"I promise."

Good. I leaned past her, reaching for the bottle of lube on the nightstand. I was still fully dressed and had decided that I wasn't going to be taking off my clothes yet.

Not until she was begging for my cock inside her.

I grabbed the glass rosebud and lubed it, listening for her gasp as I pressed the tip against her little hole. Her back arched, a moan escaping her as I began to gently work it into her.

"That feels good," she huffed. "*Cam.*"

She took it fully, the glass rose gleaming.

"Get comfortable with your legs still spread," I said, giving her a moment to adjust herself. I reached for a pillow, sliding it under her hips for more support.

"What are you going to do to me?" There was so much anticipation in her voice.

I grinned like the devil. "Make you beg me to stop. Are you comfortable?"

"Yes," she breathed out.

I took a moment to collect myself before I came in my pants from seeing her like this. Her ass filled, her body waiting for me, her thighs spread, and her dark pink pussy shining.

I reached for the vibrator and felt more satisfaction with the way she gasped, as I turned it on, than ever had before.

"*Cam.*"

Her raspy plea turned into a cry as I held the vibrating head to her clit. A dark chuckle escaped me as her voice lifted, her muscles tensing. I reached up, holding my thumb to the little rose as I held the vibrator in place.

"Fuck!" she gasped.

I pulled it back for a moment. My cock was so fucking hard.

Every little noise she made just turned me on more.

I waited before holding it back to her. Her shout was one of pure ecstasy. I watched as she gripped the blankets, groaning as her first orgasm overtook her.

I loved watching my sunshine come.

She melted against the bed, her pants ragged. I reached down and dragged my fingertips down her back, enjoying the way she purred. I then flipped on the vibrator again, holding it back to her clit. She cried out, and I watched as she realized that I wasn't done with her yet.

She groaned my name as I edged her. I held the vibrator to her clit, watching as she responded. She gripped the blankets all over again, her entire body coiling up as I drove her to the edge.

"That's my good girl," I said softly.

My cock was so hard, my own need became stronger and stronger. I wanted to just unzip them and shove my cock inside her. I wanted to fill her over and over again.

But not yet.

Not until my sunshine came again for me. I angled the vibrator, and she cried out, her back arching.

"I'm gonna come again," she groaned.

I kept going, keeping her there, forcing her to take the pleasure. She finally let out another cry, another orgasm tearing through her.

She relaxed again, letting out a soft moan. "Cam," she whispered. "Fuck."

"How do you feel?" I asked, setting the vibrator down. Her pussy was dripping with her release, her skin flushed.

"Like I've been needing to release for a whole fucking week."

I chuckled, my hands falling down to my belt buckle.

"Please," she whispered.

She already knew the moment she heard me pull it off. I swallowed hard as I moved off the bed, stripping slowly, making her wait for me even though it was torture for me too.

My cock sprang free, and I reached down to stroke it. My head fell back with a groan, a curse leaving me.

I needed to fuck her.

"Cam," she rasped. "Please. Please. I need to feel you inside of me."

Fuck. I couldn't hold out anymore. I climbed back onto the bed and dipped two fingers inside of her, feeling how fucking wet she was. She let out a low groan, pushing back against me.

I pressed the head of my cock against her, huffing as I stayed there.

"You're fucking killing me."

"I know," I grunted, but I didn't move.

"Cam. *Fuck* me."

I thrust forward, giving her every inch. She gasped as she took me, her pussy clenching me. I gripped her hips as I dragged my cock back out and then filled her again.

I fell into a brutal rhythm, fucking her harder than I ever had. Her cries and groans edged me on, the sound of our skin slapping together filling the room.

She gripped me, a shudder working through her body. "I'm going to come again. *Fuck.*"

"Come, baby."

Haley gasped, and I felt her come around me, her tight pussy a vice around my cock. I didn't stop. I kept fucking her all the way through her orgasm, going until I felt myself getting closer.

"Fill me," she moaned. "I want you to breed me like your own little slut."

Fuck. I pumped into her harder until I growled, giving one last thrust as I started to come inside of her.

I gave her every drop until every muscle in my body relaxed. I stayed there, sweat shining on both of us.

I reached for the little glass rose and pulled it out at the same time I pulled my cock free. She gasped as I did so, her body collapsing against the bed.

I set it on the side table with the vibrator and then collapsed next to her, breathing hard.

"That was..."

"Mind-blowing," she said.

"Yes," I agreed, still panting hard. "I think we're due for a shower and some food."

"And sleep," she chuckled.

"And a good night of sleep."

"In our bed."

"In *our* bed."

Tell her now.

I should have. I thought about the ring I'd bought a few days ago tucked away in my dresser, hiding for the perfect moment. It would have been such an easy thing to whisper in the dark.

By the time I worked up the courage to say it, though, Haley's soft snores drifted around me.

CHAPTER THIRTY-ONE

cameron

THE SUN WAS JUST NOW STARTING to rise. I decided when I hadn't been able to fall back asleep at 4:00 a.m. that I'd go to the winery for a couple of hours just to try and get a sense of normalcy.

Last night was incredible with Haley. One would think that meant I would have slept well, but all I could think about was how I needed her to be safe. How I needed all of this to end.

We had to find the killer. And we had to find Andy.

Citrus Cove was so damn small you'd think it would be easy. And maybe he'd left town. But even so, there was still someone out there hunting the woman I loved more than anything else in the world.

I couldn't take it anymore.

Maybe we'd missed something on the security cameras. Maybe there was *something* that I'd overlooked.

"I'm going to go to the winery for a little bit," I whispered to Haley. "Hunter is on his way over with coffee and donuts."

She cracked open an eye, pulling the blankets tighter

around her. She blinked at me, processing what I'd said. "It's like 6:00 a.m.," she protested.

"I know. I just want to go check on things. I just... Maybe we missed something."

"You're a monster," she sighed dramatically. "How did you get Hunter to come over this early?"

"I bribed him," I chuckled.

"With what?"

"Naming our future child after him."

She swatted me with a sleepy chuckle but nodded. "Be careful, cowboy."

"Always, sunshine." I planted a kiss on her forehead before heading downstairs and out the door.

I would be careful, of course, but I wasn't worried about myself the way I was worried about her.

The police hadn't made any progress in finding out who killed that poor woman. I was starting to get antsy and wanted to go over to the winery to take a look at the footage again.

I'd replayed that night in my head so many times. Part of me wondered if me fighting Andy was the reason he'd killed that woman.

If it was him.

There was no way to know for sure. I had a hard time imagining him doing it, but I didn't know him. I didn't know what he was capable of.

Maybe he was the killer.

The idea that he stalked Haley all the way from Baltimore infuriated me.

The drive over was quick, I was lost in my thoughts. It was early in the morning, the sun peeking over the hills, highlighting the Texas Hill Country. We were due for more rain soon, which was a good sign before rolling into the brutal heat of summer.

262

I slowed as I drove up. Everything looked normal.

I pulled into the parking lot, my eyes drifting over to the spot where Haley's car had been left. The police had it towed in for forensics, but I wasn't sure if she'd ever even want to see it again.

New pole lights had been installed, so at least at night, the entire parking lot would be illuminated.

I sat still, taking it all in. Finally, after a couple of minutes of just letting my mind rest, I got out of my truck. I unlocked the front door and slipped into the cool air. It felt strange being back, almost normal.

It was silent. The only sound was my boots on the floor, echoing as I went to the back toward my office, where I set my things down. I took a seat in the chair, leaning back and thinking about the things that Haley and I had done in here that night.

A little slice of paradise amongst the hell that our lives had become. It had to end. We had to catch the killer.

We couldn't keep living like this.

Haley deserved happiness, and I wanted to build a life with her. We had a future to look forward to, one that didn't involve a killer stalking her.

My phone dinged in my pocket, I pulled it out, seeing Hunter's text.

Hunter: *At your house, drinking coffee with Hal. I don't think that she's a morning person.*

I chuckled. She most certainly was not. I shot him a text back and told him I'd be home within the hour. I set my phone down and logged on to my computer. There were emails from customers, some social media posts that I needed to check on. I perused it all until I finally decided to do what I had come for.

I pulled up the security camera system, logging in the dates for that Saturday night, and scrutinized the footage.

Frustration rolled through me as I watched the same footage of the scene over and over again. I'd watched it with Bud. I'd watched it with Haley. I'd watched it with Hunter and Sammy and Colt. All of us looked it over, looking for anything that might have been a clue.

I zoomed in on one of the cameras, selecting a square to magnify. It was the closest to the spot where Haley parked.

It infuriated me that I couldn't see what happened. I watched it once, and watched it twice. Still nothing. Nothing helpful, no clue to the identity of the serial killer or even Andy.

I spent a few more minutes looking over footage before I let out a sigh and leaned back in my chair. This was pointless.

Everything was fucking pointless.

I groaned, leaning forward and rubbing my eyes.

I was worried about her. Worried about everything that had happened. I couldn't stand the thought of it being her in that car instead of Darlene.

My future was with Haley. Between all of the crazy moments this week of us dealing with everything happening, I thought about proposing to her. What I would do. How I would plan it. Wondering if she would be crazy enough to say yes.

Hell, I still had to tell her I loved her first. But, it was nice thinking about a proposal and wedding amidst all of the bad things. The idea of her walking down the aisle to meet me... It would be a dream come true.

I smiled, my shoulders relaxing. We just needed to weather the storm. Eventually, all of this would blow over, and we'd be able to move on with our lives.

The scent of smoke drew my attention. I scowled, looking up.

"What the fuck?"

It became stronger.

I stood, my eyes on the doorway. The air was quickly

turning hazy, becoming stronger as I stepped out into the hall-way. A cloud of smoke billowed at the end, filling up the space. I coughed, my eyes watering.

Panic rolled through me. This place was my dream. I'd spent countless hours working, countless hours worrying.

What the hell was happening? A million thoughts ran through my head. Why hadn't the sprinklers gone off? Why hadn't the alarm? Why was my winery on fire?

I rushed down the hall and out into the main part of the winery. I pulled my shirt over my mouth and nose, shock following.

Fire licked at the walls, crawling toward me. It was spread-ing, moving fast, consuming anything and everything in its path. I stood, frozen. Staring.

My whole damn life was going up in flames.

The scent of gasoline filled my nostrils, something that hadn't been here earlier.

Someone had done this.

My blood ran cold.

I stood still, my heart pounding.

Someone had been here.

I had been so fucking focused in my office that I hadn't even noticed. Daydreaming and hyperfocusing on the footage, all while someone had waltzed in and set this place ablaze.

What if they were still here?

My adrenaline finally kicked in. I ran for the front door, going as fast as I could. I kicked it open, running out into the open air, dragging in breaths as I looked around.

A black car sat in the parking lot, still parked.

I looked around wildly, pulling my phone from my pocket. I texted Hunter.

Me: *Call 911. Someone here. Set place on fire.*

I then tucked it away, jogging over to the car.

265

Whoever the fuck they were, they had to come back here, right?

I knelt behind it, my heart pounding as I watched my dreams go up in flames. It hurt in a different kind of way, an ache so deep that I was losing something I might never recover. Smoke billowed in the baby blue Texas sky, the puffy white clouds marred.

I felt my phone buzzing in my pocket, but I ignored it. I hunched down, waiting for whoever had done this. I heard the sound of boots on gravel, rushing toward the car. Right as they reached for the driver's side, I jumped up, rushing toward them and grabbing them by the jacket they wore.

I yanked them back as they turned, throwing them to the ground. Their hood fell back.

"Andy," I snarled. "You son of a bitch. What the fuck is wrong with you?"

He jumped to his feet, his face contorted with rage. "It's what you get. You ruined my life!"

"Did you kill that woman?" I snarled. "Are you the serial killer?"

"No, but I'm going to kill you," he growled, reaching for me.

It was clear that he'd been holding back the other night when I'd fought him. He grabbed me by the shirt, kicking my feet out from under me and slamming me onto the ground. The gravel dug into my back, sharp pain tearing into me. We rolled together, and I felt a little bit surprised that he was as strong as he was. I kicked him back, managing to roll back to my feet.

I punched him hard, feeling my knuckles crack against his nose. He managed to land a blow to my face, my ears ringing from the impact. I staggered back and then gasped as I felt something sharp stab into my side.

The fucker had a knife.

266

He yanked it out, tackling me to the ground. I clutched my side as he hit me again and again, the pain excruciating.

I curled in, protecting my head and neck and stomach, despite the pain radiating from the stab wound.

He stopped, hovering over me. "You should have never interfered. I would have taken her home and did whatever I wanted if you hadn't. Guys like you always think they deserve the whole world. She wanted me and you interfered."

Disgust rolled through me. "She never wanted you. You're a fucking killer."

"I am now," he snarled.

My hand covered the knife wound, blood hot against my skin as I stared up at him in a daze.

He was going to kill me.

I was pissed about that. I didn't want to go. I didn't want to lose out on living a long happy life with Haley.

I hadn't even told her I loved her yet.

Regret rolled through me. I was stupid. I was so fucking stupid. Why had I waited so long to tell her? I loved her. I loved her so much.

Sirens made his head whip around.

"You're lucky," he said. "If I had more time, I'd make sure you died too."

He turned and ran, getting into his car. I lifted my head, glaring despite the fact that I was lying in the parking lot of my burning winery, bleeding out.

I maintained the glare as he drove off, peeling out and kicking up gravel behind him.

My head throbbed as I lay back down. Haley was going to kill me if I didn't die. Fuck.

A police car pulled up to a stop next to me. I heard a shout, my vision starting to darken and splinter into dots.

This sucks.

"You idiot. You fucking idiot."

I blinked, seeing Sammy hovering over me. I heard my mother's voice too, shrill above the fire truck siren.

Sammy gripped my face, his eyes burning with rage. "Who did this, Cam?"

"Andy. He brought a knife to a fistfight," I breathed out. "Wasn't fair."

Sammy shook his head and was soon replaced by someone I didn't recognize. I closed my eyes, sending up a silent prayer.

I love you, sunshine.

CHAPTER THIRTY-TWO

I STORMED INTO THE HOSPITAL. Hunter tried to keep up with me, but even with his long legs, it was difficult for him.

Bud was already standing at the reception desk, and I marched right up to him, seething. Very few things brought my mean streak out, but I was done.

"If you don't find this son of a bitch, I am going to—"

Bud grabbed my shoulders, his voice firm. "We got him."

Everything in me deflated. "You got him?"

"We got Andy," Bud said again. "He's in custody. And we'll talk in a bit, Haley."

"Haley," Hunter said, his voice gruff.

I was about to lose it. I could feel myself unraveling, a spool of thread let loose. Hunter steered me away, leading me down one of the halls. He paused, shoving his hands in his pockets.

"Take a deep breath," he said.

The look I gave him made him wince.

"He's still passed out," Hunter said. "They stitched up the

knife wound. It missed anything vital, but he lost a lot of blood. But he's alive, Haley."

"How can you be so calm?" My voice trembled. "This is all my fault."

"It isn't," Hunter growled. "Haley, I swear this isn't your fault."

"Hey."

We both looked up, seeing Sammy and his mom rushing toward us.

"I'm so sorry," I blurted out, my voice breaking. "I'm so sorry, Mrs. Harlow—"

"Oh, honey," she said. "This isn't your fault, darlin'. Come here."

My eyes teared up, and she spread her arms, pulling me into a big hug.

"Oh, baby doll," she said, holding on to me as I started to sob. "Cam has told me some of what you've gone through. You're stronger than me. No one blames you for what happened, but this isn't your fault, and don't you go thinking so."

I didn't even know this woman, but the instant comfort I felt broke me. I held on to her as I fell apart.

"Hunter, go get her some water."

"Yes, ma'am," Hunter responded, disappearing.

I felt Sammy's hand on my shoulder and drew back, wiping my eyes. "I'm so sorry. Fuck. I'm a mess. Hunter got that text from Cam, and then you just happened to call Sammy, and I just—I can't lose him. I can't. *I can't*," I repeated.

The tears wouldn't stop.

"He's tough," she said. "And the doctor said he'll be okay. My husband is waiting for them to let us all into his room once he's out. He knows the surgeon here."

Hunter came back with a Styrofoam cup of water and handed it to me.

"They caught Andy," Hunter told her and Sammy.

"Good. I want that son of a bitch behind bars," she said, her voice taking on a fierce edge. "Also, you can call me Lynn," she directed to me.

"Thank you," I said, taking the cup and drinking. "I'm Haley. I'm sorry I haven't come for dinner yet."

"Don't be," she said, patting my arm. "We'll have plenty of time for that."

I needed to pull myself together. I drew in a breath, mentally steeling myself with every sip. By the time the water was gone, I could breathe again.

I hadn't lost him.

That was the most important thing.

I drew in another breath right as a nurse came toward us, the same one that attended to me the other day. She winced when she saw me.

"I'm starting to get used to seeing you here," she said.

"Unfortunately," I sighed. I wiped my eyes again, trying to pull myself together. Hell, I'd had a lot of practice doing so over the last few weeks. "I mean, not unfortunate to see you, but being here."

She smiled. "Well, I have good news for y'all. He's out and doing fine. Dad's already sitting with him. He's starting to wake up."

"Good," Hunter said. "Thank you."

She nodded and turned, pointing down the hall. "He's in the room down on the right. He might be a little out of it."

I was already moving. I practically ran down the hall, stopping when I came to the doorway.

Cam's eyes were open. He turned his head and grinned when he saw me. "There's my wife," he said proudly.

My knees felt weak.

His dad snorted and came toward me. I could see where his sons got their looks. He winked. "Hey, Haley. I'm Bob. I'm gonna hold off the troops and give you two a moment."

"Thanks. It's so nice to meet you. I'm sorry it's under these circumstances."

"He gave us all a scare, but he's tough."

I went to Cameron's side, the tears falling again. His face was covered in bruises and he was definitely out of it, but he was alive. The idea of losing him and knowing that I hadn't changed something in me.

He looked horrified at the tears.

"Fuck," he sighed. "Yeah, I was an idiot."

"Yeah, you were. What were you thinking?"

"I was thinking I could catch the killer and we could live happily ever after, Hal."

I shook my head and sniffled, leaning down and planting a kiss on his forehead. "Please don't ever scare me like this again."

"I'll try not to," he said.

I closed my eyes and kissed his forehead again before grabbing one of the chairs and dragging it to him. I sat down, my hand sliding into his.

He squeezed it. "I kept thinking while I was laying there that that was it. That was my end. I was going to die without ever telling you the truth."

"The truth?" I whispered.

"I love you. I love you so fucking much. I want to marry you. I want to make love to you."

"Cam," I hissed. "You're on drugs."

"I might be, but I'm telling you, I love you more than anything else and I was a dumbass for not telling you sooner. I could have died without telling you."

I didn't fight the tears this time. "I love you too," I whispered. "So much. So fucking much."

He grinned, giving my hand another squeeze. "I want a big wedding."

"Oh my god," I snorted. "Alright, mister. You are too drugged up for this right now."

Cam shrugged and his smile faded. "I think he was the killer. He killed that woman, Hal. I think it's finally over."

I breathed out. "You really think it was him?"

"We'll have to see what they say. But whoever killed her left those words on your car. It had to be him. That's why he was trying to get you to go with him."

"Don't worry about any of that right now," I whispered. "I'll talk to Bud later. Okay? But for now, stop worrying."

A soft knock interrupted the two of us "Alright, the troops would like in, if that's okay."

I looked up at the doorway, Cameron's dad standing there. "Of course," I said.

Everyone came in. Cameron rolled his eyes as Lynn yelled at him about being the hero. His brothers kissed the top of his head, and followed it up by giving him the finger.

"When you're better, I'm gonna fight you for scaring the shit out of me," Hunter said, crossing his arms. "And scaring your girl."

Cam chuckled and then sighed. "How's the winery?"

Everyone was silent. He winced.

"We can rebuild," Hunter said.

"You have insurance, but if push comes to shove, we could do a fundraiser," I said.

"That's a good idea," Sammy said. "Raise some funds to build it back."

Cameron's eyes softened. His hand was still in mine, and

he gripped it a little harder. "It was the family barn. It's been around for a long time, and now it's fucking gone."

My heart hurt for him.

"It was just a building," Lynn said, her voice firm. "I'm thankful that you got out. Today could have been a lot more tragic."

"I just don't know how I didn't hear him." Cam sighed. "I was watching footage of the night he killed that woman."

"So it was him?" Sammy asked.

"Maybe? I think so," Cam said.

I pressed my lips together and slowly pulled my hand from his. "I'm going to go talk to Bud."

"I'll go with you," Hunter said. "Colt is on the way, by the way."

"Figures," Cam said. "You'd think I'd died."

His mom hissed at him. I kissed his forehead as she started to scold him, then slipped out of the room and into the cool hall. Hunter followed, the two of us heading back toward the front, where Bud still was.

"Why are you here?" I asked him as I walked up.

"I need to talk to Cam," Bud said seriously. I'd only seen him a handful of times, but right now, he looked like he'd aged fifteen years. "But wanted to give y'all some time."

"Tell us what's going on," Hunter said.

Bud looked like he was going to hold back, but then gave in. "We have him in custody. He did admit to killing that woman but claims he's never been to Baltimore and says that something in him snapped that night. He did, however, have pictures of you, Haley, where he was staying. But they were all photos from your social media accounts."

My blood ran cold. Hunter crossed his arms, giving me a reassuring glance. "We have lawyers."

"Do we?" I echoed.

"Yep."

Bud chuckled, giving me an apologetic look. "Your boyfriend's brother seems to know everyone in the whole damn world sometimes."

"I've got connections," Hunter said, shrugging. "So he's the killer, then."

"He hasn't admitted to anything else and claims he hadn't heard of Haley prior to running into her at the bar."

I shook my head, my gut twisting. It still didn't feel right.

"I think it's him though. I really do," Bud said. "He's new to Citrus Cove. He claimed he was a jeweler, but his business is bankrupt. Sounds like he's been running around and avoiding paying fines and taxes. And he killed Darlene. It all makes sense."

"Maybe I'm just unable to accept it right now," I whispered, my thoughts whirling.

"Probably," Hunter said. "You've been through a lot, Haley."

I nodded, frowning. Was that it, then? Was Andy really the person who followed me from Baltimore? Who killed my neighbor and then threatened me? Who destroyed my apartment?

"I think if Cam is feeling okay, I might try to talk to him. I'd just like to confirm what happened."

"You can try," Hunter said. "I can take you to the room."

Bud nodded. "Thanks. Oh, and I reached out to Baltimore. They actually got some footage, so we should be able to confirm everything soon. You can rest easy, Haley."

"I'll join y'all in a few minutes," I said, giving Hunter and Bud a nod.

Hunter hesitated but then gave in, the two of them heading down the hall.

I just needed a moment to myself. I darted the opposite

way, running for the bathroom. I pushed open the door and went into a stall, slamming it shut. My heart hammered in my chest, my head spinning.

Breathe. Breathe.

I forced myself to take in deep breaths, swallowing back the tears. For a moment, I relived everything.

That night in Baltimore.

What he said to me.

You're next.

Coming here. The text messages, the picture of Cam and me. My apartment.

The murder. The car.

I'd lost almost everything because of this person.

Breathe.

My heart rate finally started to come down. I opened my eyes, feeling a heavy exhaustion fall over me.

We were finally free of the monster that had been trying to kill me.

CHAPTER THIRTY-THREE

I HELD my phone to my ear as I opened the fridge, listening to Sarah talk.

"The house has been great. You and Cam should come over for dinner if he's feeling better. The boys would love to see you. They talk about you all the time."

"How are they doing with everything?" I asked.

"Hanging in there," she sighed. "I didn't realize how much they hated their dad, Hal."

"Has he found you or anything?" I asked, feeling my stomach twist.

I pulled out a pitcher of sweet tea and kicked the fridge closed, pulling down two glasses. Cam was in the living room, relaxing on the couch and waiting for me to join him for snuggles. It was moments like this that I thought *what the fuck?* It felt so...normal. Even with everything that had happened.

And it was those moments that kept me going.

I smiled, glancing up at him out of habit.

Sarah let out a long sigh. I could hear her exhaustion. "No. It's like he's just gone. Maybe he had a work trip."

I frowned. "What even is his job?"

"He works for an insurance company and travels a lot."

"Does he? How is he doing that and being drunk?" I winced at my own words. "Sorry. That was harsh."

"No, you're right." Her voice was firm, her tone weary. "I don't know, Hal. I stopped asking questions. I just... stopped. I guess I gave up. Does that make me a bad person? A terrible mother? It does, doesn't it?"

"No," I said. "You've done the best you can."

"It wasn't enough."

"It's going to work out, Sarah," I said. "It will. You're doing the right thing. You've made changes. I just hate that you had to deal with him."

"In some ways I guess it hasn't been terrible. Most nights he spent in the basement anyways when he was home. He'd leave us alone then..."

"When do you see the divorce lawyer?" I asked. I wanted those damn papers signed ASAP. The longer her last name was Connor, the longer I felt like her and the kids were being dragged through the mud.

A few loose curls fell in my face, loosening from my bobby pins. I fought them for a moment, and then held the phone to my ear with my shoulder as I readjusted the pins.

"Sarah?" I asked.

"Tomorrow." She was quiet, her sniffle audible. "Haley, I can't thank you enough for everything. You don't owe me shit, but you've still pulled me out of a bad situation. I couldn't have done this without you. For the first time in years, I feel like myself again."

"I'm just happy I can help." I sighed. "We've both been through a lot. I just want to rebuild my life now. I can't believe I ended back up in Citrus Cove."

She laughed. "Speaking of *why* you're staying. How's Cam?"

"He's okay," I said, pouring us each a glass of tea. "He keeps trying to hide when he's in pain, but I can tell. It's like he's forgotten he got stabbed yesterday and wants to do everything himself."

"I can hear you," Cam called from the living room. "I have ears."

I grinned. "But he's doing good."

"Good," Sarah laughed.

"Is Colt still sleeping on your couch?"

She sucked in a breath. "Yes. He doesn't want to leave for now. I can't say the boys mind having him around though. If anything, he's kept them distracted. Sammy has stopped by a couple times too."

I narrowed my eyes. "Hmm."

"Don't *hmm* me."

"I'm not saying anything."

"You don't have to." She sighed. "Colt is just a friend."

I fought the urge to snort. The way he looked at her was a lot more than *friend*. "Alright, then. Well, I'm glad he's there."

"Me too. I'm gonna go though. I need to run to the store."

"Be safe," I said. "I'll talk to you tomorrow."

We ended our call, and I left my phone on the counter, putting the pitcher back in the fridge. I grabbed our glasses and took them to the living room.

"Hey, sunshine," Cam chuckled, beaming at me as I handed him his glass. He was sitting up, which was good.

"How are you feeling?" I asked.

"Better now that you're in here."

I rolled my eyes but leaned over the couch and kissed him. He hummed with satisfaction.

"How are Sarah and the boys?" he asked.

"Well, it sounds like Colt is guarding them dutifully. That man is a golden retriever, I swear."

"He is. Come sit with me."

I raised a brow at him, kissing him softly again. "You mean, sit next to you while you lie down."

"Maybe I can lay my head in your lap, Nurse."

I laughed and went around the couch, sitting at the very end. I set my tea down on the coffee table, then patted my lap, raising a brow at him.

He grinned and started to lean forward to put his glass down and then winced.

"Fuck," I said, jumping up.

"I'm fine, I'm fine."

"Clearly not," I hissed, taking the glass from him. I felt a flash of worry. I kept forgetting that he was good at hiding the pain until he did something like that. "Babe, we should probably move you upstairs where you can lie flat."

"I don't like being hurt. I do like you calling me babe, though."

"Shut up," I mumbled. "I know you don't like it, but you are hurt, and we need to make sure you don't strain yourself," I said. "You took care of me when I was hurt. Now it's my turn. Come on."

No amount of begging was going to make me budge on this, and he knew it. Cam made a noise of protest but ultimately gave in to my demand. I helped him up, slipping my arm gently around his side. We went to the staircase, and I helped him up, thankful when we made it to the bedroom.

"So eager to get me into bed, I see," Cam mused. There was a strain in his voice, though, one that was far too telling.

I hated seeing him in pain. I pressed my lips together, trying to smother the rage I felt about everything that had happened. We'd already been through so much.

"Hey," he whispered. "Hal, I'm okay, baby."

I held his gaze, breathing in deep. He was right. He was okay. He was alive and here with me. "I'll get your pain medicine. Should be time for you to take it."

"Just lay with me for a moment," he said. "Please."

He got onto the bed slowly, wincing as he leaned back. I shot him a dirty look as I climbed in next to him, trying to ease myself down.

"Don't give me that look," he growled.

"You worry me," I said. "That you'll push yourself or do something you shouldn't and then tear open the stitches."

He sighed—a long, dramatic one. "I'm a bad patient."

"I can kiss it better," I said, leaning over and kissing his cheek.

He smirked. "I think a kiss on the lips might work a little better..."

"Hmmm. Let's see." I grabbed his face and planted a kiss on him. "I don't know, let's try again." I kissed him again, and his hand slid behind my head, pulling me into a deeper one.

He drew back, relaxing against the pillows. "There. I'm healed. My body and soul are all new again."

"Nice try," I whispered, curling up next to him. "I'm going to lay here for a couple minutes and then run downstairs for your meds. They're on the counter."

"Fine."

I smiled and relaxed next to him. "Still haven't heard from Bud today."

"Don't even think about that right now," Cam murmured.

"It's hard not to," I admitted. "But you're right. I should start thinking about my life again. I...I've been meaning to talk to you, Cam. About everything. I love you."

"I love you too," he said.

"I want to stay here."

His eyes lit up. "Here?"

"Yes. If you want. I mean, I can always move out, but I—"

"I want you here. I want you here forever, Haley."

I grinned at him. "Back in Citrus Cove. Look at me. Emma may or may not be considering moving down too...she could live with Sarah and the boys. At least temporarily."

"Perfect," he whispered. "Perfect. Fuck. I love you so much. I can't stop saying it."

I teared up. After everything we'd been through, I didn't want to stop saying it either.

I could see it all now. If Emma moved down, then I'd have everything I needed. A life with Cam here sounded perfect.

"I've been thinking too..." Cam said.

"Oh yeah?" I asked.

"Yeah. Well, I was thinking that we should plan a trip somewhere. You have so many recommendations and I'd like to see the world. Especially if it's a place you love."

That made my heart flutter. "We have the winery though."

"It can wait," he said, his hand slipping into mine. "We'll rebuild it from the ground up. But a mini vacation sounds nice right now...and then we can come home."

Home.

I liked this idea a lot.

We could have the best of what we both wanted. Travel and then coming home to our small town where we had our family and loved ones.

"Okay," I said. "Yes. I want this."

"Me too," he chuckled.

"Where would you want to go?" I asked.

"What's your favorite place in the whole world?"

"I should say Citrus Cove because that's where you are."

He laughed and then groaned. "Fuck. This wound is a bitch. But what place, really?"

"I'd take you to my favorite beach in Queensland. We could go to the shops that are in the Daintree Forest. Get some fresh ice cream. Eat amazing fish and lounge in the sun."

"Sounds like a dream," he said. "Let's do it. Let's book our tickets right now."

"*Right now?*"

"Yes. Why not?"

I lifted my head, looking at him.

I couldn't think of one damn reason as to why not.

"You really want to?" I asked.

"Yes," he said. "Truly. Let's get the hell out of here. Let's restart everything, okay? Enjoy some time away from everything and when we get back, we can start everything up."

"I don't know if you can travel like that..."

"I'd be fine in a couple weeks," he insisted. "I'm sure."

I studied him a few moments longer. It wouldn't hurt to at least look at booking tickets.

And the idea of Cam on the beach shirtless was certainly appealing.

"My life is with you," he said. "Wherever we are. Wherever we end up. I'm in it forever, Hal. I'm yours."

He had a way with words. I felt my heart melt and leaned forward, giving him a sweet kiss.

I broke out in a grin, and so did he. "Well, my phone is also downstairs," I said, already rolling out of bed. "And your medicine. I'll be back."

I went back down the stairs swiftly and went to the kitchen, grabbing my phone off the counter. If we booked our tickets so last minute, we might actually be able to get a deal. And I liked deals. That was part of why I liked writing travel articles, because I liked finding such things.

Cam's medicine was sitting on the edge, so I snatched it up, turning to run back up—

And froze.

My brother-in-law stood in front of me, his gaze fixed on me.

"David," I said, taking a step back.

But...

This wasn't David.

There was something slightly different about him. This was the man that I'd seen at the gas station, or that I swore I saw at the winery. Someone who looked like David, but wasn't him...

The two of them looked almost exactly alike, but the way he smiled made every part of me freeze. His nose was slightly more crooked, and his clothing was pressed and starched.

"I'm not David," the man chuckled.

His voice.

I knew that voice. I knew that fucking voice. The night of the murder came back to me, the snarl that I'd heard from the man that killed my neighbor.

You're next.

"David is an oaf. I love him, but he's not intelligent. Just a drunk." He moved his hand up, and I realized there was a gun in it. "If you scream for help, I will kill you. And then I will go upstairs and kill Cameron Harlow."

"Who are you?" My heart thundered in my chest, my adrenaline spiking. "Why are you in my house?"

"Not *your* house, last time I checked," he said.

Fuck.

Fuck.

My heart pumped, terror icing my veins.

"What are you doing?" I whispered.

"Doing what I wanted to do so long ago, Haley. Now, go to the door. Leave the items you're holding."

"Haley?" Cam's voice came down the stairs. "Everything okay?"

I stood still, unmoving. "I'm not going," I said. "I don't know you. I don't—"

He pulled the trigger, my ears ringing as the bullet whizzed past me, grazing my arm. "You know me. Go to the fucking door."

I heard Cam's shout, but he was already moving. I reached for the knife block on the counter, but he grabbed my hair and slammed my head forward hard enough that I saw black. Pain burst through head, my ears ringing.

This couldn't be happening.

This wasn't supposed to happen.

Everything was supposed to be over.

"Fucking bitch."

"*Haley!*"

David dragged me out of the kitchen and down the hall, straight to the front door. Pain blinded me as he threw me out onto the front porch, waving the gun.

"Get in my car, or I will kill him."

"*Haley!*"

Cam's cries were like knives through me. But the thought of this man killing Cam made me move. I got to my feet, staggering. I went down the steps, tears streaming down my cheeks as I stumbled to the car. I got into the passenger side, shutting the door as blood trickled down my face.

What am I doing? I could run.

But I couldn't let him hurt Cam.

He followed behind me and got into the driver's seat. He slammed the door and pointed his gun at me, cranking on the little car. It was the electric one I'd spotted before. It came to life and he put it in reverse, peeling out of the drive as Cam came to the front door.

His expression broke me.

Cam, Cam, Cam.

He'd broken open his stitches. I could see the blood.

I let out a sob but then swallowed it as I felt the cold nose of a gun against my neck.

"Stop fucking crying."

"What are you doing?" I asked, trying to keep every word level and calm.

I still trembled.

David let out a low laugh. "Taking you someplace I can take my time with you. I've been wanting this for so long. There's just been so many fuck ups along the way. I should have just taken you before, but my brother had all these plans."

I felt sick. "Brother?" I asked.

He hit my face with the gun, pain splintering through my cheekbone. I gasped, curling against the door.

"Cam will just follow you," I sobbed.

"Not with slashed tires."

The nausea increased. "Why are you doing this?"

"You talk too fucking much," he snarled. He jerked the steering wheel, stepping on the gas until we came to the road that led back into Citrus Cove. "*You're next*. I meant what I fucking said. To think it was supposed to be you to begin with anyways. You've ruined my fucking life. And my brother's life. David marrying your sister was just to help me get closer to you, and then of course, you just never came back here. Why would you do that? Abandon your family like that?"

"David's your twin," I said. Things were starting to click into place.

"He is."

"Why didn't anyone know?"

"My mother always kept me home. She swore the devil was in me. Maybe she was right. She should have kept her mouth shut, though. You look like her. Your blonde hair. The curls."

"I've never done anything to you," I rasped. "Just let me go.

Let me go and leave me alone and we can put this all behind us."

"David married your sister and took a job that allowed him to travel, which was very convenient for increasing my radius and access to women since we look alike. He could go drink for days and I'd pretend to be him. It paid enough for me and my brother to change positions."

I thought about the boys. They were twins. It certainly ran on that side of the family.

"I've been doing it since high school, experimenting, playing, killing. Our parents didn't really care for us right. And well...they're no longer alive."

Fear rolled through me. I looked up at him, wiping at the blood that continued to drip down my swelling face.

His breathing was heavy, erratic. His eyes darted back and forth on the road as he spoke. "It's the sounds of their terror I enjoy most. You were supposed to be my first—I would have killed you that night so long ago if Cam hadn't interrupted us. Do you even remember?" He glanced over at me.

I glared at him, even if it might cost me my life.

"I was at a party at his house and he slipped his arm around you. Cameron Harlow and his friends were always ruining things. I had been planning it for weeks. If you wouldn't have taken off that night, I might have been able to get you to the car. David was already drinking by then and didn't go to the party and everyone is too dumb to tell us apart. Cam picked a fight with me though. Son of a bitch."

For once, I was glad that Cam was an asshole in high school.

"When you left Citrus Cove, David married Sarah because she was weak and naive, and she was easy to manipulate. She doesn't know about me. Doesn't know that those kids could be his or mine. But she just kept talking about you all the fucking time. All the goddamn time. I finally decided to go back to where it all started. Your neighbor looked like you, you know. Her hair, the curls. Like an angel."

"You killed an innocent woman," I whispered.

"Yeah. That was your fault, Haley."

My eyes fell down to the door, to the handle. I wasn't buckled. Maybe I could jump out and live.

"Put your head down."

I hesitated for a moment, but he shoved me forward. My head hit the dash, my vision blurring.

I felt the butt of the gun on the back of my head, and everything went black.

CHAPTER THIRTY-FOUR

cameron

IT WAS DAVID.

Panic washed over me as I ran back inside, ignoring the pain ripping through me. Blood wet my shirt from where I'd torn open my stitches rushing downstairs.

I'd been too late.

I ran upstairs and grabbed my phone from the nightstand, calling Bud. My heart pounded in my chest, blood rushing in my ears.

"Hello?"

"He took her, Bud. He took her. I was here, and he took her and—"

"Cam? What's going—"

"It was David. David took Haley. He had a gun. He took her from the house and is driving in a small black car I haven't seen before. Fuck," I rasped, leaning over the bed. I was breathing hard.

"I'm sending people your way and notifying everyone. Cam, don't leave the house."

"I'm calling my family." I hung up before he could argue. I hit Hunter's number as I went back downstairs, pacing.

I'd seen the look in his eyes. He'd never looked like that before.

"Cam—"

"David kidnapped Haley—he's the killer. It was him. It was him this whole fucking time."

Hunter let out a growl. "Fuck. *Fuck.*"

"He just took her. I'm too weak. I wasn't able to stop him, and now she could be dead." My breathing became harder, my vision dotting. I looked down, cursing. "And I'm bleeding because I tore open my fucking stitches."

"Sammy, Colt, and I are on the way. If you're passed out, you can't help her. We will find her. This town is small."

"What if she's dead? What if he kills her?"

"Stop," Hunter growled. "You have to take a deep breath. He won't kill her."

"You didn't see him. You didn't see his eyes."

"Cameron. I need you to breathe. I'm on my way, brother."

He hung up, and I stood there, frozen.

I should have moved faster, should have responded quicker. I never should have let her out of my sight.

Fuck.

I stood there until I heard the sirens. I turned right as Alexa came through the front door, her eyes falling to the blood on the floor.

"Why are you here? Instead of out there finding her."

Alexa held up her hands as if she were approaching a wild animal. "Cameron, everyone is out looking already. Everyone that we have. I'm here to make sure you're okay. And you're not, by the looks of it."

I felt myself falling apart. He'd taken her from me. From

290

my home. From our home. I'd tried to move as fast as I could, but it hadn't been enough. I hadn't been enough.

Alexa winced as she approached, her eyes falling to my side.

"We need to get you patched up."

"No. Not until she's found. We need to go."

"Cameron," she said, grabbing my arm before I could rush past her. "Where did he go? Do you even know?"

"No," I said. "I have no fucking clue. I've never seen him like this before. It was like he was a different person. He will hurt her."

"Cam!"

Hunter rushed through the front door, followed by Sammy, Colt, and Sarah.

"The kids are with Honey," Sarah said, her voice trembling. "David was supposed to be out of state for work until tomorrow. He really..."

"Yes."

Alexa turned, her gaze hardening on Sarah. "You really had no idea he wanted to kill your sister?"

"What the fuck, Alexa?" Colt growled.

"She has a point," Hunter said, his voice gruff.

Sarah's eyes widened. "Do you really think I would have stayed if I had known?"

"You'd be shocked what people will do for their abusers."

The silence that settled between us all was harsh. But meanwhile, Haley was out there in danger with a killer.

"This isn't helping," I said. "We need to get out there. Where would he have gone?"

"Has your husband killed anyone before?" Alexa asked.

Sarah scoffed. "No!"

"Are you certain?"

Sarah shook her head, her mouth open but no words

coming free. "This is absurd. David has never hit me. He's never threatened to kill me. He..." Her voice broke.

Sammy held up his hands. "Alexa, I think we need to focus on finding Haley. I'm going to call your neighbors. Hell, I'm going to call everyone I can."

"And I'm going to stitch Cam up," Hunter said.

"I'm going to check in with the other units. Don't leave the house," Alexa said, turning and storming off.

"We'll find her," Colt said to me. "She's strong. She'll be okay."

She had to be. Because if she wasn't, I would never recover. I could barely stand the fact that I hadn't been strong enough to get to her in time. He'd taken her from *our* home. We were supposed to be booking our trip for a vacation, not dealing with a crisis. She'd been through too much, and it wasn't right that this was happening.

Hot fury rolled through me again.

Hunter pushed me toward the living room. I sat on the armrest of the couch as he retrieved a first aid kit from the bathroom. I'd always kept supplies for stitches in it, a habit from growing up on the farm.

"I can't do this right now," I growled. "I would have followed them, but he slashed my fucking tires."

Maybe I should've tried anyway. I ran through the scenario over and over in my head, trying to figure out what I should've done differently. Because right now, she was gone. She was gone, and I was helpless.

"He thought it through," Hunter said, lifting my shirt up. "Shit, Cam. You tore this fucker wide open."

"I don't care."

"I do. I need you in one fucking piece. Haley needs you in one piece. This is going to hurt."

It did hurt, but I could barely feel it as my mind raced. Her expression killed me. Fuck. I kept replaying watching him leave with her over and over again. Pain clawed at my chest, my eyes watering.

"We have to find her," I whispered.

"We will. I'm almost done. We really should take you in."

"No."

"Figured you'd say that," Hunter sighed. "Alright." He placed a bandage over the wound and then wrapped my waist with tape, grimacing at the job he did.

The moment he was done, I stood up, going back to the front porch. Alexa paced, talking on the phone. There was another cop with her, one talking to Colt and Sarah.

I walked over to them, interrupting. "I have questions for you," I said to Sarah.

She looked up. Her eyes were red with tears. "I'll answer anything."

"He was driving a black electric car. Have you seen it before?"

Sarah frowned. "He doesn't own an electric car. This is David we're talking about."

"Well, he was driving one. Why would he have been driving one?"

"I don't know. One of his friends supposedly got an electric car recently but that's all that comes to mind."

"What friend?" I gritted out.

"I don't know, Cam. I don't know his friends."

"How have you been married to him for so long and don't know his friends? Do you know anything about him?"

"Cam," Colt warned.

I ignored him. I wasn't holding back my words.

She winced. "I'm sorry. I'm trying my best."

"Did he go to Baltimore recently?"

"He never told me exactly where his trips were to."

I shook my head. I couldn't handle this.

"Cam."

I turned, looking up at Alexa. Her eyes were burning with fury.

"The killer isn't David."

We all stared at her like she'd lost her mind.

"What?" Sarah whispered.

"The killer isn't David. Baltimore confirmed it. They finally found fingerprints in Haley's old apartment, and they recovered footage from a parking garage down the road from her. We have plates, but the fingerprints don't match David's."

"I saw David with my own eyes," I snarled. "Do they know who the killer is?"

"They matched with someone named Thomas Connor."

"I—I thought it was Andy," Sarah whispered. "I really did. I thought they caught the killer. I... But it's not David?"

"Does David have a brother?" I asked. "A twin brother?"

Colt paled. "Fuck. Haley asked me that recently. If he has a doppelgänger."

Fuck.

My head whipped back around. "Where would he take her, Sarah? Where?"

"I don't know! David doesn't have a brother!"

"Apparently he does!" I shouted. "Where would he take her?"

"Cameron," Colt growled, stepping toward me. He put his hand on my chest, pushing me back. "She doesn't know."

"She was married to David for over a decade!" I snarled. "She has to know something!"

I was losing it. I was losing my mind, losing my patience. I was stuck at my house while Haley was out there. And not even with the person we thought.

She was probably so scared.

Fuck.

I ran my fingers through my hair, turning, thinking. Pacing. I'd been in their house. I'd seen glimpses of David. But I hadn't seen glimpses of Thomas. How were we going to find her now?

I ran through everything, trying to find anything out of the ordinary. Anything that stuck out to me.

If this was David's brother, maybe he kept things for him. Or information. Something.

"The basement," I whispered.

The basement.

"What was in the basement?" I asked, turning to look at Sarah.

"I was never allowed down there," she said.

My jaw ticked. I spun back around to Alexa. "Take me to Sarah's house."

"They've already checked there," Alexa said. "His car wasn't there."

"Did they check inside? In the basement?" I asked.

Alexa frowned. "I don't know."

"Check," I demanded. "I'm telling you, that's where she is."

"You're still hurt—"

"Either you drive, or I will," Hunter threatened, already moving toward his truck. "We might as well fucking check instead of hanging around here. We're not doing any good sitting."

"Someone has to be here if she comes back," Alexa growled, although she sounded doubtful that would be the case.

"Thomas isn't going to just let her go," I said. "And you don't need to come. Hunter and I are perfectly capable of going."

Alexa gave me a sharp glare. "I can't let you go there alone, Harlow. Don't be an ass."

295

I bit my tongue. Part of me wanted to blame a lot of this on departments and people not doing their jobs, but now wasn't the time.

Alexa cursed as she headed towards her cruiser. I followed, getting into the front seat. She slammed the driver's door and rolled down the window, shouting at the other officer. "Stay here in case she comes back."

She cranked the engine and flipped on the lights, peeling out of the drive.

I ignored the pain in my side, silently hoping that we found Haley in the basement. Because if we didn't?

I didn't have a clue where she might be.

CHAPTER THIRTY-FIVE

Cameron

HUNTER FOLLOWED BEHIND US. I glanced in the side-view mirror as Alexa sped down the road, her lights and sirens blaring. My body felt cold as I thought about the house. About the stench in the basement.

If Thomas was the killer and David's brother, then maybe it wasn't a dead animal causing that smell...Maybe David had been helping him all along and we hadn't realized it.

The thought made my gut twist. There had been so much death in this town recently, I couldn't help but wonder if there was a body down there. But surely Sarah or the boys would have noticed something like that. There was only so much one could do to ignore things.

My gaze raised to the clouds. A storm was rolling in, a dark wall in the distance promising rain and thunder. It was the type of weather during which I should have been snuggled in bed with Haley.

Not trying to find out if she was still alive.

Another steady breath. One that would keep me from falling apart. One that made my side burn with pain, pain that I pretended didn't exist. I had to stay together and ready for anything.

"I hope she's there," Alexa whispered, her knuckles whitening on the steering wheel. "If she's not, we'll figure it out, Cam. Thomas isn't that smart. And now that we know it's him, he can only hide for so long before we find him. An electric car in a small town in Texas? Someone will have noticed."

"She has to be there. When Haley and I moved Sarah and the boys out, there was a stench. Like a dead animal. I thought that's what it was at the time, but now that I know he's a murderer..."

"Oh god," Alexa breathed out. "Do you think there are bodies down there?"

"I don't know," I whispered. "All I can do is hope she is down there alive."

Alive and unharmed. That we'd get there in time to save her. If she wasn't...

My heart pounded faster in my chest.

I thought about Thomas, about the man who had been in this town for so long. What happened to make him into a killer? Why Haley? Why didn't we know about David's brother?

Obviously David and I never got along, but I never knew him to have siblings.

"It's gonna be okay," Alexa whispered.

"Don't promise anything," I said. I glanced in the side mirror, seeing Hunter. We were hauling ass. "When are you taking Bud's job?" I asked, trying to keep us talking.

Alexa laughed as she swerved around a car in front of us that was going too slow. I tensed in my seat, ignoring the flare of pain in my side. I looked down, seeing the blood staining my shirt.

Later. I would deal with my wound later. I drew in a long breath, trying to steady myself.

I glanced at Alexa. "I'm not joking. You seem to keep the whole department together."

"I do," she answered. "And when he retires, maybe I'll take over. But for now, I'm fine with not being the boss. Because otherwise, I'd have to be coordinating with the others instead of taking off like this."

She took a sharp turn, heading down the main road into Citrus Cove. Right before we hit Main Street, she took a right, entering the neighborhood close to where Sarah's old house was.

Thunder rolled in the distance.

"I'm going to park a block over, and I'll go in on foot. I have a gun. You don't. So you're staying put. I'm going to check the premises, and then if it looks like she's here, I'll call the other units in. Okay?"

"I'm not staying here," I argued. "I'm coming with you. I'm already here. And I know how to handle a gun."

She glared at me. "You're just a civilian, Cameron, not a superhero."

"And? I'm coming with you. You already said the department is stretched thin looking for her. It's a small town. Hunter will come too."

Alexa glared for a moment, her gaze flickering back to where Hunter was behind us. She cursed under her breath and lifted her radio, sending off her location as she stopped the car. "I go in first. I'll handle Thomas if he's there, and you find Haley. I call the shots."

"Deal."

My adrenaline was already pumping. She got out of the car and popped the trunk. I followed her, and she handed me a Glock 19. Hunter came up to us, his brows pulling together.

"We're going in?"

"We're checking to see if we think she's there," Alexa said. "And both of you should stay here, but—"

"No," Hunter snorted. "First of all, my brother is bleeding. Second, his girl might be in there. We're going in."

"Are you sure you know how to use a gun—"

"Yes. We need to go," I said. "Stop with the protocol bull-shit. We're going in."

She shut the trunk and nodded. "Fine. We go in. If it looks like she might be there, we alert the other officers and wait for Bud."

Yeah, no. I wasn't waiting for anyone. I didn't say that aloud though.

She led the way, leading us around the neighborhood block. I glanced at the houses, wondering if some of the neighbors were watching us. If they were, no one came out.

We looked around a white picket fence, peeking to see if the car was in the driveway of Sarah's house.

It wasn't in the driveway.

Pain split through my side, but I ignored it. None of that mattered right now. What mattered was getting Haley back and away from that monster.

"The car could be in the garage," I said.

Alexa nodded. "We're still going in. Follow me."

She ran across the yard quickly, and I followed, the two of us rushing to the front door. She motioned for me to be quiet as she reached for the knob, twisting it as silently as she could.

The door was locked.

"Here," Hunter whispered. "I grabbed this from Colt the other day when we were moving and forgot to return it." He pulled out a copper key.

"Great," Alexa said.

She took the key and unlocked the door, slowly turning the knob and opening it.

300

She stepped inside, the two of us following. The house reeked and looked nothing like how we'd left it. The furniture was destroyed, broken bottles littering the floor. Blood stained the rug in the living room.

Nausea rolled through me. Hunter cursed under his breath.

Alexa shook her head, glancing back at us. "The two of you check the rest of the house. I'm going to check the basement. Okay?" Her voice was barely above a whisper.

I didn't like it, but I nodded. Hunter slipped past me and led the way toward the kitchen. Alexa left us, all of us doing our best to be as silent as possible.

The house had truly been destroyed. The kitchen was just as bad as the living room. Rage was evident in every smashed dish and mangled piece of furniture.

It chilled me.

The sound of boots had the two of us pausing. I turned, expecting to see David. The kitchen connected to the hall, and I watched as Alexa stood at the top of the stairs that led down to the basement.

A grunt echoed through the house.

"Fuck," Hunter snarled.

Suddenly, all three of us were moving.

"Alexa!" I called, but she was already down the staircase and swinging open the door.

I ran down the staircase after her, Hunter right behind me. Right as I hit the bottom step, a gun went off.

"Who the fuck are you?" A slurred voice shouted.

I hit the basement just in time to see Alexa shoot David Connor in the leg. At least, he looked like David. Beer cans littered the floor around him and he had a gun, one he'd fired into the doorframe, narrowly missing Alexa.

He howled as he went down, blood gushing down his leg.

Rage pumped through me as I stormed past Alexa, grabbing him by his collar and shaking him.

"Where is she?" I snarled. "Where is Haley?? Where did your brother take her?"

He looked up at me, his eyes lighting up with amusement as he panted through the pain. "He got her, then? I tried to tell her to leave. Such a stupid whore."

I punched him hard enough to break his nose.

"Cam," Alexa growled.

I ignored her. "Where is Haley?"

"I don't know. Don't know where he took her."

I punched him again, my hand going numb this time. Hunter let out a curse. "You're bleeding everywhere, brother," he growled.

I didn't care. "Where is she?" I asked again.

David smiled, his teeth bloodied.

Thunder shook the whole house now. Hunter pulled me back from David as Alexa took over, making a call in.

All while he kept grinning and grinning.

All while Haley was still out there with the killer.

CHAPTER THIRTY-SIX

MY ENTIRE BODY HURT. My eyes slowly opened. I was met with the golden glow of a swinging light, the sound of water dripping, and a musky, rotten smell.

I drew in a breath, my heart already racing. My head was throbbing. Blood crusted along my face.

I listened for him. I hadn't even asked his name. I heard no other movement, no breathing, nothing. I slowly raised my head, looking around.

I had to get out of here. I had to escape before he came back.

The look on Cam's face haunted me.

I was worried and scared, but I wasn't going to go down easy. I started to lift my hand and realized that I was hand-cuffed to metal pipes.

I cursed under my breath, nausea rolling through me. The smell in this room was rancid. I slowly sat up, awkward as I adjusted with the handcuffs.

My wrists burned as I yanked at the cuffs. I pulled hard,

trying to break them, to break the pipe I was trapped against. It was old and rusty but still wouldn't give.

"Fuck," I whispered.

I was in a small room with brick walls. It was clearly a basement. Boxes surrounded me, stacks of them filled with god knew what. I focused on one of them, seeing that they were case files.

What kind of hell had I ended up in?

A door opened and closed. I trembled as he came in, his gaze falling on me. "I figured you'd be waking up," he said, smiling.

"Just let me go," I whispered. "Please."

"No," he said, creeping closer. He stopped in front of me. "No, I'm not going to let you go. I'm going to kill you, Haley. And I'm going to enjoy every second of your torture."

"I never did anything to you!" I shouted.

He backhanded me hard enough that I saw stars. I leaned back, but there was nowhere to go. Nowhere to run. I was stuck, a rabbit in a trap.

"You're nothing but a whore," he whispered. "It took a long time to train your sister to stop talking about you. A long fucking time. Pretending to be David was hard too. All these things I've done just for you, and you don't appreciate me at all."

He reached up to touch my face. I jerked back, kicking out at him, but he only chuckled.

"How does it feel knowing your neighbor died because of you? That you're the reason that poor woman is dead. I really thought she was you. I grabbed her first before I realized it wasn't you. But the way she begged...god, that was my favorite part. It was too good not to kill her."

"I'm not begging you for shit," I hissed. "And if you kill me, I'm going to haunt the fuck out of you."

He smiled, an eerie smirk slashing his face that made my entire body tense. "I'd like that," he said softly, touching my face. "You say you won't beg, but I'm certain you will. They all do, Haley."

I yanked my head back from him, pressing my lips together in a firm line despite the panic I felt.

"Why me?" I asked.

"It's always been you," he said. "Always."

"But why? We didn't even know each other in high school. You never spoke to me. I don't even know your name."

"Thomas," he whispered. "We met plenty of times, even if you didn't realize it. You were too damn blinded by the Harlows."

"You just..."

"Watched you," he said, his eyes darkening. "Watched how Cam treated you. And yet you just let him. And then you come back years later and sleep with him? Let him touch you?"

"He's changed," I said. "He's not the stupid boy from high school anymore. And what about you? You're a murderer. Your brother is a drunk. Hell, maybe you are too."

"I'm not a drunk," he said. "All a ruse. It's a lot easier when the town you live in thinks you're worth nothing. All they do is pity you. My brother *is* a drunk, and pretending to be him? Easy. So fucking easy. They'd never believe that every time I left town for work, I was leaving to kill another pretty blonde girl that looked just like *you*."

"You're sick," I whispered, doing everything I could to keep the fear out of my voice. "They'll know it's you. They're going to catch you. You'll go to jail for the rest of your life. What's the point?"

"Why do you care? You'll be dead."

He stood up at the same time I moved. I yanked against the pole right as the tip of his boot hit my ribs right where I'd been

305

kicked before. The breath was knocked out of me, my knees collapsing under me.

He kicked me again and again, each time harder than the last.

By the time he stopped, my vision was blurry. His breathing was heavy, his hands curled into fists.

"I'll come back in a bit. We're going to take this nice and slow, Haley. I've been waiting to do this for years. I'm going to savor every moment of it."

I panted as he left, the sound of his shoes shuffling. A door shutting.

Pain. It was too much. Everything hurt. Things were broken. I could barely breathe without feeling a thousand knives stabbing my body.

I have to get out.

I didn't have the bandwidth to sob or scream. Everything went numb, including my emotions. Everything but the desire to survive.

I had to break the handcuffs, even if it meant breaking my own wrist.

My eyes swept the floor, looking around for anything. Anything that could help. Anything within arms reach.

I reached up and felt my head, working my fingers against my scalp. I sucked in a breath when I felt a bobby pin.

I'd forgotten about them.

My breaths quickened as I pulled one out, my curls tumbling free. My fingers shook as I twisted, pain radiating through me. I stifled a cry as I twisted, trembling as I pulled the bobby pin completely open. I worked the tip of the bobby pin in the handcuff keyhole and bent it to the side, and then did it again, fiddling around with it.

Please, please, please.

The sound of wood creaking above made me freeze. I

looked up at the ceiling, hearing his footsteps. Silent tears streamed down my cheeks, every muscle on fire.

My eyes closed. The pain was too much. Every breath was too much.

Don't stop. Don't stop.

I kept twisting the bobby pin until I heard a soft click. I was able to pull it free, the metal clinking against the pipe. I tried to lower my wrist and the handcuffs as silently as possible.

Could I even stand? I wasn't sure. I had to try.

A pained cry left me as I leaned forward. I grabbed onto the pipe, using it to slowly haul myself to standing. I wavered on my feet.

I needed a weapon. I needed something to hit him with. That was the only way I'd be able to surprise him.

My gaze swept around the basement again. All of the boxes full of files and papers. I limped forward, clutching my waist as I searched for something I could hit him with. There were no windows, but I could hear rain outside. It had to be really coming down.

A shine caught my eye and I hobbled towards a set of boxes. On the floor next to them was a glass beer bottle. That was it. I picked it up and I limped towards the staircase that led to the basement door. I forced myself up them and tried the handle.

It was locked.

I closed my eyes, finding strength. I needed to call for him. I needed to get him down here, strike him, and then get out. I needed to move as fast as I could the moment I could, even if the pain was excruciating.

My legs shook as I went back down the stairs and crouched behind boxes out of sight of the door, but within a range I might be able to get past him or hit him.

"Thomas!" I screamed, my voice cracking. "Thomas! Get down here you son of a bitch!"

What if he ignores me?

"Thomas!"

I heard his feet shuffling. I readied myself, wiping the tears as I heard him come to the door. The jingle of keys.

The door to the basement creaked open and he came down the steps. I peeked around the boxes as he went towards where he'd chained me up.

Now. NOW.

I used everything I had to take off up the stairs.

"You stupid bitch!" he shouted.

I slammed the basement door behind me as he shoved against it, his wrist getting caught. He growled, letting out a short yelp. I slammed his hand again by bumping the door with my shoulder, holding onto the glass bottle still. I spun around and went up another set of stairs, coming out in a dark living room.

He was right behind me.

I kept moving, rushing towards the front door. I yanked at the locks as he slammed into me and I turned, smashing the glass bottle against his head.

It shattered and he stumbled back long enough for me to get the front door open.

Run. RUN.

The rain was pouring in heavy sheets. I didn't recognize the field this house was in, but I still took off running, running as fast as I could.

Thomas' shouts echoed behind me. Getting louder. Closer.

Don't stop.

I kept pushing. The rain made it hard to see in the distance, but I swore I could see a dirt road.

I'd either die out here or make it out.

That settled over me. My lungs burned as I kept moving, my shoes sloshing in the mud. The grass became waist high, making it harder to move fast.

My heart pounded, every breath becoming harder.

"*Haley!*"

He kept shouting my name. Over and over. It echoed across the field, becoming meaner and more desperate. It only scared me more.

A gunshot cracked like thunder.

Don't stop. Keep going.

A bullet flew past me as I screamed, forcing myself to keep moving through the fields. The rain pelted my skin, the pain of every step making me scream louder and louder.

Headlights flashed, interrupting the constant gray darkness. Hope flooded me as they came closer. Had they found me? The lights blurred, more following.

I raised my hands, waving them as I kept moving.

"You stupid bitch!" Thomas shouted.

Another bullet went past, grazing my arm. I cried out, stumbling forward as I heard sirens.

Lightning snaked through the clouds, flashing above. A heavy body tackled into me, slamming me into the muddy ground. I cried as I fought, using the last of my strength and adrenaline to do anything I could. I rolled over, shoving at him.

"You stupid bitch," he snarled. "You ruined everything. You're going to die."

I dragged my nails across his face, digging them into his skin.

I never stopped screaming. I couldn't stop.

Thomas' hands slipped around my neck, squeezing hard. He shook me, his face wild with hatred.

"They found us," I wheezed. "They got you."

He roared and squeezed tighter, cutting everything off.

I couldn't speak.

I couldn't breathe.

This can't be it.

I jammed my thumbs into his eyes. He cried out and fell back. I got to my feet, staggering as he did the same. He reached behind him, pulling out his gun and aiming at me.

"You're going to die."

I closed my eyes, waiting for the bullet. A shout echoed across the field, along with a gun firing—but it wasn't at me. My eyes flew open right as a figure running towards us went down.

Another was sprinting towards us.

Cam.

Thomas growled and turned towards me again, pointing it at me. I stared at Cam, unable to move. *Everything hurts.* Everything hurt too much. And I was frozen with fear that Thomas would turn the gun on him instead.

His gaze met mine for a split second.

"I love you," I whispered.

Thomas pulled the trigger right as Cam tackled him with a shout.

The bullet hit my shoulder, taking me down. I fell back, hitting the ground hard. The rain washed my blood into the dirt, more lightning flashing above.

Everything hurt. I was so tired of the pain.

I drew in shallow breaths, forcing my eyes to stay open. Above the thunder and pouring rain, I heard more shouts and cars and sirens.

I'd escaped him.

I closed my eyes. So much was happening, but it was getting harder to pay attention.

Harder to stay awake.

Everything hurts.

"*Haley, Haley. Baby girl.*"

I felt his hands touch me, gripping my face.

"*No, no, no. You have to wake up, sunshine.*"

I forced my eyes open, seeing Cam hovering over me. He cupped my face gently, one of his tears falling on my cheek. Or was it the rain? I wasn't sure anymore.

"I love you," I whispered.

"You're going to be okay. You're alive. You're alive and..."

My eyes closed again, his voice growing further away. I could feel myself slipping under the tide.

But at least he was safe.

CHAPTER THIRTY-SEVEN

Cameron

I PACED the hall back and forth. *Waiting, waiting, waiting.*

Waiting for news.

Waiting to know if she was going to make it.

Everything was a nightmare. Alexa was dead. She'd been the first across the field and Thomas shot her before shooting Haley. She'd died instantly. I'd never seen someone die before, and prayed I never did again. If I wasn't thinking about that, then I was thinking about how I'd been too late in stopping him from hurting Haley too.

He'd just missed her heart.

She wasn't out of the woods yet though.

Grief washed through me. I'd known Alexa for a long time. I couldn't shake the nightmare of the storm and her just going down. It happened so fast. She'd died trying to save the woman I loved.

Alexa hadn't been the only one though.

The house where Haley was taken belonged to David's parents, who were long dead. After we'd gotten him, Hunter forced info out of him. I didn't ask how. The house was on the outskirts of Citrus Cove, pretty much in the middle of fucking nowhere. But we'd made it.

We'd made it just in time.

Several of the files in the basement were filled with pictures of women Thomas killed. All of them had been blonde, like Haley, about the same height. Same color eyes. All over the country, too.

The smell down in the basement. The foul stench that I had sworn was an animal the day we moved the kids out. It belonged to an animal. It seemed that while David wasn't a serial killer like his brother, he did sometimes kill things.

I felt sick knowing that Thomas had done this. Even more so finding out that there had been times he'd pretended to be David. It was a mind fuck for all of us, especially Sarah.

I didn't know what Sarah would do. It had broken her in a way that I wasn't sure could be mended. All of us were doing our best to keep things from the boys, but it was hard with the news trying to cover everything.

How many women had Thomas Connor killed? His obsession with Haley made me feel sick. My stomach twisted, my thoughts going through the cycle again.

Grief. Worry. Fear. Pain. Sadness. Horror.

Over and over.

I couldn't stop it.

And above it all was the very real thought that I might lose her. I might lose Haley. I loved her so much that it made me feel weak, and losing her would destroy me.

"Cam, honey, you need to sit down. You're bleeding again."

I ignored my mom, the same way I'd ignored everyone else. Everyone was waiting too. I was still covered in her blood, her expression haunting me.

I love you.

She'd whispered the words right before she'd passed out. I

thought then and there that she had died in my arms. I'd never screamed like that before.

"Cam."

Hunter grabbed my shoulder, forcing me to look at him. He wore that big-brother face right now, his muscles tense.

He'd seen Alexa go too. He'd been the one to check Haley's pulse, to keep me from completely falling apart. He and another officer had been the ones to uncover the basement, the photos, everything.

"You got to stay together, man," Hunter said. "And in order to do that, we need you well."

"Leave me," I whispered.

"No. I won't. I got the nurse. She needs to look at your wound. We should have word on Haley soon."

"I'm not leaving until I know," I said, my voice soft but firm. I needed to know. I needed to know that she was okay.

She was still in surgery. They were removing the bullet.

The bullet was just part of the problem. He'd hurt her. He'd hurt her badly. Between broken ribs, her concussion, being shot, and the blood loss, it didn't look good.

I couldn't lose her.

"Hey, Cam."

I looked up to see my nurse from when I was here only days ago. It felt like that was ages ago, when in reality, this was just the longest week of any of our lives.

She stopped in front of us, folding her hands together.

"Do you have anything?" I asked, wincing at the desperation in my voice.

"Haley is out of surgery," she said, holding up a hand before any of us could speak. "She is stabilized. They lost her for a moment, but she is alive. We won't know more until we get through the night. And if you plan on being there when she wakes up, you've got to let me look at your stitches. She wouldn't want to see you like this."

My knees felt like they were going to buckle. Hunter gripped my arm, holding on to me.

I felt a different hand pat my shoulder and looked to my left. Honey stood there, more exhausted than I'd ever seen her before. "Please let her look at you."

I couldn't say no to her. I sighed and nodded.

"Thanks," Hunter murmured to her. "I also brought you new clothes."

He handed them to me. I followed the nurse to a room, my thoughts whirling. I kept replaying what happened in my mind. "Lie back on the table. We'll get you restitched up and cleaned up. By the time we're done, I'll take you to Haley."

* * *

Three days passed.

I laid my head on the edge of the hospital bed, listening to the beeps of the machines. I listened to her breathing.

Tears slid down my face again. My eyes were tired from crying.

I'd prayed. I'd begged. I'd sobbed.

All three on repeat for hours, and I'd keep doing it until she woke up. I slipped my hand into my pocket, feeling the outline of the engagement ring in my pocket.

I reached in and pulled it out. Mom and Colt helped me pick out the perfect one. There was a single diamond in the center surrounded by a dozen smaller ones and a twisted vine silver band.

It was perfect.

There was a knock at the door, but I ignored it, tucking the ring back in my pocket.

"You have to eat."

It was Sammy. I drew it a sharp breath and leaned back, looking up at him. "Not hungry."

"Cam," he whispered. "We're all worried about you. Almost as much as you're worried about her."

"I'm not hungry."

"If you don't eat, then I'm going to have them kick you out. Hunter and I will drag your ass back home and force-feed you."

"I'd fight you."

"You'd lose." He stepped closer, shoving a brown bag at me, followed by a water bottle. "Eat. Drink. If not for us, for her. She's going to need you when she wakes up."

I nodded, reluctantly taking the food. He left as I pulled out a burger. I looked up at Haley, tears welling again.

Her face was still covered in bruises. Her chest rose and fell, her eyes closed.

The first day, I'd been so angry. So fucking angry at David. And then Thomas. Angry that he'd killed Alexa. Angry that all of us had never paid more attention.

I'd always hated David. We'd all known there was something not quite right, but I never would have imagined that maybe it was because his twin brother was a serial killer.

Sarah had been in and out. She wouldn't look at me. I felt a flicker of guilt over that, but I couldn't worry about mending that fence right now.

My anger drained me, leaving me feeling hollow and scared. Scared that Haley would die.

I'd gotten my chance to love her. To be a better person. To be the best man I could possibly be, to give everything I could to her. I wanted to create a life with her. A future.

I couldn't imagine a world without her in it.

I ate the burger and washed it down with water. I knew my body appreciated it, but I still felt empty.

My head fell back, my eyes roaming over the ceiling tiles

again. I'd counted them at least twenty times, but what was once more?

I counted them once. Twice. And then leaned forward in my seat, slipping my hand back into hers. I waited, hoping she would squeeze it. Some sort of sign that she was there. That she was fighting.

I laid my head on the edge of the bed, looking up at her.

My eyes started to close. I fought myself but could feel the exhaustion starting to take over.

And then I felt her hand.

And I heard her voice.

"There's my husband."

CHAPTER THIRTY-EIGHT

CAMERON GENTLY EMBRACED ME, careful not to jar me. I held on to him, tears streaming down my face as he kissed me over and over again. I was groggy, and my body ached, but I was alive.

I was safe.

He cupped my face, letting out a soft sob. "I thought I was going to lose you, sunshine."

"Never," I croaked.

He kissed my forehead, his touch turning gentle. I blinked a few times, taking everything in. Memories washed over me, the last moments coming to my mind.

Thomas.

The gun.

The person that went down in the field. I hadn't been able to make them out.

"Who died?" I whispered.

Cameron's eyes softened. "Alexa died, Hal. Thomas shot her, and it was almost instant."

"Oh my god," I whispered, more tears falling.

"He's in jail right now. He'll never get out. He'll never hurt you or anyone else again. It's really over this time, baby. It really is."

Sadness and relief. I felt them both, equally potent.

Andy was done for, and so was Thomas.

It really was over.

No more death. No more pain.

I drew in a shaky breath, my head falling back against my pillow. Cam slipped his hand into mine, squeezing.

"I love you," he said. "More than anything. Anything, sunshine. I thought I was going to lose you."

"I'm sorry," I whispered.

"What are you sorry for? Don't be sorry. None of this is your fault, Haley."

"I still worry that I brought this home. That somehow I caused this..."

"You didn't do anything," Cam rasped. "*Haley*. Look at me."

I did look at him. I held his bright blue gaze, feeling him. Seeing him.

"There was something wrong with him. He was a murderer. And he became obsessed with you. None of that was your fault."

"He told me it was always supposed to be me," I croaked. "I barely even remember him, Cam. I need to talk to Sarah."

"Sarah will be around in a bit, I'm sure. Remember when your sister dragged you to a party at my farm, and you punched me in the barn? All those years ago?"

"Yes," I said, raising a brow. "That's why I dumped my beer on you. Back then, I swore up and down I'd never have anything to do with you again. And yet here I am..."

Cam smirked, a glimmer of the man I knew under the exhaustion. "I'm charming. Won you over."

"I think it's more like you fell in love with me."

"Baby, I've been in love with you since you came to Citrus Cove." He chuckled, kissing my hand. But then his expression turned more serious. "I seem to vaguely remember him being there, and my dumb and drunk ass interrupted a pass he was going to make. And I can't help but wonder if that's when this all started. I've been thinking back, thinking about who he was growing up. A little bit older, quiet. The adult he became was nothing like that kid. I don't know what happened."

"Me neither," I breathed out. "And maybe it wasn't him to begin with. Maybe it was his brother. None of us know."

He nodded, pressing his lips together. "It's scary to think about it."

"It is. Is Sarah really okay...? The boys..."

"No," he answered honestly. "No. They'll need us. They'll need therapy. My mom is actually helping set Davy and Jake up with a therapist. She's friends with a child psychologist."

"I swear your family knows everyone," I said.

"Perks of a small town," he said. "But we didn't know David or Thomas."

"No one did."

He nodded, leaning back in his chair. "Part of me wonders if Sarah knew..."

"There's no way that she did," I whispered, my stomach clenching. "Surely not."

"I knew she was awake."

A new voice startled us. I blinked back tears and looked past Cam, seeing Honey in the doorway. She was clearly exhausted. Every wrinkle that lined her face looked a little deeper, circles under her eyes a little darker. The same circles that haunted Cam too.

"How long have I been out?" I asked as she crossed the

320

room to me. I reached for her as she went to the other side of the bed, her hand clutching mine.

"Three days, sweetheart. And this man hasn't left your side once."

I looked at Cam, feeling everything inside of me melt. He offered me a soft smile.

"You need to rest, then," I said.

"You don't need to worry about me, sunshine. I'm doing just fine."

Honey snorted, squeezing my hand. "I'm going to let everyone know you're awake. And the nurse. They probably need to check on you."

She leaned down, kissing the top of my head. "I'm so sorry this happened. But you're safe now. Thomas and David will never get to you again."

My throat closed up. I wondered what the outcome was with David right now, but didn't ask.

"We don't need to talk about him again right now," Cam murmured, glancing at Honey.

Honey nodded. "I'll be back with everyone else. The boys have been asking about you."

"Have they?" My heart squeezed. "Do they know..."

"They don't know everything right now," Honey said, her voice softening. "I wish it could stay that way. But you know how people talk in our town."

I nodded as she left the room, sinking back into the bed. Cam rose from his chair and leaned down, kissing me on the head.

"Get in with me," I murmured.

Cam hesitated. "I don't want to hurt you."

"Get in the damn bed."

He snorted and carefully pulled the blankets back. I moved over, sucking in a breath. My body felt like it was made out of wood, but I wanted to be held by him. He slid in next to me, the two of us shifting until we were comfortable.

He kissed the top of my head. I laid my ear on his chest, listening to his heart.

I closed my eyes and exhaled, feeling every muscle in my body relax.

Within a couple of minutes, he let out the softest snore. I smiled, feeling a wave of exhaustion too. But it was different. It was the feeling after running a marathon, a heavy relief settling in.

I heard a shuffle in the doorway and opened my eyes, seeing his mom poke her head in.

"We'll come back later," she whispered. "He's barely slept. Y'all get some rest."

My heart squeezed, and I nodded. "Thank you," I whispered.

"Of course, sweetheart."

She left, and I closed my eyes again, already feeling the comfort settling like a soft blanket. I'd been through a lot, but he'd been right there with me. Holding me, loving me. My ray of sunshine through the storm that followed me home.

And that's what this place was.

Home.

With Cam, it was home.

CHAPTER THIRTY-NINE

One Month Later

IT HAD ALREADY BEEN a month since everything came to an end. The whole town had been covered on the news over and over again, but it finally felt like the storm had passed. There was still the sting of sadness. Thomas was in jail, which was where he would stay indefinitely. Alexa was dead. She'd saved my life, and I would forever be grateful to her. David was still being questioned about everything, and while we weren't sure if he would end up in jail, he wasn't staying in Citrus Cove. He was out of our lives for good.

"Are you ready?"

I glanced up in the mirror, seeing Emma behind me. Her dark brown hair was pulled back into a chignon. Her lilac maid-of-honor dress hung perfectly on her curvy frame, and she wore four-inch heels that she'd "compromised on" because the wedding was outside.

She came up to me and pulled me into a hug.

Ever since she'd arrived, I hardly let her go. It was either her or Cam that I seemed to hold on to.

"You look stunning," she whispered. "Look at you."

"You helped me find the dress," I said, grinning at the two of us.

"I've had this dress picked out since I've known you," she laughed. Her smile softened. "He's the one."

"He is. I love him so fucking much."

"I know. And he loves you even more. I've run my tests."

"Oh yeah? The three Emma tests."

"Mmhm. And he passed. His brother, however, is an absolute nightmare of a man, and I despise him."

"Well, I hope you can keep that to yourself since he's officiating the wedding," I giggled. "Hunter isn't that bad, Emma, I swear. I like him a lot."

She rolled her eyes but let go of her protests. "We're ready when you are. I'd bet you fifty dollars that Cam cries."

"No," I hissed. "He won't cry."

Emma snorted. "Then we have a bet."

"Deal."

"Deal," she giggled.

I took one last look at myself.

I looked happy. Truly happy.

I smiled and let her lead me out of my in-laws' home. Emma had taken over at 8:00 a.m. for all of the preparations.

I stepped out onto the front porch. Cam's father was waiting there wearing a tuxedo. He gave me a soft smile. "He's a lucky man," he said, offering me his arm.

"And I'm a lucky girl. Thank you for walking me up."

"I'm happy to," he chuckled.

We made our way through the vineyard, winding our way up the path to where my future husband waited.

I walked through the tall grass, my wedding dress trailing behind me. The Harlow oak tree stood strong, chairs split into rows filled with friends and family.

I didn't see them. I didn't see how beautiful the sky was or how perfect the weather was.

All I saw was him.

Cameron stood under the tree, wearing a tux. The moment our gazes met, I fought the tears that wanted to fall. The tears of happiness, of gratefulness, of love.

His eyes widened, and damn it. *He* started crying.

"You can't cry!" I called as I came to the aisle, looping my arm into Honey's.

Emma snickered as she took her spot under the tree.

Colt slapped Cam's back, everyone beaming. Bob gave my hand a squeeze as Honey came up to me. Honey was going to walk me down the aisle.

"You're a beautiful bride," she said, her voice wavering.

"Thank you, Honey," I whispered.

The music started, the wind picking up gently. Honey walked me down to the man who loved me so much he was crying.

"You're so beautiful," he said as we came to the end.

Hunter stood in as our officiant, because of course he had a license to do so. I turned and kissed Honey's cheek and then went to him.

Cam reached out, taking my hand. I squeezed his, smiling at him. "Hi, baby," I whispered.

"Hi," he whispered. "I love you so much."

"I love you too."

"You're supposed to wait until I've officiated," Hunter teased.

"Okay, well, hurry up and marry us so I can kiss my husband," I said.

Hunter chuckled. "We are gathered here today..."

I tuned him out as he went through the ceremony, my eyes on Cameron. Everything felt like a blur, my heart beating faster. This man had seen me at my absolute worst and loved me through every moment of it.

He smiled as we looked at each other, both of us saying the words.

I do.

Hunter handed Cameron the tool for carving our initials into the tree. He tugged me close, his body pressed to mine as he held the blade to the bark, whittling in *HB + CH* encased in a heart. I blinked back tears, whispering under my breath.

"I'm yours forever, Cam."

He kissed the top of my head, his hand cupping the back of my neck. "I'm yours too, sunshine."

citrus cove continues...

clio's creatures

Hello Creatures!

My name is Clio Evans and I am so excited to introduce myself to you! I'm a lover of all things that go bump in the night, fancy peens, coffee, and chocolate. If you're reading this, then that means you've joined me on my small town romance adventure!

For updates and more, make sure to sign up for my newsletter.

Clio's Creature Newsletter

also by clio evans

Not So Much Appreciated

FREAKS OF NATURE DUET

Doves & Demons

Demons & Doves

THREE FATES MAFIA SERIES

Thieves & Monsters

Killers & Monsters

Queens & Monsters

Kings & Monsters

GALACTIC GEMS SERIES

Cosmic Kiss

Cosmic Crush

Cosmic Heat